When I Bury Mr. Snow

When I Bury Mr. Snow

Judith Johnson

Kismet Mysteries

Library of Congress Control Number: 2025914431

ISBN 979-8-9896511-2-2 (paperback)

ISBN 979-8-9896511-3-9 (ebook)

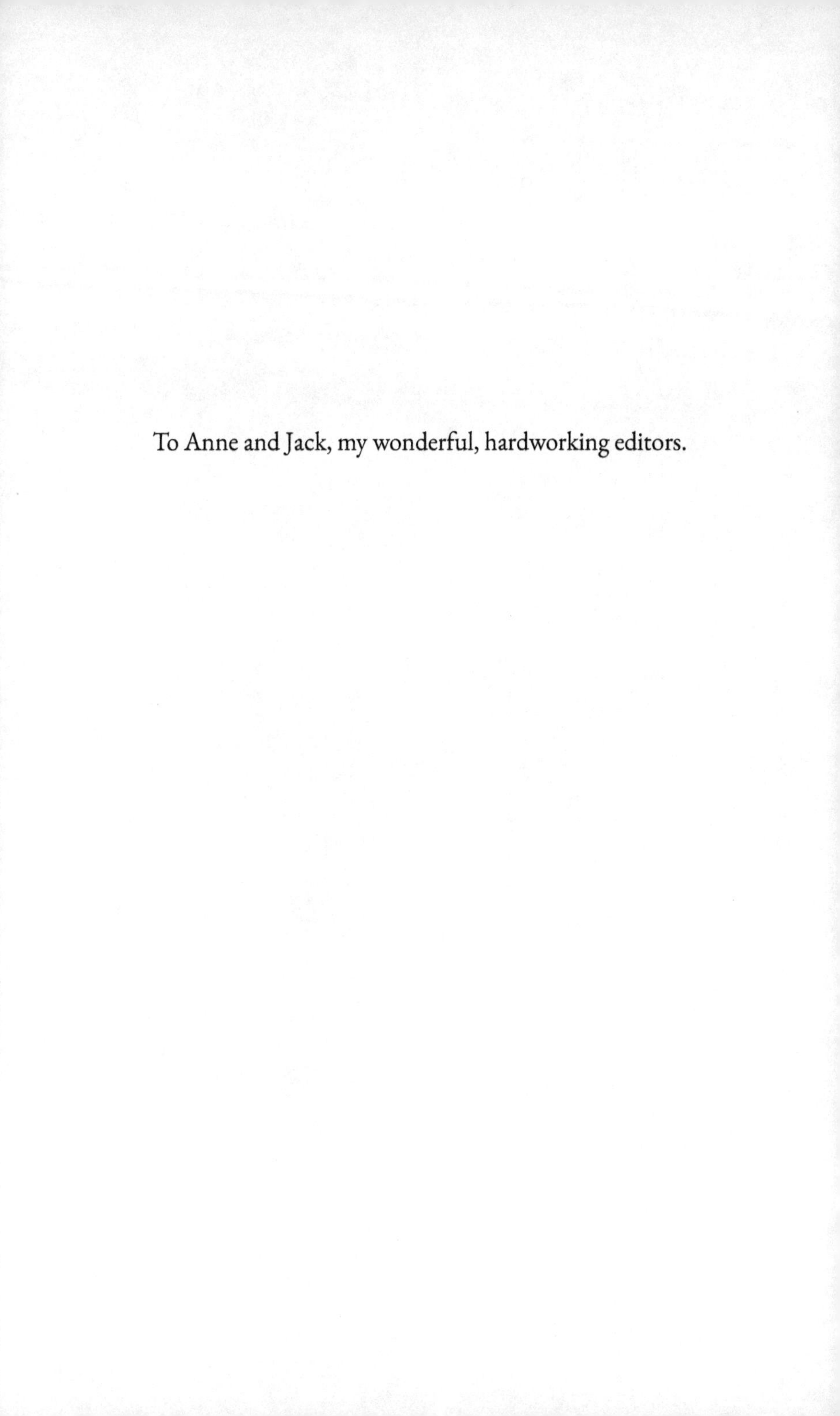

To Anne and Jack, my wonderful, hardworking editors.

Chapter 1

On the Road to Grand Marais

RUTH CARSON MAYS KEPT her eyes firmly on the narrow road that wound its way northward along the shore of Lake Superior. She tried not to think about the hundred-foot drop to the rocks and crashing waves at the bottom of Silver Creek Cliff.

"Gram," whispered her granddaughter from the back seat of their beige Toyota, "they really need to build a tunnel on this part. This is scary!"

"We're almost past it, sweetie. Just close your eyes."

"But then I won't see Lake Superior. And Gram, that is one awesome lake!"

"Yes, indeed," said Ruth, slowing down as she carefully navigated the strip of US Highway 61 that hugged the cliffs about an hour north of Duluth. "And you're right about a tunnel. That would be a good idea. Maybe they'll put one through here someday."

It was 1991, and pleasantly warm for early August in northern Minnesota. Not too hot. Ruth could feel her heartbeat return to normal as she completed the curve and eased her car into a straighter stretch of road.

"Did you have a good nap?" she asked her granddaughter, who had been sleeping off the lunch they'd had at the McDonald's in Duluth.

Annika Marie Lindstrom stretched her arms over her blonde head and leaned back in the seat. "How long was I sleeping?"

"About an hour, I think. We have a couple more hours to go before we reach Grand Marais."

"Don't you wish Grandpa Del was up here with us?" Annika said wistfully.

"I sure wish he was driving!" Ruth laughed. "But you know he'd be here if he could."

In her sixties, Ruth had been a widow for five years, when she met Delancy Mays, himself a widower. He was an opera singer who'd been taking an extended break from his usually busy performance schedule. They had met last summer when both were in the musical *Show Boat* at the Como Park Pavilion in St. Paul. Ruth recalled their falling in love.

He was so handsome, so gracious, and Lord! I'm so happy I met him! And now I'm happy to be Mrs. Mays.

She smiled.

"He told me when he left for Boston, he'd rather be with us," Ruth announced.

Annika looked out the window. "Are we going to be in Grand Marais pretty soon?" she asked.

"No, sweetie, like I said, it's about another couple of hours." She briefly looked at her granddaughter in the rearview mirror. "Do you need a potty break?"

"Not right now, I'll let you know," the girl told her.

They drove on for a while, in silence.

"You're so quiet, Gram," Annika said. "Are you thinking about Grandpa Del?"

"You're a mind-reader!" Ruth laughed as she kept her eyes on the road. "I wish he could have come up here with us, but the opera in Boston makes us a living." She was glad that her granddaughter had so readily accepted Del, who was Black. She had worried about it needlessly. Ten-year-old Annika Marie Lindstrom absolutely adored her new grandpa. Like most children, she was color-blind.

"I know he has to sing opera in Boston," the girl said. "He said he'd be home by the time we get back from Grand Marais. He promised to take me fishing."

Suddenly she shook her blonde braids in an *oh no!* gesture. She put her hands over her eyes and cried out, "Gram! Why do people have to run over the poor little animals?" A dead skunk could be seen ahead on the road. Ruth was on a tight curve and couldn't go around it without leaving her lane. It was mangled and bloody. Ruth winced when she felt her tires run over it.

As the pungent odor entered the car, she tried to comfort Annika. "Sometimes animals just dart out into the road and people can't avoid hitting them. Sometimes they're sick and they just run out without thinking. Maybe this one had rabies. I've heard that many skunks have it."

They rode in silence as the car gradually aired out. "I know a song about dead skunks in the road," she told the girl. "I taught it to your mom when she was just about your age. I learned it when I was in Girl Scouts."

Annika wrinkled her nose. "You know a song about dead skunks?"

Ruth proceeded to sing the little campfire ditty in a lusty voice, trying to make light of what, in her granddaughter's eyes, had been a tragic encounter on the highway.

"Poor dead skunk, a smellin' up the road. Poor dead skunk, his life's a heavy load! His smell is in m' nose, and I'd rather smell a rose, than a poor dead skunk, just a smellin' up the road!"

"Gram!" Annika laughed in spite of herself. "That's gross! I bet Grandpa Del would never sing something like that."

"Sure he would," Ruth laughed. "Only he'd sing it like an operatic aria."

Annika changed the subject as the highway again skirted the lake. She peered out her window. "It looks really steep down to the lake, doesn't it, Gram?"

"Don't worry, sweetie," Ruth said, edging her car closer to the center line. "I'm a careful driver. We'll be farther away from the lake soon, and driving through woods in another mile or so. And then, before you know it, we'll be in Grand Marais!"

They sang the "gross" skunk song together a few more times. Ruth was glad to see Annika smile in spite of worrying about the road kill.

"And by the way, your mother *liked* that song. She thought it was funny."

Annika started looking through her small white cotton sack of rocks. They had stopped at the Rock Shop in Beaver Bay and purchased some agates. Ruth remembered when she and her late husband, Tom had driven up here with their kids. Hannah and Robbie had loved the Rock Shop. The kids had insisted they stop there every time they came up north. The store had two show rooms and case after case of interesting rocks from around the world, as well as the north shore—agates, quartz, gemstones, crystals, geodes ... and also things made of rocks. There was something for everyone.

"I think this Lake Superior Agate is my favorite," Annika said as she held up a large, polished agate with radiant white and rust-colored stripes. It had been tumbled until the surface was smooth as silk.

"That was a good choice," Ruth told her. "You can play with it now, and when you're older you can use it on your desk as a paperweight."

"I don't have to wait until I'm older, Gram. I have a desk right now. It's used, but it's very nice. I kept using my mom's desk, so a couple of weeks ago she went to a garage sale and finally got me one of my very own. It even has a matching chair."

"That was a good idea," Ruth told her.

"Mom says school is my job. You know I get bonuses when I get A's?"

"I did that with your mom, too," Ruth said. "Your mom really liked those bonuses."

They rode on in silence for the next half hour or so ... past the little towns of Lutsen and Tofte ... past weathered cabins and stretches of lonely, pebbled beaches ... past the last vestiges of northern wildflowers—gold and white and bright blue—that dropped like splashes of paint in the tall weeds by the side of the road. Forested ridges, dark and thick, bordered their left window. Out of their right window was the immense lake. It seemed to go on forever as it glimmered behind mile after mile of birch, aspen, and spruce.

The sun was getting lower in the western sky. Long shadows from tall pines fell across the road. Annika gazed at the passing landscape. "This is so beautiful," she whispered, her eyes scanning back and forth between the woods on her left and the lake on her right. "Isn't it beautiful, Gram?"

"As many times as I have driven up here, this scenery has never failed to amaze me. I never tire of it. This is your first trip up the North Shore, isn't it?"

"I've never been this far north. Duluth is as far as Mom and Dad ever took me."

All of a sudden Annika again pointed to something she saw on the road ahead of them. "Gram, look at those people. Are they in trouble?"

Four people—two adults and two children—were standing next to a blue sedan. The car was pulled off on the shoulder, on the lake side of the road. As Ruth got closer, she saw a man staring into the open trunk of the car. A woman appeared to be ushering two children—a boy and a girl—away from the vehicle. Ruth slowed down and pulled off the highway in front of them.

"Having some trouble?" she said as she exited her car. Annika followed her.

Suddenly Annika yelled excitedly and ran up to the girl. "Andrea! What are you doing here?"

Both girls laughed and hugged each other.

"We're going up to Grand Marais to see my grandma," Andrea told her. "What are *you* doing up here?" They both laughed excitedly.

"I'm on a vacation with my grandma," Annika explained. "We're going to paint pictures of Lake Superior."

Ruth looked at the group. "You know this girl?" she asked her granddaughter.

"Yes! We were in a church thing together. You remember, Gram, when we packed those meals for the starving kids?"

The wife smiled as she stepped up. "Your granddaughter and my Andrea were buddies. They were in charge of the rice bags. They hit it off so well, I always meant to find time to get them together for a play-date. I just never got around to it. Maybe while we're up here they can get together?"

Ruth smiled at the woman. "I think we ought to. I think it's meant to be."

While the two girls were chatting away, Ruth looked at the man, who had stepped up closer to her.

"Thanks for stopping," he said with a smile. He was slender, dark-haired and slightly balding, wore wire-rimmed glasses, and he looked tired. "My left rear tire went flat and it seems I don't have my jack." He sighed. "You wouldn't happen to have one I could use, would you?"

"I'm sure I do," said Ruth. "Just a second, I'll get it." After a brief search, she returned with the jack she kept in her trunk. "Here, see if this will help." *I wonder why a man, traveling with his family, wouldn't have a jack in his trunk?* Ruth thought briefly, as she handed it over.

"Thank you! By the way, I'm Roy Foley," the man said as he took the jack. "This is my wife, Janet. And your granddaughter seems to already know our Andrea. And this is Norman, our son." He indicated the boy, who looked slightly younger than the girls. He was thin and dark-haired like his dad. He didn't look at Ruth, but stared out at the horizon. He was rocking back and forth, humming to himself.

The woman, who was plump, pretty, and blonde, put a protective arm on the boy's shoulder.

Andrea, a carbon copy of her mother, smiled. "Norman's special," she chirped. "He has autism. But we love him to pieces, don't we, Mama?"

The woman nodded and leaning over, kissed her daughter's forehead. "We love you to pieces too," she whispered.

"Did I hear you are going painting up in Grand Marais?" the man asked as he maneuvered the jack under the back of his car. "There's sure lots of beautiful scenery up there."

"Yes we are," Ruth answered. She was trying to keep from staring at the rocking boy, unlike Annika, who couldn't take her eyes off him. "I'm Ruth Mays, and I'm taking my granddaughter up for a little vacation. She's never been this far north. We're going to take the boat to Isle Royale tomorrow."

"That's a wonderful place," said the woman. Her daughter and Annika were looking at the rocks Annika had run back to the car to get.

"Are you staying in Grand Marais?" Ruth asked.

"Oh yes," said Janet. "The kids and I, we're going to stay at my mom's house. But Roy has to work. He'll be driving between here and Duluth every week."

The boy continued rocking and his mother touched him again, protectively.

Ruth looked at the woman more carefully. "Your name is Janet?" she asked. "You wouldn't happen to be Sally Merritt's daughter, would you?"

"Why yes." Janet smiled. "You know my mom?"

"We went to high school together," Ruth told her. "We weren't that close in high school, but we did have home economics together. The first time I came up here to paint, I ran into her by accident, and we went out to lunch and became reacquainted. We've had lunch a couple of times since then. I hope we can get together again, this time."

"She'd love that. And the kids and I just might join you."

"That would be great. And I know Annika would love it too." She saw the girls talking excitedly about the rocks.

Mr. Foley worked fast and soon replaced his tire with the spare he kept in his trunk. Wiping his hands on a rag, he handed the jack back to Ruth.

"So, you know Sally Merritt?" he asked Ruth. "Sally's a great lady. And thank you so much for being a Good Samaritan. I hope you and your granddaughter have a wonderful time up here."

"Yes, thank you!" echoed Janet as she dug a piece of paper out of her purse and wrote on it. "Here's my mom's phone number, in case you want to call her. Why don't we all get together as soon as you get back from Isle Royale?"

"Let's plan on it," Ruth said as she and Annika turned to leave.

As they were walking back to the car, Ruth stumbled over something.

"*Oof!*" she said as she almost fell. "What the … ?" Then she saw a hand sticking out from the weeds. "Oh my God!" she screamed, pushing Annika to the side.

"What is it, Grandma?"

"Get back in the car, honey, right now!" Ruth called to Roy Foley, "Mr. Foley! Please come over here quick! I think it's … a … a *body!*"

Chapter 2

The Body by the Beach

Roy Foley lifted some dried brush and leaves off the body of a young man.

Ruth told Annika to stay in the car.

"Is it a dead person?" Annika called from the car, her eyes round and frightened.

"I'm afraid so," her grandmother called back. Just then Ruth saw a white truck coming down the highway. She waved it down. A burly, ruddy-faced truck driver rolled down his window.

"You folks having difficulties?" asked the man, adjusting his glasses over a bulbous nose.

"Yes," Ruth told him. "Are you on your way to Grand Marais?"

He nodded. "Yup, I'm making a delivery to the hardware store. What's up?"

"We just found a body. It's over there, in the weeds." She pointed toward Roy, who stood staring into the nearby brush. "We need the police to come and look at this," Ruth asserted.

Janet took her kids to their car.

The truck driver jumped out of the truck (very agile for such a big man) and went to take a look.

"Geez, looks like he's been dead for a few days. Anybody know who it is?"

"We haven't a clue," Roy told him. "We pulled over to change a tire, and this lady here"—he indicated Ruth—"just found him."

"I'll call the sheriff's office on my CB. It'll probably take them twenty minutes to get here from Grand Marais."

The man climbed into his truck and made the call.

After a few minutes he rolled down his window and said, "I've got to be on my way, but they're comin'. Are you folks gonna stay here?"

"Yes, I think we had better stay until they come," Roy answered.

"Thank you so much for your help!" Ruth called out as the trucker began to drive off.

Ruth and Roy stepped away from the body and tried not to look at it.

Roy shook his head. "Not a great way to start your painting holiday."

"You're right, but it's always been a painter's paradise up here. Artist's Point is one of my favorite places. I've been here many times, and I know Annika will love it."

"I don't know much about art," Roy replied. "I sell industrial kitchen appliances to restaurants and food service operations. Stoves and coolers mostly. There's a new restaurant opening up in Grand Marais—a big fancy one, I'm told, right in the middle of town, by the wharves. Gonna bring in a lot of new tourist business."

"By the wharves?" said Ruth anxiously, hoping this new development wouldn't spoil the town's picturesque features.

"Yep. *Some*body up there has a lot of money. I'm on the road a lot, which is why I can't stay with Janet and the kids. Wish I could." He put his arm around his wife, who had left the kids in their car and come back to join them.

"I wonder if my mom knew him?" Janet said quietly.

"The new restaurant owner?" asked Ruth.

"No. The young man ... in the grass."

After about fifteen minutes or so, they heard a siren.

When the wailing car pulled up, two uniformed officers got out of a vehicle marked Cook County Sheriff. One was a tall, beefy older man, the other a young, slender, pony-tailed brunette.

"So, what's going on here?" the man asked Roy.

"We stopped here because I had a flat tire. But I couldn't change it because I didn't have a jack. This nice lady here stopped and lent me hers." He nodded toward Ruth. "And then, just by accident, she noticed a body in the bushes. It's over there." He pointed toward the spot.

"I'm Bob Norstrand, the sheriff. And this is my deputy, Roberta Norstrand ... also my daughter."

"I'm Roy Foley, and this is my family. Nice to meet you."

"Let's take a look at what you found." They walked over to where the body lay.

The younger officer put on a pair of rubber gloves, got down and brushed a few more leaves from the face of the body that lay on its back, its eyes staring vacantly into the air.

"It's him, Dad," she said quietly, looking down at the face and shaking her head. "We can quit searching. Let's call Coroner Morris."

Sheriff Norstrand walked back to his car, got on his radio, and instructed a dispatcher to contact the county coroner. "It's Joey-Frank Jurak," Ruth heard him say.

The younger deputy asked Ruth and the Foleys to stand aside as she began unspooling yellow crime-scene tape around the area.

"You know who this is?" Ruth asked the deputy.

"His name is Joey-Frank Jurak," she answered. "We've been looking for him. His sister reported him missing when he didn't come home from work two nights ago."

"How do you think he died? Is this a murder?" Ruth asked the deputy.

"Don't know yet. That's for the coroner to find out."

"But he was all covered up with brush," Ruth retorted. "Someone must have done that after he died."

"What?" Sheriff Norstrand said as he rejoined the onlookers. He looked sharply at Ruth. "He was covered? Who uncovered him? Don't you know you're not supposed to tamper with a crime scene?"

"I'm sorry," Roy Foley told him. "I'm afraid I pushed brush off the body." He shifted uncomfortably. "I had to see what it was ..." His voice trailed off.

"Well, that sure changes things," the elder Norstrand sighed as he lifted his cap and ran his hand through a thick gray mane of hair.

"Murder," his daughter said, more to herself than to anyone else. "Way up here. First all the drugs ... and now murder. What next?"

"*Drugs?*" said Ruth.

The sheriff shot a stern glance at his young deputy, who said nothing more.

After giving their statements and telling the officers where they were staying in Grand Marais, the sheriff smiled and told Janet, "I know your mom. She's a real good lady."

Ruth and Roy then pulled their vehicles back onto the road and continued northward toward Grand Marais. The sky had turned gray and Lake Superior began to look cold and unwelcoming. Ruth switched her headlights on and watched carefully for darting deer. Annika was quiet. Ruth wondered how she should try to explain what had just happened, but it was the girl who spoke first.

"Gram, I heard that lady policeman say something about drugs. Do you think that dead man was a druggie ... or a *dealer?*"

"Who knows?" Ruth answered uneasily. She didn't want to say the word *murder* to a ten-year-old.

They drove in silence until Annika continued processing what had just transpired. "Is Andrea's brother retarded? Oops! I mean, *mentally challenged?* That's what our teacher says instead."

Ruth answered carefully. "Well, she said he's autistic. The fact that he moved like he did tells me he probably is, because that's what autistic people sometimes do ... rock back and forth. It's a brain thing, honey. They can't help it, and I don't really understand it.

"Doesn't he ever stop rocking? Does he talk?" Annika wanted to know.

"Well, I suppose he stops rocking when he gets tired," Ruth told her. "And many autistic people talk, but I don't know whether Norman talks."

"But why?" Annika wanted to know. "Why is he that way?"

"I don't know, sweetheart. When something like autism happens to people, they're usually born with it. Autism is kind of a mystery. Some people with autism rock back and forth like that boy. Some of them are very normal-acting. And some are quite gifted in a certain area, like playing the piano, or doing math. I don't think anyone really understands what causes autism. Like I said, it's a 'brain thing.' Kind of a mystery."

Annika gazed out at the passing scenery. "I wonder if that boy does something special?"

Ruth looked over at her and said, "Maybe. I hope it's something really good."

Annika nodded. "Me too."

Chapter 3

Welcome to Grand Marais

As Ruth drove over the hill on the edge of town, she wanted to make their entrance into Grand Marais a happy experience.

"Watch now. Right after this hill," she said. "It's coming right up ... there it is ... Grand Marais!"

As their car began its gradual descent into town, Annika got her first glimpse of their destination, nestled snugly against the backdrop of Lake Superior and the green, sometimes rocky surrounding hills. The quaint harbor came into view. Some sailboats bobbed in the dark and choppy water. Ruth always felt good at this terminal point in her drive north, not only because the long trip was finally over, but because she so loved the little town itself.

"But it looks so small," Annika said with a hint of disappointment. She strained forward in the seat, pulling against the seat belt to get a better view. "Is this it? There's not much here, is there, Gram."

Ruth laughed. "All right, city girl, be patient. Grand Marais is a wonderful little town! You'll see more of it tomorrow."

She drove past the campgrounds, past the old fishing shacks, past the marina, past the bear cubs statue, and onto a "Main Street" (actually Wisconsin Street) lined with simple but colorful buildings, such as the World's Best Donuts bakery with its brightly painted signage and gingerbread trim. They pulled into a small parking lot adjacent to the East Bay Inn.

"We'll leave our bags in the car," Ruth said. "It's getting late. Let's check in first."

The inn, which anchored the east end of town, was built in the 1920s right next to the lake. They walked up a couple of steps and entered an enclosed porch with large windows on three sides. The porch contained two comfy white wicker lounge chairs with brown pillows, and a little white wicker table displaying a half-completed jigsaw puzzle. An elderly brown lab lay on a colorful rag rug near the table. He thumped his tail in welcome.

From the porch they stepped into a small lobby with a blue sofa in front of a bay window next to the main entrance. To their right was a stairway that went to the rooms upstairs and a hallway to some rooms on first floor. In front of them was a large dark wood counter, along with a display of brochures. In back of that was a hallway that led to the dining room.

From the large counter, Loris Biederman's curly gray head was looking up at them and staring. Her family had owned the hotel for as long as Ruth could remember.

"Mrs. Carson! I mean, *Mrs. Mays.* You're here." The woman shook her head. "I'll have to get used to your new name. How was your trip up?" Then, as if realizing there was someone with Ruth, she said, "And who is this young lady?"

"This is Annika Lindstrom, my granddaughter—Hannah's daughter," Ruth said.

"Oh, my." Mrs. Biederman put her hand over her heart. "Your Hannah has one that old?" She pointed to Annika's long blonde braids and exclaimed, "Of course she's Hannah's girl. She looks just like her mama did at that age."

Ruth answered her, "Yes, she does, doesn't she? And my 'little Hannah' is all grown up now. Robbie is too. So, how are you? How's your family?" *I wonder if she feels okay,* Ruth thought. *She looks 'off,' as if she's not feeling well.* Ruth reached over the desk to pat her hand and try to put her at ease, but Loris just started and moved backwards, out of Ruth's reach.

"Oh we're fine, all of us are … just … fine …" Loris looked up at the old pendulum clock on the wall, which signified 7:30. "I thought you'd be here by suppertime. What happened? Did you get a late start?" The woman looked addled.

Ruth began explaining about the young man found dead by the side of the road to an obviously upset Mrs. Biederman. Annika, sensitive to the fact that her Gram was talking "adult talk," returned to the entrance porch and fiddled with the unfinished puzzle. Seeing her, the lab thumped his tale again, without moving his body. Annika reached down and patted his head.

After Ruth described what had happened at the side of the road, Mrs. Biederman just looked horrified.

"Joey-Frank? I knew him," she told Ruth. "He used to hang around my eldest daughter, Pam." She shook her head as if to get rid of the memories. "I was glad when she broke up with him. The guy was just plain no good." Then Loris asked Ruth if they wanted supper because the kitchen was about to close.

"Thank you, we do, if it's okay," Ruth told her. "I know we're late, so maybe I can just get our bags and leave them here? Ruth indicated a space near the front desk. Then she poked her head into the porch where Annika was working intently on the puzzle.

"Annika, why don't you go into the dining room and find us a table?"

"It's right through those doors there," said Mrs. Biederman. She pointed to a hallway to her left as the girl re-entered the lobby. "Tell them I said it was okay for you and your grandma to ... uh ... to go in and order something to eat."

Something's definitely off, thought Ruth.

Annika paused to look at a large painting of an old church before walking into the dining room, where she stopped in her tracks, embarrassed. A waitress with long dark hair pinned high on her head was having an argument with a rough looking young man in a leather jacket. Annika could see the girl was pretty. She could also see the young man's hand on the girls' hip, and that he was pulling her towards him, as she was pushing him away.

"Get out of here!" she hissed. "I broke up with Joey-Frank weeks ago, but that doesn't mean I'll go out with *you*. And I certainly don't owe you any money! I don't care what Joey-Frank owed you." She glanced back at the kitchen. "And how did you get in here, anyway? The back door is supposed to be locked!"

Annika quickly turned and went back into the lobby. "I think I'll wait for my grandma out here," she told Loris.

"Suit yourself," Loris Biederman told the girl. "I'll just buzz the kitchen and let them know there will be two more people for supper tonight."

When Ruth entered the lobby with their luggage and painting gear, she was helped by a tall older man with a shock of white hair and a muscular build.

"Thank you so much for your help, Mr. ... Mr. ... ?"

"Haakala. Arvid Haakala," the man replied in a thick Iron Range accent. "Glad to be of help."

"Thank you, Arvid," Loris added. She turned to Ruth. "Ruth, this is Arvid, a friend of ours. Arvid, meet Ruth Carson ... ah ... I mean, Ruth *Mays*. As a matter of fact, why don't you just cart all their stuff down to room 101? We need to get them into the dining room before the kitchen closes up."

"No problem. Nice to meet you, uh ... Mrs. Mays," the man said with a nod and a shy smile to Ruth, who nodded and smiled back.

"Thank you so much," she responded.

He picked up all the suitcases and bags and started down the hall.

Ruth got her purse, and turned to Loris. "Should I"—she whispered—"tip him?"

Loris snorted. "Oh God, no, he'd be so embarrassed. He's Arnie's best friend and helps out from time to time. And believe me, we pay him plenty!"

Just then, a white-faced Janet Foley charged into the East Bay lobby, followed by her husband Roy and a frightened-looking Andrea pulling a reluctant Norman. Janet's long blonde hair had come loose from its bun. She was obviously distraught.

Loris Biederman looked surprised.

"My mother's house has been broken into," she rasped, "and she's not there! She's gone! And her phone was off the hook!"

"You're Sally Merritt's daughter, aren't you?"

"Oh, I'm sorry, yes. My mom is missing. We came here to visit her for a few days and when we went to the house it was wide open and her living room looks as if someone ransacked it! We called the police, and they said they would come and take a look. I know you two were good friends, so I thought ... I thought maybe you might know where she is."

Loris didn't seem worried, much to Janet Foley's consternation.

"Well, I'm pretty sure I know where she is." She leaned across the wooden counter. "And you don't need to worry. Tonight's the big dress rehearsal for our Grand Marais little theatre production. Sally's probably up at the old church where they're doing the show. She made all the costumes for it. They're doing *Carousel,* and it wasn't easy. I know she's been scrambling to get everything done by tonight. I'm not surprised if her house looks like a tornado hit it."

"What?" Janet snapped, throwing up her arms. "Costumes? Some play? She never mentioned anything to me."

"Maybe we should go up to the old church and see if we can find her," Roy said quietly, attempting to calm his distraught wife. He turned to Loris. "Thanks for letting us know what Mom is up to. We really had no idea."

"No problem. I don't think there is anything to be concerned about," Loris said with a reassuring smile. "It's just up the hill—the old Lutheran church, near the art center. Janet, you remember where it is, don't you?" Loris looked again at the wall clock. "They'll probably be there until late tonight. It's quarter-to-eight now. I can just about guarantee that's where she is. She'll be fitting costumes."

Loris caught Ruth's attention and rolled her eyes as they watched the Foley family exit the hotel and head back to their car. Roy seemed to be talking softly while Janet, still obviously upset, was gesturing excitedly with her hands.

I hope those poor kids get their supper tonight, Ruth thought.

Chapter 4

Where Is Sally Merritt?

LORIS TURNED TO RUTH and said, "That Sally, she's really something. How a woman that age can do all the things she does is beyond me. Like agreeing to make all the costumes for this town's community theatre. I used to do it. Did it for several years. But the job kept getting bigger and bigger and I couldn't keep up. I heard it's a really big production this summer. Everybody involved is a volunteer, you know."

"I know what you mean," Ruth interjected. "I've done just a few costumes for our summer theatre productions in St. Paul, and it's a lot of work. Sounds like your town lucked out when your friend agreed to do it."

"Hmph! On top of that she juggles two, maybe three, men. She's got both Arvid and our esteemed sheriff at her beck and call. And who knows who else she's got on her hook?" Loris Biederman lowered her voice to a whisper. "That woman can put a spell on any man she gets near. We used to be pretty tight, Sally and I, but we don't see each other as much anymore. I guess we don't agree on, let's see, um ... certain moral areas, if you know what I mean?" The woman looked down at

her wedding ring, then back up at Ruth. "I'll say this for her, though: wherever she gets her energy, I sure wish I had a little of it!" She laughed ruefully. "She's almost as old as I am, but you'd never know it from the way she acts!"

Ruth pursed her lips and looked at the woman, and then at Annika, as if to tell Loris that this sort of conversation was not appropriate for a child to hear. She decided to change course.

"So, when is opening night?" Ruth looked over at her granddaughter, who was now sitting on the floor getting better acquainted with the Biederman's chocolate lab, 'Odie.'

"It opens tomorrow night at 7:30—up at the old Lutheran church on Maple Street. You remember, don't you? They converted it several years ago into a little theatre? It's small, but we're a small town." She gave Ruth a flyer from a stack she kept on the registration desk. "Ten dollars for adults and five for kids under sixteen. That's a bargain if you ask me."

"It certainly is," Ruth said as she looked at the hand-lettered flyer. "I've always loved that musical. My daughter Hannah and I were in it together. We sang in the chorus of that community theatre group in St. Paul. That's the one I sewed costumes for. We performed in the summer, in a big pavilion on Como Lake."

"Well, you know how much work that kind of thing is, then," said Loris. "Say, we'd better get you some supper. The kitchen staff usually starts closing down this time of night."

Loris led Ruth and Annika down a short hallway to the dining room. She pushed a side door open for them. "If you'd like, you can use my own private bathroom to wash your hands first."

"Thanks," said Ruth. She let Annika go in before her. "I always thought this was a closet."

"It used to be a coat closet but, as I got older, I needed a bathroom nearer the front desk, so Arnie made it into a 'water closet.'" She grinned at her own pun.

When Ruth and Annika entered the dining room, it was empty except for the waitress, who was sitting at a table near the kitchen, counting the day's receipts. The woman looked up with a visible sigh.

Ruth ushered her granddaughter to a table with a white table-cloth by a window with a commanding view of Lake Superior. The sun was low in the sky, and the lake glistened.

The waitress rose slowly from her seat and took their orders—wild rice soup for Ruth and a grilled cheese sandwich with french fries for Annika. Ruth apologized to the waitress for being so late.

"Gram!" Annika whispered after the woman disappeared into the kitchen with their orders.

"What is it, sweetie?"

"That waitress was fighting with a guy when I came in here before. A mean, bad-looking guy who was trying to make her his girlfriend. Or get money from her. I couldn't tell which." She made a face. "That's why I came back in the lobby to wait for you."

Ruth grimaced. "Well, don't get involved."

"I wouldn't, no way." Then Annika changed the subject. "Don't forget to call Mom and Dad and tell them we got here."

"Oh, I completely forgot!" Ruth exclaimed. "Thank you for reminding me. Let's do it right now." When the waitress returned with two glasses of pop, Ruth said to her, "We need to make a quick phone call. But we'll be right back to eat."

The waitress nodded and gave them their beverages.

Loris let Ruth place a collect call to Annika's parents from a phone at the front desk. They had been waiting for the call. Ruth explained how they had stopped to help a young family with car trouble and got to the hotel later than planned. (She didn't tell them about the body.) Then she passed the phone to Annika. "Your mom wants to say good-night."

Annika, who had picked up on her grandmother's stark omission, went along with it.

"Mom!" she gushed, "Lake Superior is awesome! ... Uh huh ... Okay ... Yeah ... Yeah ... We're going out on a boat tomorrow to this big island. Sure ... Of course I'll stay with grandma the whole time ... *Mom*, it's not like I'm some little kid! ... I know ... okay ... yeah ... I love you too ... love Dad, too ... Okay ... yeah ... I will ... Bye!"

The girl rolled her eyes at Ruth. "Mom is such a worry-wart!"

"Your mom loves you so much," Ruth told the girl. "I'm sure she's already missing you."

"I know." Annika made a face. "But geez! She acts like I'm going to fall off the boat or get lost on the island or something. I'm smarter than that."

Ruth hurriedly placed her next collect call to Del's hotel room in Boston, but there was no answer. "Grandpa Del is probably in rehearsal," she said to Annika. "I'm sure he'll call me back in our room later tonight." Ruth wished she could have reached him. *I miss that man already,* she thought.

Their food had arrived by the time they returned to their table. While they ate, Ruth told the girl about the Grand Marais Little Theatre.

"They put on all their plays in an old church that isn't used as a church anymore," she explained. "We can walk there from the hotel. Grandpa Tom and I went to a couple of plays there. They were so much fun!" Ruth smiled at the memory.

"What's this one about?" Annika asked, munching on her french fries.

"Well ..." Ruth hesitated as she tried to think about how best to describe Rodgers and Hammerstein's *Carousel* to a ten-year-old. "Um ... let's see now. This young woman falls in love with a man who works at a carousel, which is another name for a merry-go-round."

"I know what a carousel is. There's one at the State Fair."

"That's right! It's like the one at the State Fair. Anyway, the girl runs away with him and marries him."

"Marries him!" said Annika, who apparently thought that was a dumb thing to do. "Does she even know this guy?"

"Uh ... not very well. And then he gets into trouble and dies. But they have a daughter. And when she's a teenager, *she* gets in trouble. She's sort of like her dad."

"Does she die?" Annika asked, more interested.

"No, she lives. But the dad—who really has a good heart—comes back to earth as a ... a kind of angel. Who can only be seen by his daughter. And, um ... he helps her." Ruth laughed a little nervously. "Not a very upbeat story, is it."

"But it's got angels and dead people," said Annika. "That's a start. So, the girl's dad comes back from the dead to help her? What happens to the girl's mom? Does the mom get to see him too?"

"At the very end," Ruth told her, "the mom sort of knows he's there because she can 'feel' his presence." Ruth broke the hard roll that had come with her soup. "And then he goes back to Heaven. Actually, it's a very touching story, and the music is beautiful!"

"Sounds dorky." Annika wiped her mouth with her napkin. "And the woman shouldn't marry a guy she just met. But I'll go to it with you—to keep you company," she added with a grin.

Just then, Sheriff Robert Norstrand and his deputy, Roberta, came into the dining room. Loris was with them as they headed straight for Ruth's table. Ruth felt her stomach lurch.

"Sorry to bother you, ma'am," said the elder Norstrand, "but we need to talk with you." He glanced at Annika. "Privately, if you don't mind. It'll just take a minute."

"Yes, of course," said Ruth. "Excuse me, sweetie," she said to Annika as she got up from the table. "I'll be right back." *What now?* she thought, as she followed them all out into the hall.

The elder officer looked to his daughter and she started to explain.

"We found another body," the young woman said very softly. "Janet Foley—the woman you met on the road today—had called earlier and asked us to check on her mother. We went to her house up by the old church to look around. We found a body in the garage, hidden behind the garbage cans."

"Was it Sally Merritt?" Ruth's question hung in the air, unanswered. Loris Biederman looked at the policemen with horrified eyes.

"Mrs. Mays, do you have any idea where the Foleys are now?" Sheriff Norstrand asked. "They weren't where they said they would be staying and ... uh, we really need to talk with them right away. Since you were with them this afternoon, we thought maybe you might know where they could be."

Loris blurted out, "They were just here! At the hotel! Less than an hour ago. They were looking for Sally, and thought I might know where to find her. I sent 'em up to the old church. Sally's supposed to be doing costumes for the show up there. Oh my God! It's Sally isn't it?"

The elder Norstrand nodded.

Loris went on, "Janet was really upset, and I sent them up to the theatre and told them not to worry. Oh, God! How terrible!" She reached out and lightly touched the sheriff's arm. He had removed his glasses and was wiping his eyes. His deputy reached over and gently took hold of his other arm.

"Dad, come on," she whispered. "Get it together. We've got work to do."

Ruth could see the effort it took for the older man to stand there and compose himself.

"I'm okay," he whispered to his daughter. "Just give me a minute." He turned to Ruth. "Sorry," he said. "After my wife died, well, Sally ... well, she became a special friend." He shook his head from side to side as if trying to understand what had taken place.

Roberta Norstrand put her arm around her father's shoulders again, with some difficulty because he was such a large man. The elder Norstrand leaned into the hug.

"Dad, come on," she said in a low voice that had begun to sound impatient, "this isn't the time or place. We need to find Janet and Roy. And anyway"—the girl lowered her voice even more—"she wasn't worth it, Dad. You *know* that."

Then the young deputy became all *business* again, turning to Ruth and Loris. "Thank you so much for your help. I'm sure we'll find the Foleys up at the theatre. And please don't mention this to anyone else yet. We probably shouldn't have given you the name of the deceased. It just sort of slipped out. We don't want the Foleys to hear about it before we've had a chance to break the news to them. I'm sure you understand?"

Ruth and Loris nodded. They were both speechless and in shock.

The sheriff's daughter took her father by the arm and guided him out through the lobby and toward the front door of the East Bay Inn. "Thank you again," she called back as they exited.

Ruth and Loris just stared at each other, stunned by what they had just learned.

"This is like a bad dream," Loris whispered. "You go in and finish your supper. I'll catch up with you later." Ruth watched her walk unsteadily back to her desk.

Ruth couldn't believe what had just happened. She was surprised and saddened by the news of the death of her high school friend, and she felt so sorry for Janet and her family. She was also very surprised to see the sheriff's reaction. And even more at his daughter's slip-of-the-tongue comment. *She's not worth it, Dad? What was* that *about? I think there's more to this story than meets the eye—that's for sure.* Then she realized Janet Foley was right to be worried after all.

She must have suspected that her mother was in some kind of danger. It was not just an over-reaction to finding her not home and a messy living room! Somehow, Janet must have known something was terribly wrong!

Ruth returned to the dining room. *I can't lie to Annika,* she thought ruefully.

"Why did the police want to talk to you?" Annika immediately asked.

"It turns out there's another body," Ruth whispered. "An older woman found in her garage."

Annika's eyes grew wide. "Gram, that's awful! But why did the police want to talk to *you*? Do they think you knew her?"

"Yes, I did know her." Ruth looked down at her lap. "It was Sally Merritt, your friend's grandma." *So much for my promise to the police.*

"Poor Andrea!" said Annika, putting a hand over her mouth.

"I guess the Foleys were up at the church, and the sheriff thought I might know where to find them." Ruth sighed. "Let's not talk to anyone about this, okay? I wasn't even supposed to tell you."

Annika's mouth turned into a grim line. Her blue eyes narrowed as she looked solemnly at Ruth and asked, "Are we going to have the same trouble that you had last summer in Como Park?"

Ruth was aghast. "What? How do you know about that!"

"Duh ... I know about it, Gram."

"B-but you were out of the country, in Sweden!" Ruth stammered.

"Mom and dad were talking about it, and I asked them to tell me about it too." She looked up proudly. "They don't keep much from me. Mom says I have a very grown-up attitude about stuff."

Ruth didn't quite know what more to say to this, except, "Yes, I suppose I shouldn't be surprised that you found out—since Grandpa

Del and I were in the middle of it all. It was pretty scary, and really big news when they found out who did it."

"I sure hope we're not gonna get mixed up in this kind of stuff while we're in Grand Marais," Annika warned. She picked up two french fries from her plate. "No 'bloody fingers' this time," she stated as she silently dipped the fries in ketchup and popped them into her mouth, her eyes never leaving Ruth's face.

Ruth recalled when she had taken Annika and her mom to McDonald's after a day of shopping. It was right before Halloween and Ruth had dipped her fries in ketchup and waved them in front of her, whispering, "Bloody fingers! Bloody fingers!"

Annika, with squeals of laughter, had immediately followed suit, dipping her own fries, and yelling, "Bloody fingers! Bloody Fingers!"

Her mom had groaned and said, "Here we are, trying to teach good table manners and her grandmother acts worse than a kid!"

Ruth remembered that day as she placed her hand on Annika's. "No, honey, I won't get mixed up in anything like that here in Grand Marais. That'll never happen again." She gave Annika's hand a squeeze as if to seal the promise.

"Mom told me to take very good care of you," Annika informed her grandmother solemnly. "I think that means *no murders!*"

"You bet! No murders!" Ruth asserted. "Maybe we shouldn't even go up to the play."

"No," insisted Annika, "I still wanna see that play, even if it's dorky. We can't watch TV every night. What was it called?"

"*Carousel*. And yes, of course, we can go see it if you'd like." *I sure hope they can get someone to take their costumer's place.* "Are we finished here?" She managed another smile.

Annika wiped her mouth on her napkin. "I'm really sorry about Andrea and her brother's grandma. Grandmas are important in a kid's life."

Ruth got a little choked up as she looked at her granddaughter. "Thank you, sweetie. And grandkids are really important too. In a grown-up's life."

Chapter 5

A Midnight Picnic

"I'M DONE." ANNIKA BRUSHED some crumbs from the front of her shirt. "Do you think I could take these rolls back to our room?" She pointed at the two uneaten homemade rolls lying in the basket that came with Ruth's soup. "I might want a snack later."

"Of course," Ruth told her. "We'll get a doggie bag. And take some of those little peanut butter containers too, to go with the rolls."

"What will we use for a knife?" the girl asked and then quickly answered her own question. "Oh, I know—a palette knife!"

Doggy bag in hand, they left the dining room and headed down the back hall, for room 101.

There were only two guest rooms on the first floor of the East Bay and both looked out on the lake. They were larger than the other rooms, and more expensive, but Ruth didn't mind the added cost. She wanted to hear the waves wash against the shore at night.

They always lull me to sleep, she thought.

As they passed room 102, Ruth noticed the door was open and that it looked empty.

"I think we're the only guests staying on the first floor," she said.

"Cool," was Annika's reply, and then she yawned a big yawn.

"Let's get washed up and into our jammies right away," Ruth said as she unlocked the door. "We can watch television or read until we're ready to fall asleep."

Annika yawned again.

The room was cheerful and spotlessly clean, with off-white wallpaper and a ceiling border of birch trees and sky. The floor was wooden. A blue rug matched the curtains. Once inside, Ruth locked the door and secured the chain.

I'm sure Annika and I are safe up here in Grand Marais.

Annika came alive when she saw their room.

"Wow, Gram! Look at the beds! They look like they're made of logs." The girl ran her hands over the rustic headboards. "I want this one!" she shouted as she made a running jump for the bed nearest the large window that looked out over Lake Superior.

Ruth pulled the curtains shut as Annika flopped on top of the blue flowered bedspread and spread her arms and legs. Ruth thought she looked like "Heidi," lying in a field of blue corn-flowers. "We can take showers in the morning if you want. I'm just going to wash my hands and face and brush my teeth."

By now, the girl had jumped off the bed and was trying to get something on the television. "Do you think they have cable? We had cable all the time, in Sweden." She scrolled through several channels and finally settled on an old science fiction movie. "I think I'll have one of those rolls now," she said as she retrieved the tin-foil packet they had brought from the dining room. Then she rummaged through her knapsack and found a palette knife to spread peanut butter on the rolls.

"Let's wash that first," Ruth suggested, and soon Annika was sitting on the bed with her legs crossed, eagerly devouring one of the rolls.

"This is like a midnight picnic!" Annika laughed blissfully, licking peanut butter from her fingers.

Ruth smiled at her.

How the young bounce back. Nothing seems to bother them for very long.

"Do you want the other one, Gram?"

"No thanks, sweetie. You go ahead and eat it. I'm getting ready for bed."

Ruth brushed and flossed her teeth, brushed her hair, and peered at a 63-year-old face in the mirror. The face that peered back had slightly wavy, shoulder-length hair. It was blonde with only a hint of gray. The cheeks were rosy and unlined. *I think I look younger than my age, but I look tired. And I'm lonesome for Del.* She shed her "day clothes"—a jeans skirt and blue plaid blouse—and donned a long pink flannel nightgown. Ruth was trying hard not to think about the day's events. *Two bodies. Two!* She shivered. *I hope Annika and I will be safe up here.*

By the time Ruth finished washing-up, Annika had changed into her Barbie jammies and was snuggled under the covers. The rolls and peanut butter were gone. The television was turned off.

"Don't get too comfortable," Ruth chided. "You need to brush your teeth!"

"Tomorrow. I'm too tired tonight." The girl yawned.

"No. Now. You want to keep those beautiful teeth, don't you?"

"Okaaay," she told her grandmother. "You sound just like Mom." Annika crawled out of bed and headed for the bathroom. Ruth could hear the water run and the toilet flush. Then more water running. When she came out she kissed Ruth goodnight. Ruth could smell peppermint toothpaste on her breath.

"Good girl," she said with a hug. "Sleep tight, honey-bunny." It was a pet name that Ruth had given her since infancy.

"You too, Gram," Annika answered with another yawn. Then she looked up at her grandma and said, "I feel so bad for Andrea ..."

Ruth kissed her forehead, and patted her cheek. "You're a good friend."

Soon Ruth saw the girl close her eyes, and within minutes she was sleeping soundly.

Ruth felt exhausted. But after all that had happened, she couldn't relax enough to fall asleep. Del hadn't called back. That bothered her. She knew he could be in rehearsal until late, but she couldn't for the life of her remember the difference between Boston time and Minnesota time.

I'll ask Annika, tomorrow. She'll know.

Then Ruth's thoughts turned again to the two deaths. She tried putting them out of her mind, but the image of that young man's pale hand kept intruding. When she closed her eyes she could still see him—his lifeless body obscured by weeds and grass just off the side of the road.

Who was Joey-Frank Jurak? What kind of person was he? And did he know Sally Merritt? Is there some connection to their murders? And ... were these murders? They must have been. And poor Sally—those kids' grandmother, of all things! Apparently Sally had been seeing both the sheriff and ... what was his name? That nice man who helped me at the hotel? Arvid ... Arvid Haakala? I wonder if those two men knew about each other. I wonder if one of them was angry and jealous enough to ... to kill her!

Ruth shivered as she got into her bed and pulled the covers over herself.

But they both seem like such nice men! But ... I guess you never can tell about people ... when there's a love triangle. And Sally Merritt is dead. My old high school friend ... murdered?

Ruth squeezed her eyes shut.

And what about this Joey-Frank? What's the connection? God, I've got to stop thinking about all of this. It's too terrible. Go to sleep, Ruth. Go to sleep. Tomorrow we're going to Isle Royale, and we're going to have a wonderful day. And maybe ... maybe we'll have supper at that new fancy restaurant Mr. Foley told us about ...

After tossing and turning for a long time, Ruth finally let go of all her dark thoughts and concentrated instead on the rhythmic sound of Lake Superior's waves, just outside her window, as they washed gently over a shoreline of smooth pebbles. Coming in ... going out ... coming in ... going out ... coming in ... going out ... coming in ... until she finally drifted off to sleep.

Chapter 6

Just a Little Favor

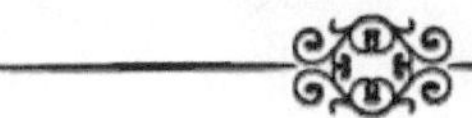

ANNIKA WAS FIRST TO wake the next morning. Seeing that her grandmother was still sleeping soundly, she wrote a note, left it on the chair near Ruth's bed, quietly slipped on her clothes and left the room. About twenty minutes later Ruth woke with a start, looked over at Annika's empty bed and called her name.

"Annika? Annika! Are you in the bathroom?"

Annika was not in the room. In a panic, Ruth hurriedly threw on her navy-blue sweatpants and sweatshirt and ran out into the hall just as Arvid Haakala was opening the door to the room next to hers.

"Mr. Haakala," Ruth was so upset she could hardly catch her breath. "Have you seen my granddaughter? She has long blonde braids, about so tall?" She indicated Annika's height with her hand.

"No, Mrs. Mays, I'm sorry. I just got here. But have you tried the dining room?"

"Not yet. Thanks, I'll do that."

Ruth hurried down the hall to the dining room and there was Annika, dressed in jeans and a pale-green sweatshirt with a Girl Scouts logo, sitting by a window. In front of her was a stack of blueberry pancakes swimming in maple syrup.

"Annika Marie Lindstrom, for God's sake," Ruth whispered anxiously to the girl. "Don't frighten me like this! Please don't leave the room without letting me know where you're going." She sat down across from her and let out an audible sigh.

"I left a note," the girl said, after swallowing a forkful of pancakes.

Ruth stiffened. "I didn't see any note!"

"I'm sorry, Gram. I didn't think you'd mind as long as I stayed in the hotel ... and you were really sawing logs. I left it on the chair by your bed."

"Sweetie, I do mind." Ruth was calmer now. "It's not like in the old days when your mom and your Uncle Robbie and Grandpa Tom and I were up here. Back then it was safer."

"'Things are different today,' I know," replied the ten-year-old. "My mom says the same thing. "'Things are different today.'" She mimicked her mom. "But Gram, I'm more grown-up now than you and my mom were at my age. Why can't I have a little freedom now and then?"

"I'm sorry, honey. I know you want to act grown-up. But when I'm responsible for you, I need to always know where you are and what you're doing. It's just the way things have to be while we're up here, okay?" Ruth was trying not to let the other guests overhear her impassioned plea. She picked up a plastic-coated menu so she could focus on that, and not on her fears for Annika's safety. She looked up with tears in her eyes. "I don't know what I'd do if anything happened to you!"

"Okay, Gram. I'm sorry I snuck out. I won't do it again. I promise."

"Thank you, honey," Ruth told her.

Just then the waitress came in and hurried to a table on the other side of the room. Ruth watched as the girl took the man's order for coffee. She noticed a stiffness of manner in the girl. She was acting as if she didn't want to take the man's order. And the man—dressed in a black leather sports coat—looked like some kind of gangster. He was leaning back in his chair, and he seemed to be leering suggestively at the girl.

No wonder she doesn't want to wait on him, Ruth thought. *He kind of looks like a creep.* The man, who had to be at least fifty, and way too old for the waitress, pushed his graying hair back from his face and then, as if he'd read her thoughts, looked intensely toward Ruth and Annika. Ruth quickly averted her eyes and studied her menu.

The waitress hurried over to Ruth.

"Your granddaughter's got a head start on you," the young woman said with a genuine smile, as she gave Ruth a glass of water. "What'll it be?"

Ruth looked at the pancakes on Annika's plate, swimming in blueberry syrup. "Those look awfully good, but I think I'll have a cheese omelet, with cheddar. Also, do I know you? You look so familiar."

"I'm Pam, Loris and Arnie's girl," she replied. Then she gestured at Annika. "I remember your daughter, Hannah. This has got to be her kid 'cause she looks just like her."

"Oh my gosh, *Pam!*" exclaimed Ruth, embarrassed that she hadn't recognized her. "Pam Biederman! Yes, this is Hannah's girl. She'll be painting with me while we're up here. This is her first time in Grand Marais. So, how are you?"

"I'm okay," Pam blurted out. "I like helping out my parents ... sometimes ..." She glanced briefly at the man.

"So, what else are you doing to keep yourself busy? Other than helping out here?" Ruth inquired.

"I teach high school math during the year," she told Ruth.

"How wonderful! Right here in town?"

"Yup. Right here in town." Pam looked uneasily around the dining room. "Sometimes I get my own students or their ah ... friends, in here as customers. That can get a little, um, weird." She glanced at the man again. "But ya know, my folks need the extra help in the summer, so I guess it works out. And hey, money is money, right?"

"It doesn't hurt to show your students some good work ethic and old-fashioned family loyalty," Ruth assured Pam. "I think it's a wonderful example for them."

"Well," she sighed uncomfortably, "that's one way to look at it, I suppose." Pam again gazed around the dining room. Then she lowered her voice. "But, to be honest, I'd rather not have my students or their cohorts as customers. The lines get blurred—especially with some people." She shook her head. "Sometimes it gets downright ... unpleasant."

"I'm sure you handle it with grace."

Pam just shrugged and tucked her hair behind her ear. "So, do you want anything with your omelet?"

"A cup of English breakfast tea would be nice, and perhaps some unbuttered rye toast?"

As Pam hurried off to put in Ruth's order, Ruth wondered *What was that all about? Something pretty serious must have happened between Pam and that man to make her that nervous.* And then she thought, *Oh well, it's a small town, and I don't think I'd want my students or some other people as customers, either. Boundaries probably do get blurred.*

She glanced over and noticed the man as he clunked his coffee cup down, put a bill near it but just sat there, looking speculatively around the room. *It looks as if he's 'casing the joint,' as my father used to say,* thought Ruth. *I wonder if he's one of the 'unpleasant' ones.*

Just then Annika piped up, interrupting Ruth's thoughts. "Gram, are we still going to that island today? When do we leave? Do we have time to also walk out to that art place—the place where you said that the artists go to paint?"

"You mean Artist's Point?" Ruth smiled. "I guess it is kind of an 'art place.' It's a popular spot just up the shore from here where artists like to paint the lake and the rocks and trees. But I don't think we'll have time for it today. We'll go there tomorrow." She looked at her watch. "We have to finish our breakfast now, and drive up to Grand Portage. That's where we catch the boat out to Isle Royale."

"But I wanted to go out there today," Annika grumbled.

"Oh, sweetie, I promise you, this week we'll have plenty of time to go out there and paint the scenery. But today we'll be spending our time on the water and on that island, which is really quite beautiful. And you can take your sketchbook, if you'd like."

Annika looked wistfully at the vast blue lake that glimmered on the other side of their dining room window. "My mom did this neat painting of Artist's Point when she was about my age. She has it in her office. I want to paint one just like it."

Ruth looked lovingly at the girl. "Are we getting a little home-sick?"

"Maybe a little. My dad said I might. He said I'd probably miss my cat." She smiled at that.

"Don't you miss your cat?" Ruth asked her. "I sure miss my two. My friend Angie is looking in on Morrie and Griselda while I'm gone."

"Well, I do a little. Nefertiti always sleeps with me."

"I know what we can do." Ruth looked toward the hallway. "We can get some postcards today, and you can write to Nefertiti."

"Yeah, like she can read!" Annika said sarcastically.

"Your parents can read, and they can read your postcards to Nefertiti," Ruth reminded her.

"Maybe I should send a postcard to my mom and dad, too," Annika mused, "so they don't feel left out."

Just then, Loris Biederman waved to Ruth from the entrance to the dining room. "There's a phone call for you, Ruth, and it sounds like a gentleman," she said, arching her eyebrow and making a circle with her lips. "You can pick it up at the front desk."

Annika jumped up. "It's Grandpa Del! Can I say 'hi?'"

"Come on." Ruth got up and hurried toward the lobby. She blushed a little due to Loris' obvious delight in telling her that a 'gentleman' was on the phone.

Ruth took the receiver from the woman. "Hello," she said breathlessly.

"Good morning, my love." Del told her, "I'm sorry I didn't call you last night. Zimmerstein kept us until eleven. By the time I got back to the hotel it was too late to call. So, how's Grand Marais?"

"Oh, it's fine, but I wish you were with us," Ruth told him. "It's wonderful to hear your voice, though." She tried to keep her voice down so that Loris, who was finding things to do near the phone, could not listen in.

"I miss you," Del said, "but I'm sure Annika keeps you from being too lonely. How's my little fishing partner doing?"

"She's right here, hoping to talk to you." Ruth handed the receiver to Annika. "Don't hang up when you're done," she whispered. "I want to talk with him some more."

"Hi, Grandpa Del," Annika said to him. "Grandma Ruth and I are going out to a big island today. On a boat!"

"Yes, I know—Isle Royale. That'll be a lot of fun. It's a beautiful island. Maybe you'll see a moose there and you can draw a picture of it."

Ruth signaled that she wanted the phone back. "I'm going to give the phone back to Gram now," Annika said. "Bye."

"Hi, sweetheart, it's me again." Ruth was still trying to talk quietly.

"Hi again ... is everything all right? Your voice sounds a little strained."

"You could always read me," Ruth answered. "We're in the lobby and I'm trying to keep it down. My nerves are a little frayed. There's been trouble in town, but I don't want to discuss it in the hotel lobby. I'll call you tonight on my room phone and fill you in. It's nothing you have to worry about, though. Really. Nothing concerning Annika or me." She was reassuring herself, more than anything.

"Well, okay, if you say so. Okay." He hesitated and then chuckled. "You just take good care of yourselves until tomorrow, 'cause I'm coming up there." He cleared his throat. "We have three weeks before we open in Boston, and I've been given some time off, so I thought I'd fly home tonight and drive up tomorrow. I could spend a few days with you girls ... if that's all right."

"Are you kidding?" Ruth laughed, overjoyed. "Tomorrow? Oh Del! That's wonderful! We will be so glad to see you! I'll get you a room here."

"Try to get me a room near yours. There's a non-stop on Northwest that takes off from Logan to Minneapolis at 6:30. I'll be able to sleep in our own bed tonight, and then I'll drive up to Grand Marais tomorrow. I should be there by mid-afternoon."

"I'll see about a room right away. Oh, I'm so glad you're able to come up here. I miss you so much! But that's a lot of traveling in so short a time. Are you sure about this?"

"I miss you too, and I love you." Del's voice softened. "I'll rest when I'm back with you tomorrow. Bye, and have fun on that island today."

Ruth kissed into the phone. "Love you, too. Bye now!"

"Bye, Grandpa Del!" Annika yelled.

"Bye. Love you both. I'll see you soon."

Ruth grinned at her granddaughter. "Grandpa's able to join us. He'll be here tomorrow afternoon! We'll have supper with him!"

"Yipee!" Annika jumped up and down.

"We'll need another room," Ruth told Loris. "Del has some time off and he's flying back to the Twin Cities tonight. He'll drive up tomorrow. You know the room next to ours?" she asked. "Would that one be available by any chance?"

"You're in luck. We haven't had anyone in that room for a week now because Arvid's been working on the plumbing and he takes his time. He told me yesterday that he was almost finished. It'll probably be ready by tomorrow; and if not, maybe your hubby could use the bathroom in your room. It's yours if you want it."

"Yes, and thanks so much."

Loris drew in a breath. "As long as I've got you here, I need your help with something."

Just then, the man in the dining room walked out. "Morning," he said, nodding to Loris.

She nodded back stiffly, saying nothing to him in return.

After he left, Loris watched him until she knew he was outside.

"See that guy?" she said to Ruth, keeping her voice low. "He's opening a real fancy restaurant right down the street on the beach." She looked pointedly at Ruth. "He's even calling it a 'restaurant and *event center*,' although the 'event center' is really just a big fancy party room." She sighed. "He's going to take business away from us. It's hard enough to stay afloat, without gangsters like Sam Guston trying to grab all our business!"

Ruth said, "That's the guy who's opening the new restaurant? I heard about that place. Roy Foley came up here to sell him kitchen equipment. He doesn't look at all what I expected a *restaurateur* to look—"

"And you know what?" Loris interrupted in a snappish whisper. "He even tried to hire Pam away from us. Our own daughter!" Loris shook her head. "Of course she told him *no.*"

"Pam would never leave you and Arnie," Ruth assured her.

"He offered her lots more money than we can afford to pay her."

"Even so, Pam is loyal."

"That she is," Loris asserted. "She's a good girl!"

"You were going to ask for my help with something?" Ruth reminded her.

"Oh, my God! Yes!" The woman shook her head as if to clear it. "That Sam Guston is driving me to distraction. His darned restaurant-event-venue is all I can think about!"

"So ... what do you need?"

"I spoke with Pastor Paul this morning—he's the one running the theatre. He called bright and early." She frowned. "He really needs someone to help with the women's dressing room up at the old church."

Ruth shook her head *no*.

But Loris held her hand up. "Just hear me out." She removed her glasses and wiped them off with her sweater. "They really need the help and I can't leave this place, what with Arnie's bad knee and all. I remember you worked with a little theatre down in the cities, so I thought maybe you could help him out. It's for a really good cause. All the proceeds are going to the West End Women's Shelter at the other end of town."

The request hit Ruth like a flying brick and it showed. Loris held up her hand. "I know it's a lot to ask, but it's for only five shows. Five nights that you'd need to be there. From about seven 'til ten, that's all. What would you guys do at night anyway? Go for a walk? Watch cable? You'd be helping the women's shelter. They do so much for the girls in this area. Arvid's daughter, Vicky ... well ..." She lowered her voice. "The folks in that shelter absolutely saved her life."

Ruth just looked at her.

"And I'll tell ya what. If you do this for us, all your meals, until the show closes—both yours and Annika's—will be on the house. And your new husband too. On the house."

"Oh, Loris, I don't know. That's really generous, but ... I'm here on vacation. And besides, that'll cost you too much."

"That's a really good deal, Gram," Annika piped up.

Ruth looked out the window toward the lake, then back to Loris. "Can I think about it? As soon as we finish our breakfast we're leaving for Grand Portage. We're going to Isle Royale today."

"Well, sure, but I'd like to be able to tell something to Pastor Paul. He's the production manager and he's really unnerved by Sally's death. The man sounded just about ready for the loony bin!"

Ruth paused. She considered Loris to be an old friend. And she felt so sorry for Sally's family, and now for this pastor ... and even the West End Women's Shelter.

"Well, okay then. Only five nights? I guess I can help you." *What am I doing? This is crazy*, she thought. "But only my meals, and Annika's, okay? Del can pay for his own. I don't want you going broke."

A wide smile spread across Loris' face. "Thank you," she said, squeezing Ruth's arm. "You are such a good person. And you won't regret helping these people."

I regret it already.

Ruth sighed as she and Annika returned to the dining room to finish their breakfast.

Chapter 7

Lake Superior Never Gives Up Its Dead

Just as Ruth and Annika sat down, Pam came back with Ruth's food.

"Mrs. Mays," Pam said, looking uncomfortable, "I have a favor to ask. Please don't say anything to my mom about me not liking it when some people come in here to eat. I just don't want my folks to be worried about it."

"I won't say a word," Ruth said, crossing her heart. "But I'm thinking that you are the best daughter anyone could have."

"Thanks. I appreciate it." Pam turned to Annika and said, "Your Grandma is a really nice lady."

"Yup, she sure is." Annika grinned. "Grandpa Del calls her a 'gem.'"

As they hurriedly finished their breakfast and then headed back to their room to get jackets for their trip to Isle Royale, Annika's buoyant morning mood seemed to shift. She became quiet, as though processing something in her head. When they walked past the front desk, Annika turned to Ruth and whispered, "Gram, do you think you should tell Mrs. Biederman about Grandpa Del?"

"I already told her he would be coming. She said he could have the empty room across the hall from us."

"No, that's not what I mean. You know … maybe you need to tell her more about him."

"What more?"

"Well, that … you know … that …" Annika was clearly uneasy.

"That he's Black?"

"Yeah," the girl said softly. "You know it doesn't make any difference to me, and I can hardly remember Grandpa Tom. So I love Grandpa Del. He's my grandpa and he's the best. But I know some people are funny about somebody's race."

Ruth looked kindly into her granddaughter's eyes. "It seems unnecessary, honey. But okay, if you think I should, I'll take care of it right now." She walked up to the desk. "Loris," she said, "before my husband arrives, I thought maybe I should fill you in on something about him."

"What about him? That he's an opera singer who sings all over the country? And that he's not, ah, Scandinavian?" She made quotation marks in the air and grinned at Ruth.

Ruth raised her eyebrows.

"Look here, Mrs. Delancy Mays," she said, pointing to the guest register where Ruth had signed in. "Believe it or not, I have heard of Mr. Del Mays, even way up here in the boondocks." Then she explained, "Actually, Arnie and I went to Chicago on a trip two years ago. We saw the Lyric's production of *The Barber of Seville*. Your husband was really something! We're honored to have him stay here. In fact I'll want a signed photo for our dining room, if he has one."

"I have a photo in my suitcase," Ruth said, laughing. "I'll have him sign it for you when he comes. And thanks." Ruth turned and joined Annika, who was waiting on the porch.

"I don't care if he's purple with green spots!" Loris called out to her with a wave. "And thank you again for helping us out at the theatre! Pastor Paul was overjoyed when I called and told him."

Oh yay, thought Ruth, as she smiled weakly and waved back.

The ride up the shore to Grand Portage and its reconstructed fur trading post was beautiful. The day was crisp and sunny, with a cool breeze blowing down out of Canada. An absolutely perfect August morning, in Ruth's estimation. When they got to the parking lot, there were few spaces left. Ruth noticed that people were already lining up on the dock to board the *Wenonah*.

"Come on, honey, we've got to hurry!" Ruth told Annika as she scooped up her purse and the knitting bag where she also stashed sunscreen, hats for both of them, cheese and crackers, dried cranberries, and two bottles of water. "Did you remember the camera?"

"Yup," Annika replied as she got out of the car with her knapsack. "I also have my sketch book and pens. And my sweater. And I grabbed your sweater, too. It's in my knapsack—in case it gets really cold out on the lake."

"Good girl!" Ruth was surprised by her young granddaughter's foresight, but then remembered her mom had been the same way.

They found two seats on the sunny side of the boat and settled in for the hour-and-a-half ride to the island. The lake was choppy and the boat lurched up and down as it pulled away from the dock and headed into open water.

Ruth looked back toward the shore. The rocks and forest looked ancient, and because the cars were parked out of sight behind the reconstructed trading post, Ruth imagined that the scene would have looked much the same to French voyagers in the eighteenth century.

I feel so lucky to be here, sharing all this with Annika. Poor Sally won't get to do anything with her grandchildren ever again. A tear rolled down Ruth's cheek.

Annika wanted to hang over the railing and look at the water. Ruth nervously let her do it once, but then got up and pulled her back. "Honey, please sit here by me. We don't want to lose these good seats."

"Lake Superior never gives up its dead," Annika told her grandmother with obvious relish.

"Where did you hear that?"

"My dad told me. He told me there are some boats in Lake Superior that sank in storms. He said the people on this one boat were never found. They even wrote a song about it."

Ruth turned to Annika. "You mean the *Edmund Fitzgerald?* That was an ore boat that sank in a big storm."

"Yeah. I think that was the one." Annika looked down into the dark waves. "I wonder how many bodies are under us?"

"Let's not talk about bodies," said Ruth. "We've heard enough bad news. It's a beautiful day, today. Let's just have fun!" She patted the seat beside her.

Annika sat down, pulling her sweater over her like a blanket. "Boy! It's getting cold!" She wriggled closer to Ruth.

"Did you know that the Indians called this lake *Gitche Gumee?* She put an arm around Annika and pulled her closer.

"What does *Gitche Gumee* mean?" asked the girl.

"Well, it's in one of the lines of that song about the *Edmund Fitzgerald.* And it's also in Longfellow's poem about Hiawatha. *'On the shores of Gitche Gumee, of the shining Big-Sea-Water ...'* So maybe it means 'shining big-sea-water.' We can look it up together when we get home."

Just then, some nearby seats were taken by a couple. The man was tall, a bit on the stocky side, with brown hair, brown eyes, and glasses. He was wearing a bright blue Norwegian sweater and dark pants. The woman was small and slight, with short dark brown hair worn in a pixie-cut. She wore sunglasses, a dark gray cable-knit sweater and gray pants.

They look like nice people, thought Ruth.

The man smiled and nodded, and Ruth smiled back. The woman however, stared at Annika, and then straight ahead out at the lake. She seemed upset. The man tried putting his arm around her. Ruth saw her shrug his arm off her shoulder. *Oh boy,* thought Ruth, *it looks like somebody's in the dog-house!*

Annika, completely oblivious to the couples' distress, was digging in Ruth's bag for the cheese and crackers and water bottles. Ruth laughed at her and said, "We just had breakfast!"

"I'm a growing girl, Gram. Oh, look!" She pointed to a small flock of gulls, which were swarming around something in the water. "What are they doing?"

"Probably someone threw food overboard from the upper deck," Ruth told her. "Gulls are scavengers. They often follow boats like this one, because people throw food into the water."

"Can I throw them some of our cheese and crackers?" Annika was excited. "Can I, Gram? We don't need them all."

"Sure, throw them some crackers. Don't throw any cheese, though. It probably doesn't float and they won't be able to find it. I don't know if gulls even eat cheese."

Annika went to the side of the boat once more, a half-dozen small crackers in her hand. "Here, gully, gully!" she cried, throwing her crackers into the blackish-green waves. Immediately one of the larger gulls swooped down to get the bounty. "Gram!" she screamed, "look at him! Look at him go! Isn't he awesome?"

Ruth was going to comment when the woman, who was watching Annika, got up and wiped her eyes and blew her nose. The man stood up, too, and was about to stop her from walking away from him, but she turned away quickly and he lost his balance. He sat back down with a plop.

"*Whoa!*" thought Ruth. *She's small, but mighty. And it looks as if she's mighty upset.*

Embarrassed, the man tried to cover up for it. He smiled at Ruth and stammered, "Sh-she always gets a bit nervous out on this lake."

Right, thought Ruth. To the man she replied politely, "It affects some people that way. Maybe her stomach is upset?" *And maybe you did something to upset her? I wonder what it was?* Ruth looked out at the water and thought to herself.

Chapter 8

Trouble On the Boat

RUTH AND ANNIKA WATCHED while the gulls swooped and dipped, cawing and fighting over morsels of cracker and rising into the sky again. Annika was transfixed. The man watched her too, smiling at her enthusiasm. The woman, who was at the railing now, looked sad. Ruth noticed the man seemed worried.

She spoke to him, hoping he couldn't sense her thoughts about what had transpired between him and the woman. "My granddaughter's a city girl," she told him. "And we're up here for a little vacation."

"That's what my wife and I are doing, getting away from it all. But only for a day, I'm afraid." He grimaced, then introduced himself. "I'm Pastor Paul Eklund, from Immanuel Lutheran down in Grand Marais. I have to be back there tonight for a community theatre group I'm in charge of. We're doing *Carousel,* and it's opening night. If you and your granddaughter don't have anything to do this evening, won't you please join us? Curtain opens at seven-thirty. We're just up the hill from the East Bay Inn, at the old Lutheran church building. We only use it for summer bible school and our little theatre."

Ruth smiled as he went on.

"And of course I invite you to attend my real church on Sunday—Immanuel Lutheran," he added, almost as an after-thought.

"You do both? Theatre and church?"

"Yes," he answered, warming to the subject. "We run our theatre during the summer tourist season, and use the old sanctuary for our shows. It's sort of our 'service project' for the community." He sat up taller, obviously proud of this. "It was an idea of mine, to give young people something positive and fun to do in the evenings, as well as involve the town. Multi-generational experiences are really big right now. At least that's the buzzword."

"Ah," said Ruth, thinking she'd better *'fess-up*, before the pastor went any further. "I've heard about your little theatre. In fact"—she smiled—"I'm the person Loris Biederman asked to replace your costumer. I'm Ruth Mays, and this is my granddaughter, Annika."

Taking Ruth's hand now, Paul Eklund shook it warmly. "Thank you so much for agreeing to help us! That was just tragic, about Mrs. Merritt." Then, as if remembering his manners, he said to his wife, "Emmy, this is Mrs. Mays. She's taking over for Mrs. Merritt to help with the costumes!" As the woman looked toward them, he said quickly, "This is my wife, Emmy."

Emmy Eklund nodded at Ruth. Quietly, she said, "It's very nice to meet you. Thank you for helping us." Then she turned again to look out at the lake.

Embarrassed by his wife's coolness, Pastor Eklund cleared his throat and said, "I hope we'll still have a theatre after tonight. Some of our more traditional council members think we should sell that old building, and close it down."

"Oh, I'm so sorry. Why is that?" Ruth asked him. *And why is your wife so upset? What's going on?*

Pastor Eklund gave his wife a glance before he moved slightly closer to Ruth. "Well," he said, lowering his voice, "just between you and me, they don't like their pastor being involved with theatre. And now, with the, uh"—he cleared his throat—"death of Mrs. Merritt ... and there was a young man who just died ... well, it puts a damper on any community events going on in the evenings." He sighed a long sigh, glancing at his wife again, who was still staring grimly out at the water.

I'm actually starting to feel sorry for him! Ruth thought. "I know what you mean," she said. "I'm involved in a little theatre back in St. Paul, and I just love it. Once you get bit by the 'theatre-bug,' it's hard to be away from it." She patted his hand and added, "I think it's good that you involve young people. It keeps them off the streets!"

"And it's not as if I don't know what I'm doing," he told her. "I was a theatre major as an undergraduate, before I went to seminary."

"Sounds like a good fit to me."

The pastor gave another big sigh. "I wish you lived up here; then I would feel as though I had an ally ..." At this gaff, his wife got up and quickly walked toward the middle of the boat.

Startled, he turned and called after her, "Wait, Emmy! Wait! I didn't mean ..." He got up quickly from his seat. "I'm sorry!" he said as he ran after her.

Ruth watched him go.

Annika came and sat down again. "Do you see that man over there?" she whispered.

Ruth looked to where Annika pointed. A gray-haired man—the one they'd seen this morning at breakfast, the one who was opening a fancy restaurant and event center in town—was leaning over the side of the boat. He was about thirty feet away, looking out at the water.

"Gram, isn't that the man we saw this morning? He just threw a gun in the lake. I saw him do it!"

"What?" Ruth whispered back. "A *gun?*"

The girl nodded. "Well, he didn't actually throw it. He just sort of dropped it. I don't think he wanted anyone to see him do it."

"I didn't see him get on the boat," Ruth mused.

"I think he looks like a gangster, like in old movies. Do you think he's a gangster, Gram?"

"I think we should just forget about this," Ruth told her quietly. "Whatever it was is gone, anyway, and I don't think Lake Superior gives up it's guns, either."

"Okay," Annika whispered back, "but it's weird."

"Yes, it is. But for your own safety, please just pretend you didn't see anything. Whatever it is, I don't want you involved."

Ruth looked up to see the man walking toward them. *Oh my God!* She thought. Then she whispered to Annika, "You just saw him feeding the gulls, okay?"

"Okay," Annika whispered back.

"Well, hello you two," The man said heartily, as he stood near Annika.

Ruth tightened her arm around her granddaughter's shoulders and pulled her toward her.

"Didn't I see you at breakfast this morning? At the East Bay?"

"Yes, we're staying there," Ruth said quietly.

"I saw you feeding the gulls," he said to the girl.

"Yup, they were hungry."

"I think you saw me get rid of something over the side of the boat?" He said to her.

"Um … some bread?" responded Annika, looking innocently at the man.

"Yes, it was bread." He seemed to breathe a sigh of relief, then turned to Ruth. "I really like the gulls. And it's nice to see kids like them too."

"Do you live up here?" Ruth asked him, already knowing the answer.

"Yes, I do uh, *business,* in Grand Marais. In fact I'm opening a new restaurant. Name's Sam Guston. Nice to meet you." He extended his hand.

Ruth didn't want to touch his hand, but she was polite. "Ruth Mays," she said, shaking hands with him. "I'm up here with my granddaughter, for a brief vacation."

"Well, enjoy your time up here. It's a nice town." His chest expanded. "Maybe next time, you can eat in my restaurant and see my new event center!"

"Y-yes. I've heard it's going to be … really something."

He gave a wide grin. "It sure is! And Grand Marais needs nice places for people to eat and … maybe celebrate a wedding! I'm building the biggest place that town ever saw. And I'll give you a good deal."

"Thank you, we can't wait to see it." *Oh Lord! No wonder Loris hates him. He's gonna take so much business away from her!*

She breathed a sigh of relief when Sam Guston finally said, "Well, have a good day," and walked away from them, toward the other side of the boat.

Then she tightened her arm around Annika.

"That was smart of you, acting innocent like you did," she whispered to her.

"Gram, he was kind of scary."

"He was!"

They both sat there, quietly, for a while. Ruth's thoughts were anxious.

Annika is going to stay right by my side every minute, until we're back home. She is not getting out of my sight! God, I hope he believed her.

Annika looked around and asked, "Where are the people who were sitting with us? That man and lady? Oh, there they are. I think she's mad at him," she whispered again. "Look at her, Gram. Look how she jerks away from him."

Ruth noticed the couple's body language on the far side of the boat, as Annika nodded sagely and said, "Yeah, she's mad at him, all right."

"Shh," Ruth warned her. "Try not to stare. But yes, I think you're right. She looks pretty angry." *The young really do know everything that's going on,* she thought.

"I overheard him say the little theatre might have to stop. Does this mean we won't get to work in it?" She added, "And what about our free meals?"

Ruth smiled and patted the girl's knee. "Oh, I don't think we have to worry about this show. I'm sure they've already sold advance tickets, and you know what they always say in the theatre?"

"Never give anyone their money back?" Annika grinned impishly.

"That, too," laughed Ruth. "No, they say, 'The show must go on!'"

"Okay, then I guess that means we still get our free meals at the hotel." Annika turned to look at the couple once more, and her eyes opened wide. "Oh gram! Did you see that? She pushed him away! He tried to hug her and she pushed him away!"

"Oh dear." Ruth drew her granddaughter closer to her. "Just don't look at them, honey. Look out at the water instead."

Ruth and Annika sat for a while, looking out at the water. Neither of them said anything. The gulls were swooping and crying, fighting over the scraps of whatever the folks on the top deck were throwing over the side.

Finally, Annika spoke in a whisper, "Gram, if you were mad at Grandpa Del would you ever push him away?"

Ruth winced and said, "Of course not, sweetie. If we had a disagreement about something, we'd talk it over." *Oh Lord! What a discussion to have with a ten-year-old.*

"That's what I thought." Annika breathed a relieved sigh. "Mom says only ignorant people resort to physical stuff."

"Yes, that's pretty much the case."

"So that lady, that guy's wife, is she just ignorant?" Annika didn't look at Ruth, but stared out at the water.

Ruth thought carefully before she spoke. "She may find it difficult to argue with a man who spends his whole working life, um, being convincing to people." *This is not coming out right!* She shook her head.

"Yeah, I think I get it. He's used to people agreeing with him, about God and all that stuff. Everyone always listens to what *he* says, right?"

"Yes," said Ruth. "Maybe she needs someone to listen to *her* once in a while."

"Shh! Here he comes!" whispered Annika. "Should we tell him about the man who dropped the gun overboard?"

"No!" whispered Ruth. "That's got to stay just between us. We can ask Grandpa Del about it, but I think he'll agree with me. We need to stay out of it."

"Okay. But can I at least tell Mom and Dad?"

"Only after you get home." *Oh Lord!* Ruth thought. *There goes any future vacations together!*

Anxious on Isle Royale

PASTOR PAUL EKLUND CAME striding over, smiling as if he hadn't a care in the world.

He's not a very good actor, thought Ruth.

"Mrs. Mays," he said, "may I call you Ruth? And please call me Paul." He sat down on the bench next to Ruth, but glanced back toward the other side of the boat. "Emmy always gets a bit, well, over-wrought, I guess you could say. Before opening night. That's why we're out here, to get away from it all!" He took a handkerchief out of his pocket and blew his nose. "By the way, I'm just the stage manager for this show. I have a musical and artistic director who's going over last minute details for tonight. He told me to 'get out of his hair,' God bless him!" He laughed nervously. "I sure hope we get back in time for some costume work."

Annika started to say something, but Ruth put a warning hand on her knee. Fortunately, the girl looked at her grandmother, who shook her head slightly *no.* Annika remained quiet.

Thank God! thought Ruth.

Finally, the girl said, "I need to use the bathroom, Gram."

"Oh honey, I'm sorry!" Ruth pointed to the interior of the boat. "It's right through there. Put paper down on the seat," she told her quietly.

"She's a nice little girl," Paul Eklund commented as she left.

"That she is," Ruth replied. "Do you and your wife have children?"

Pastor Paul hesitated a moment before he said quietly, "Unfortunately, no. I mean, not yet." Then he sighed. "Ruth, I need to ask you, do you think you can come early tonight? We have three costumes that need re-fitting. Our leading lady, well, she's um ... gained some weight since the costumes were made." He looked down at his shoes.

Ruth kept looking toward the bathroom, not wanting to have Annika out of her sight. *Come on, Annika, hurry up, I need to see you!* She looked toward the pastor and thought, *He looks embarrassed. I wonder what this is all about?* To him she said, "I think we can, if this boat gets back on time, and Annika and I can get our supper first."

"We should get back around four. Will that give you enough time?"

"When do we need to be up at the church?" Ruth asked him.

"We?" The pastor looked puzzled, then said, "Oh! Your granddaughter, of course! I'll put her to work folding programs." He was his smiling self again, then appeared to think a moment. "Can you come around six? She has three costumes. All of them are going to need some adjusting."

"Is there a sewing-machine at the church?" *And I'll need scissors, thread, needles and pins,* Ruth thought.

"No, Mrs. Merritt always worked at home, but I can ask one of the other ladies in my congregation. I'm sure someone will lend us what we need. I'll make sure to have it there for you." He rubbed his hand over his hair. "I'm really so very grateful for your help, Ruth. You are a Godsend!"

"I think we can eat an early supper. When does the curtain open again?"

"Seven-thirty," the pastor told her.

"And your leading lady—will she'll be there with her costumes? At six?"

"I'll see to it. Thanks so much! You really are a life saver for us!"

By the time Annika returned from the bathroom, Pastor Eklund had said his good-byes and had gone back to the other side of the boat where his wife was now sitting. Ruth looked anxiously around for Sam Guston, but couldn't see him. Then she craned her neck to see how the minister's wife received him, but there was a pillar in the way.

Just as well, she thought. *Don't be a busy-body, Ruth!*

"It looks like we're working on some costumes tonight, before they open," she told Annika. "We need to get to the variety store, as soon as we're back to Grand Marais. I need some sewing supplies."

"Oh good!" chirped the girl. "I love that store! Can I get some comic books and candy? And some Cheetos?"

"I suppose." Ruth smiled, putting her arm around her.

The rest of the trip had Ruth keeping a close eye on Annika, while also watching out for Sam Guston. The day, which was sunny with a brisk wind out of the north, was energizing. After the boat docked at the small marina that served as the "official" entrance to Isle Royale, the passengers went up the couple of steps to the dock. They merged—quietly but quickly—into the building that was a combination museum, store, and park-ranger's office. It was a simple building, immaculately clean, with wooden floors and large windows looking out at the lake.

They all sat in folding chairs at long tables facing the front of the room. A brief slide presentation was given by a tall, lanky, red-haired and very freckled park ranger. She was wearing a khaki shirt, with rolled up sleeves and long matching pants. Around her neck she wore a green and red plaid scarf. Ruth thought she looked like a Girl Scout leader. She told them about the population of wolves on the island (Annika's favorite part) and about the local flora. She instructed everyone to not pick berries, flowers, or mushrooms, or strip any bark off birch trees. She warned them not to litter. She seemed very strict about keeping the island as they found it: pristine and untouched.

Some of the passengers, the Eklunds and Mr.Guston among them, purchased sandwiches in the little store which was connected to the park headquarters. Ruth noticed, as she purchased two cheese sandwiches, two apples, and two more bottles of water for herself and Annika, that Emmy Eklund was now sitting next to her husband. She also noticed the woman's nose was red, as if she'd been crying. The couple appeared to have settled their differences however, because she was allowing her husband to put his arm around her shoulders as they sat and ate.

Mr. Guston was talking to an older couple.

He's probably telling them about his new restaurant and event center, Ruth thought, as she saw him finish what he was saying and start to move on to other groups. *I guess it pays to advertise,* Ruth mused. *And I'm sure none of those people know about the gun he brought on the boat.*

Ruth steered Annika away from the group and they went outdoors to the picnic area. The picnic tables were in a lovely place, shaded by large balsam fir trees. Ruth looked around for Sam Guston, and was relieved that he was still inside.

As they ate their lunch, Annika asked, "Did you ever come here with Grandpa Tom?"

Smiling at the memory, Ruth told her, "Yes, honey, we were here several times. Isle Royale was one of Grandpa Tom's favorite places in the whole world."

"I can see why." The girl looked around. "It's really pretty here!"

"I think so too."

"My mom says she remembers being here a couple times."

"Yes, she was, and she really enjoyed it." Ruth breathed in the fresh air as she listened to the wind blowing through the fir trees. She looked up at the sunlight coming through the branches of huge trees that sheltered the picnic area. And she felt the worn wood of the table, smooth, under her hands. *This is a good place*, she thought.

"Has Grandpa Del ever been here?" Annika asked.

"Yes, he was here with his first wife, Elaine, and Auntie Liz. He remembers that Liz absolutely loved it."

"I love it, too," said Annika. "You know that my mom calls Auntie Liz, 'The Lizard.'"

Ruth laughed. "That's from when they were kids, doing Fritz's shows at Como Park."

"I know, and Auntie Liz called my mom, 'Hannah-Banana.' Mom told me all about it. I just love Auntie Liz!"

"I love her too," Ruth assured her granddaughter, thinking about Del's only child, and how Liz and her daughter, Hannah, had already known each other from Fritz Gerhardt's community theatre productions. They had already been "theatre besties." *That was certainly a wonderful surprise in our relationship!*

Ruth and Annika finished their lunches and Ruth looked around, thinking, *It's so remote here. And with those two deaths, and Mr. Guston who seems to be trying to hide something, I hope Annika and I will be safe.* Ruth was trying to quell the feeling of unease that was creeping into her thoughts. *I'm sure Grand Marais is usually a safe place,* she kept telling herself. *We'll stay away from Mr. Guston. Del will know what to do about him. Del will keep us safe!*

She tried to think positively.

After lunch, Ruth and Annika joined about a dozen people who went on the short "nature walk" offered by the same park ranger, who now wore a large-brimmed khaki hat. Ruth was relieved that Sam Guston did not join in the walk, but she did wonder why the Ecklunds weren't going.

If they're stressed, it would probably be good for them.

The walk was supposed to take about an hour and, in Ruth's mind, an hour was almost too much. *Any more,* she thought, *and I wouldn't be able to finish it!*

They all walked together through the forest. Ruth could see the ranger's hat and red pony-tail getting farther and farther ahead of her. The path went up and down hills and wound around some smallish wetlands. Ruth looked up at the huge pine trees overhead that blocked out much of the sunlight. She looked down and saw several varieties of mushrooms, and some wild flowers. She recognized a showy lady slipper—the Minnesota state flower.

She would have told Annika about them, but the girl was skipping ahead. She was so eager to see everything. Ruth tried to keep up, but was favoring her arthritic left knee and being very careful not to trip over the roots that sometimes showed up in the path. She always kept Annika in her line of sight, however.

As if sensing her grandmother's worry, Annika frequently ran back to tell Ruth about what she had seen. "Oh Gram!" she exclaimed, "isn't this place just awesome?"

Ruth smiled gamely and replied, "It sure is, sweetie!" All the while, Ruth sneaked little peeks at her watch, hoping they were nearing the end of the hike.

When the walking path finally veered back toward Lake Superior, and they came in sight of the docks, Ruth sighed in relief and hurried her pace to catch up with Annika.

"There's our boat," she said, pointing to the Wenonah. "We'd better get on it; we don't want them to sail off and leave us!"

"Oh Gram ... as if!" Annika laughed.

Ruth noticed that Pastor Eklund and his wife were among the first to embark. He had his arm around her waist and she was leaning her head on his shoulder.

I suppose they just waited by the building ... at least she seems more friendly now. I guess they must have made up. Oh, and there's Mr. Guston. Ruth spotted the man shaking hands with another couple before getting on the boat. *More schmoozing, I suppose?* She tried to not think about the gun Annika had seen. *Was it a gun? And more importantly—did he know Annika saw it?*

Annika slept during most of the trip back to Grand Marais. With her feet on the bench, her head in her grandmother's lap, and covered with a sweater, she slept the untroubled sleep of the young.

She woke only once, when Ruth gently informed her they were passing over the famous sunken ship, the *SS America.*

At that point in the voyage, the captain came over the loud speaker and told everyone that the *SS America* had fortunately no fatalities, because all the folks on it had been rescued. You could hear the murmurs of people who thought that the passengers of that boat were very lucky indeed!

Annika looked down through the water at the sunken bow of the hull, nodded, yawned, and returned to sleep on Ruth's lap.

How I wish I could sleep that peacefully! thought Ruth.

After seeing the SS Amerika, Ruth did nap, however. The nature hike and the lake air were too much for her. She woke only a couple of times: once as the captain came over the loud speaker to tell everyone about the "sleeping giant." This was the name given to some hills in distant Canada which looked like a huge man lying down. Finally, she woke again when the captain announced they were coming into Grand Portage.

"Here we are, honey. Wake up." Ruth gently shook Annika awake. "The boat is going to dock."

Ruth was stiff and a little sore from sitting in one place so long, but she picked up their bags and sweaters and followed the rest of the people off the boat and onto the dock. Annika quietly walked by her side, leaning on her.

"What's the matter, sweetie, don't you feel good?" Ruth asked the girl

"I'm okay," she said listlessly, "just a little tummy ache."

Trying to remember what the girl ate that day, Ruth felt Annika's forehead. It was cool to the touch. *Probably too much excitement, and not enough fruit. She only had a bite of her apple.*

"Come on," Ruth told her, "let's get back to the hotel and have some orange juice, and maybe a dish of blueberries."

"You're just like Mom." Annika sniffed. "Fruit juice and fruit cures everything."

As they walked to their car, Paul and Emmy Eklund came up to them. Paul looked hopeful as he said, "See you two tonight ... at six?"

"I hope I can." Ruth frowned slightly and said, "My granddaughter has a tummy ache, and ... well ... I need to see if she's okay first."

"Oh gosh!" Paul looked horrified. "How sick is she?"

"Oh, just too much excitement, I expect. You know, a kid's digestive system sometimes gets a little off when they travel away from home. I'm really sorry, but I can't leave her alone."

Emmy Eklund, who had been standing next to her husband, blurted out, "I'd be happy to take care of her for you. I can bring her some books I'll bet she would just love!"

Not wanting to hurt the woman's feelings, but not wanting to leave her granddaughter with a stranger, Ruth smiled and told her, "We'll see. I'll take her back to our room and get her something to eat and then ... we'll just have to see how she is."

"I can come by at a quarter to six," the pastor's wife told Ruth.

"Emmy is wonderful with children," Paul Eklund added. "She taught in our Sunday school for years. The kids just love her!"

"We'll just have to see how it goes," Ruth asserted again. *I don't want to leave Annika with anybody!* she thought anxiously, looking around for Sam Guston.

Chapter 10

Get Me to the Church on Time

Back in Grand Marais, Ruth decided not to go to the *Joynes Ben Franklin* for sewing supplies. *Maybe I can get some from Loris,* she thought.

At the East Bay Ruth immediately put Annika to bed.

"You just rest and I'll get something for that tummy ache," she told her, shutting the door and locking it, then going to the front desk to see what she could find for the girl. She told Loris Biederman about Annika's upset stomach.

"Travel can do that to a person," said Loris.

"I know," Ruth responded. "They want me up at the old church to work on costumes tonight; but if Annika doesn't feel well, I don't think I can go."

"I'll keep an eye on her for you. I bet all she needs is a nap and some fruit!" Loris straightened out the papers on her desk and came around the front to stand by Ruth.

"That's exactly what I thought. We must have read the same child-rearing books." *Loris won't let Mr. Guston near Annika, she already dislikes him.*

"Books? Who had time for *books?*" Loris laughed. "I'll go get her some fruit and a glass of juice and bring it to your room." She pocketed her keys and added, "I'll be there in a minute to take over."

"I want her up at the church with me, as soon as she feels better. Can you bring her?" Ruth asked the woman.

"Of course I can," Loris assured her.

"Are you sure? Don't you have to watch the desk?"

"Auph!" she snorted. "There's no one new coming in tonight. I might as well help you out." She started toward the dining room. "I'll also grab a couple turkey sandwiches and some tea for us and meet you in your room. We'll have a picnic!"

"Okay. I could use something a little more substantial, though. How about adding a piece of your famous lemon meringue pie?"

"If there's any left." Mrs. Biederman seemed to be her old self again.

When Ruth got back to the room, she saw that Annika was sleeping peacefully, her arms thrown over her head. She was snoring lightly.

Mrs. Biederman arrived with a tray, and Ruth put the dish of blueberries and orange juice down on the desk, motioning for Loris to sit in one of the big chairs. Ruth sat down on her bed.

Quietly, Loris Biederman held out a sandwich to Ruth, along with a mug of hot tea. She motioned to a large slice of lemon meringue pie on the tray she'd brought from the kitchen.

"I had to wrestle it away from the kitchen staff," she whispered.

They ate in silence, sipping their hot tea and enjoying the quiet.

"This is just what I needed," said Loris. "I could just lean back in this chair and take a nap myself. With Arnie's bad knee, I've had to take on so many more duties. *Uffda!* If I didn't have Arvid Haakala around to help out, I don't know what I'd do!"

"Do you think he'll finish Del's room in time?" Ruth asked, quietly.

"Oh, yes. You'll have your handsome hubby next to you, don't worry." Loris grinned. "Arvid's a hard worker. You know those Finns."

"I know some, but not too many, I'm sorry to say."

"Do you know how to tell when a Finn really likes you?" Loris had a twinkle in her eye.

"Okay, I'll bite. How do you tell when a Finn really likes you?"

"They look at your shoes instead of their own!"

Ruth laughed silently, shaking her head. "I'll have to remember that one."

"Yup, that's a good one," Loris assured her. "Arvid's a good one, too." She shook her head. "I'm kind of surprised Pastor Eklund talked him into being in *Carousel.* But I think he really wanted to support that women's shelter ... I guess for his daughter, Vicky's, sake. They really helped her, you know."

"It's a wonderful thing for him to do. What part is he playing?"

"Two parts: the star-keeper, and the doctor," said Loris, "so he doesn't have to sing." She checked her watch. "You should probably get up to the church."

Ruth looked at Annika and said, "I hate to go before she wakes up." Just then, the girl turned in her bed and opened her eyes.

"Go where, Gram?"

"Up to the old church, remember? I'm fixing their costumes," Ruth told the girl. "But I hate to leave if you're not feeling well."

"I'd feel a lot better if I could get a hamburger," Annika said. "I'm starving!"

"Well, come on, then," said Mrs. Biederman, getting up from her chair. "Let's go see if we can rustle you up a burger!" She patted Annika's back. "After you eat, I'll drive you up to be with your Grandma."

"Do you mind if I go to the church before you?" Ruth asked the girl.

"Go ahead, I feel okay. I just need food."

Ruth turned to Loris and said, "By the way, I didn't have time to get any sewing supplies. Do you have a scissors, and a needle and thread I could borrow? And maybe some pins?"

"There's a bunch of stuff in the big drawer in the front desk," said Loris. "It's a hot mess, but just rummage around in there and take whatever you need." She patted Ruth's arm. "Keep anything you want. Most of it's stuff we found in people's rooms after they left."

Ruth thanked her and hugged them both, saying, "Ok, I'd better run then, see you in a little while." And then quietly she said to Loris, "That Guston guy you don't like was on the boat. He was talking to us, and I don't want him anywhere near Annika, okay?"

"I'll watch out for him, don't you worry. That man is a real scumbag." Loris got very close to Ruth and whispered, "There's a lot going on with Sam Guston. He took old man Sanderson's property on the lake, after he died last spring. I guess Sanderson owed him all kinds of money, and his daughter couldn't repay it out of the estate. Guston got that property for back taxes and a song." She sniffed. "We woulda bought it ourselves, but Arnie said no. Too much trouble. He said it's all we can do to keep *this* place up. *And* ... there's some local gossip that maybe old man Sanderson didn't die a natural death, if you know what I mean."

"Oh!" said Ruth, thinking of the gun.

"So don't worry. Sam Guston won't get near Annika!"

Then Loris and Annika went to the dining room together, Annika munching on the blueberries Loris had ordered for her. Ruth hurried to dig out the sewing supplies she needed from Loris' extremely messy front desk drawer. She pondered what she'd just heard about Sam Guston.

I wonder if he killed the old man to get his property? And if he'd do that, what might he do to Annika and me, to keep us quiet? Ruth shuddered.

As she was going through Loris' junk drawer, Ruth did smile to herself as she recognized some of the same hoarding tendencies in Loris Biederman, that she herself had.

Eventually Ruth found what she needed—scissors, pins, spools of thread and a needle—and put them in an old cloth bag she found in the drawer.

As she went outside to her car, she almost ran into Emmy Eklund, who was coming in the front door, her arms full of children's books. Her short brown hair was plastered to her head in perspiration, as if she'd rushed to get to the hotel. Her blue eyes were wide and she looked anxious.

"Oh, I'm so sorry!" said Ruth, noticing Emmy's books. "Are you here to look after Annika? She's so much better now. She's with Loris Biederman, in the dining room, having her supper."

"But I just thought ... I just ..." Emmy looked stricken.

Ruth instantly felt sorry for the woman. *She must really need to have children, poor thing!*

"I've got an idea," Ruth told her. "Mrs. Biederman is looking after her right now, and maybe you could sit with her and show her your books while she eats her supper?"

"Oh! Thank you!" Emmy smiled at Ruth and seemed to brighten up considerably. "I loved these stories when I was her age."

Ruth saw *Winnie the Pooh* on the top of the pile of books and thought, *Yikes! That's a little young for Annika. I sure hope she'll be nice to the poor woman.* To Emmy she said, "I'm sure she would enjoy seeing them." Ruth hoped Annika would at least be polite. "You go on in and tell Mrs. Biederman you're there to help her. She's driving Annika up to the old church after she eats. Maybe you can sit with Annika and me during the play?"

"I would just love to!" Emmy gushed.

The woman smiled and nodded as she hurried past Ruth.

I wonder if she's still upset. She looks so uncertain and worried, and yet she's so eager to help us.

Against her better judgement, Ruth left Emmy Eklund and hurried to her car. She was a bit late, and decided against walking. As she drove up the hill to the church she thought, *There is something* off *about that poor lady. I can't put my finger on it. Maybe she wants kids* so *badly she pours out attention on any who come near her. I wonder if she can even have kids?*

Ruth thought about turning around and going back to the hotel. But then she decided against it.

If I went back, it would seem as though I didn't trust Emmy with Annika. And after all, she's a pastor's wife!

As Ruth continued driving up the hill to the old church, she thought about Del and how glad she would be to have him up in Grand Marais tomorrow. *I really need his help with Annika. I won't worry so much if he's with her. Two grandparents are certainly better than one. And oh, how I miss that dear man! And he'll know how to deal with the creepy Mr. Guston and that weird Emmy Ecklund!*

Chapter 11

Costumes, Costumes Everywhere!

RUTH'S MUSINGS CAME TO an end as she pulled into the old church's parking lot. It was already filling up, and Ruth had to park some distance from the door. She saw a few people, some of them looking as if they were in costume, laughing and calling out to one another.

Ruth took her purse and bag of sewing supplies and hurried inside.

I remember opening nights at Como. Now, what did we all say about opening nights? "Nothing more exciting ... and ... nothing more terrifying?"

Right inside the door, Paul Eklund sat at a small table with the money box and tickets. He'd been waiting for Ruth and got up immediately.

"Ruth!" he called to her. "Am I glad you're here!" He motioned for one of the older women from the chorus to take over the tickets for a moment. Then he took Ruth's arm and hurried her down some steps and through a hallway, which was full of playbills taped up on the walls. "We have a *situation,*" he told her in whispered tones.

"The leading lady?" Ruth whispered back.

The pastor nodded.

"And you think I can take care of it?"

"I certainly hope so."

He ushered Ruth down another hallway, to a green-painted door with a homemade sign that said, "Women's Dressing Room—Men KEEP OUT!" Underneath that someone had penciled, *"Unless you are carrying a bouquet of flowers!"* Ruth smiled to herself as Pastor Paul knocked on the door.

"What do you want?" came an irritated-sounding voice from inside.

Oh dear, thought Ruth. *It sounds as if she's in a really bad mood.* She looked at Pastor Eklund and shook her head, her mouth set in a grim line.

The man knocked on the door, more softly this time. "Amy? Amy? It's Pastor Paul and Mrs. Mays, our costumer. May we, uh, please come in?"

"Whatever," came the sarcastic reply.

As the man edged the door open, Ruth looked in dismay at the room. Costumes were thrown everywhere—across chairs, over a table and makeup mirror. Some were even littering the floor.

"Oh, my goodness!" whispered Ruth. More loudly she said, "Hello, Amy?" She extended her hand. "It's so very nice to meet you."

The sullen teenager, who was lounging across a worn sofa, did not even extend her hand. She merely looked warily up at Ruth and said, "You're the new costume lady?"

"Why, yes." Ruth decided to be cheerful in spite of Amy's attitude. "I'm Ruth Mays. I'm taking Mrs. Merritt's place. I guess we'd better get to work if we're going to make a seven-thirty curtain!"

"Fine," the girl said, rolling up to a sitting position. She reached back to pull a black plastic clip out of her hair, releasing a long mane of curly dark-brown hair, shot through with red highlights. "Oh, and please call me *Amy Birdsong*. That's my stage-name."

"Okay, Amy Birdsong. I like that name."

Amy was stunningly beautiful. She shook her head, letting her hair spill over her face, and then she got up and quickly started to take off her shirt.

Pastor Paul gave an alarmed glance and made a hasty retreat.

"You've got an hour and fifteen minutes until *curtain,*" he called back. "The blue dress is the one she uses in the first act, the green one for the second, and the black one for the finale. The sewing machine is on the table, and I threaded it with gray thread. You should be able to use that color for all three dresses. And I plugged it in," he called to Ruth from the other side of the door.

Ruth noticed that Amy was looking toward the door and making a face, as she slipped her jeans off.

"Okay, now ..." Ruth took out Loris' sewing things from the bag and laid them on the card table with the sewing machine—a ripper, scissors, some pins, a needle and thread. "Let's see if we can make these costumes fit better ..."

Amy stood in the middle of the room, still as a statue, her tee shirt and jeans in a muddle at her feet. Clad only in some white panties and a pink chemise-like undershirt, she was tall and slender, with olive skin and ruddy cheeks. Ruth noticed that her breasts and mid-section were decidedly swollen.

I knew it, she's pregnant! Ruth thought as looked at the girl.

Ruth brought the blue dress over and tried to slip it over Amy's head. It stuck when she got to her breasts. "Are you married, Amy?" Ruth asked her gently.

"No," the girl answered. "Why?"

Ruth paused before saying, "Oh ... no reason, really. You're about the right age, and so pretty ... I just thought maybe ..." Ruth stammered.

"Yeah, I'm pregnant." Amy patted her stomach protectively. "Everybody knows, and I have to have all my costumes taken out. And no, I'm not married." She sniffed.

Wincing inwardly at Amy's state, Ruth looked with sympathy at her and said, "Pastor Eklund didn't tell me anything except that you needed some adjustments on your costumes." Ruth slipped the blue dress back off, over the girl's head. Then she began to rip some of the stitching in the side seams, which were wide *(thank goodness).* They could easily be let out.

Ruth asked quietly, "Does the baby's father know?" as she began to rip the stitches out in the waistline.

"The baby's father ... is dead."

"I'm so sorry."

"He was a druggie, anyway," Amy sighed, almost to herself. "My baby and I are probably better off without him."

"You've got to stay healthy. For the baby's sake."

"Yeah, I know," the girl replied quietly.

Ruth went to the sewing machine to work on the blue dress, while Amy put on her makeup and fixed her hair.

After a bit, Ruth told her, "Okay, this should fit better now. Do you know where your other dresses are?"

"Do you think my baby will be okay?" Amy asked hesitantly, as she pulled on the dress.

Ruth was thankful it seemed to fit the girl, with even enough room to expand a little.

"I mean," Amy continued, "if the baby's father used drugs, but I didn't ... will it be okay, do you think?"

When Ruth stood up and put her arm around Amy's shoulders, the girl leaned into her and started to sob.

"That's something to ask your doctor, sweetie. But I think as long as the mother is healthy, the baby is usually healthy too." Ruth squeezed the young woman's shoulders and then said, hoping to stop her from worrying, "Now, how many other dresses do we need to fix?"

Amy wiped her eyes on her sleeve and said, "There's only two more: that green one"—she pointed to a chair nearby—"is for the clambake scene." She sniffled. "And that dark gray one"—she pointed to a dress hanging over a screen—"that's for the final act." Then, as if she finally decided she could trust Ruth, she said, "It was Joey-Frank, you know. He was the guy they found down by the lake."

"Oh, Amy." Ruth shook her head, remembering how she'd found the body. "I'm so very sorry! Is anybody helping you?"

"I live with my mom. But I haven't told her yet, because she'll just freak out." She shook her head. "She hated Joey-Frank. Actually, I was just about to break up with him when I found out about the baby. Tommy Sherman says I should just tell her it's his."

"Is Tommy Sherman a good friend?" Ruth asked.

"Tommy Sherman is the leading man!" crowed a wiry young man from inside the doorway. He'd apparently been listening to their conversation. He burst into the dressing room. Dressed in a red and black striped muscle-shirt that showed off a multitude of tattoos, and a black beret that did nothing to hide his pale-blond receding hairline, he called out, "Hey, Ms. Birdsong!" and sauntered over to Amy. "Ready for our big night?" His light gray eyes surveyed Ruth and he said, "Oh, uh, hi! How d'ye do?"

Ruth's answer was crisp. "I'm doing just fine, young man. And would you please excuse us? We're fitting costumes here, and we do need some privacy." She stood up between Amy and Tommy, trying to shield Amy's state of undress from his eyes.

"Oh, uh, whoops. Sorry!" He laughed nervously and backed himself out the door. "Didn' mean to ... uh, I mean ... later, Amy!" He waved to the girl as he made an awkward exit out of the room.

As soon as Tommy left, Amy confided to Ruth, "He wants us—me and the baby, I mean—to live with him. Says he might have a line on this apartment in Duluth ..."

"Hmmm ..." Ruth took the pins out of her mouth. "And how well do you know him?"

"Not too well, not as well as he'd like. I mean, with the baby and everything ... well, I mean"—she sighed—"I haven't even slept with him yet."

"Good!" Ruth told her. "You don't want to catch anything that could harm your baby." *Out of the frying-pan and into the fire,* she thought.

"Yeah, that's exactly what I thought." Amy frowned as she looked at the door. "He seems okay, but you never know for sure. And he was friends with Joey-Frank. What if he's into the same stuff? He says he isn't, but I don't know if I can believe him." She looked worried.

"Your instincts sound pretty good," Ruth told her, smiling. "Trust your instincts. If it's real love, he'll wait." She noticed the dark circles under the girl's eyes. "Honey, why don't you lie down over there on the sofa, and take a little nap? I'll just work on these other costumes and have them ready in half-an-hour." Ruth moved a bunch of costumes from the old brown sofa to a matching chair. She took a worn pillow from the chair, to put behind Amy's head.

As the girl settled down on the sofa, Ruth noticed a multi-colored afghan on the chair. She pulled it over Amy and gently tucked her in.

The girl closed her eyes and murmured, "I wish my mom was as nice as you."

Ruth reached down and patted her shoulder. Then she sat quietly at the sewing-machine, ripping out stitches and sewing new ones. Soon she heard soft snores coming from the girl.

That poor kid. What is she going to do? How can she support a child? And that awful Tommy ... God protect her from him!

She sewed on in silence for another half-hour, finally finishing the three dresses. She was just starting to straighten up the room when the other cast members began arriving at the women's dressing room door.

Chapter 12

Who Took My Friggin' Kleenex?

SOON THERE WAS PANDEMONIUM in the room, and Amy woke up from the noise. The girl looked around groggily for a few moments, and upon seeing a friend, got up from the sofa to greet her.

"Mrs. Mays," she called Ruth over to her. This is Willy Guerin, who's playing *Carrie Pipperidge.*

Willy Guerin was as fair as Amy was dark. She stepped forward, her white-blonde hair piled up and bobbing on her head, with ringlets falling like snakes around her face.

"Boy! I'm glad you're here," Willy said, her blue eyes wide. "With Mrs. Merritt gone, I thought they'd have to close the show for sure!"

Hmm, that's not quite how I'd expect someone to act when a person is murdered, Ruth thought. But she looked at the girl and said, "I'm glad to meet you, Willy, and I'll do what I can to help everyone."

Ruth had hung Amy's completed costumes up on one of the screens. Amy slipped into her dress for the first act. She smiled and mouthed a *"Thank you"* to Ruth.

Willy grabbed her dress from the floor and put it on. The two girls then hurried to the makeup table to get two of three mismatched chairs in front of a long mirror. They started chatting and putting on their makeup.

Ruth did what she could to straighten up the room. Finding some hangers on the floor and a long clothes rack for costumes, she hung up what dresses she could, in plain view, so the actresses could find them. The rest of the young women—eight in all—looked as if they might be in the chorus. They were already in costume and carrying baskets. When they entered the dressing room, they looked briefly in the mirror to check their makeup and hurried out again.

"Pastor Paul wants us on stage for warm-up in fifteen!" one of them yelled over her shoulder as she exited the room.

Ruth found a broom behind the chair, and started sweeping the floor when a heavy middle-aged woman bustled in. She wore a tight maroon dress, trimmed with off-white lace that helped make the low-cut bodice *slightly* less revealing. And she carried a huge basket that she dropped on the floor by the makeup table.

Plopping herself down in the extra chair, she spritzed her obviously dyed red hair with Final Net and yelled, "Who took my friggin' Kleenex?"

She must be playing the part of Mrs. Mullin, the carousel owner, thought Ruth. *Good type-casting.* Ruth found a box of Kleenex on the floor near the back of the sofa and brought it over to the table.

"Thanks," muttered the woman. "Sorry for the language, but someone always takes my damn Kleenex!"

"Have my 'kids' got here yet?" Willy asked her.

"Your kids?" said Ruth. She thought the girl looked far too young to have children. "Oh!" She laughed and said, "You mean your children in the show!"

"Paul's got the kids all lined up by the piano," interrupted the older woman. "Norm's ridin' herd on 'em!" She laughed. "Norm and his first wife raised four of their own; he sure as hell—oops—I mean *heck*—can watch the kids in this show!"

Ruth looked at her and smiled. She was starting to get used to her earthiness.

"I'm Ruth Mays," she said as she held out her hand to the woman. "I'm taking over costume duty."

"Glad to meetcha!" The robust woman pumped Ruth's hand vigorously. "I'm Edna Fuerling, Norm's better half. He plays piano for this shindig, and helps direct the musicians and singers ... if they show up."

"Oh, he's the musical director."

"His kids are all grown up and moved away. I don't think they liked me much." She sighed. "So it's nice to be around young-uns again, even if they do take my friggin' Kleenex." She snorted as she started rubbing rouge on her pudgy cheeks. "I play Mrs. Mullin, in case you haven't figured it out." Then she pointed at her bust and said, "I know it's low, but she's supposed to look kinda sexy. I wear my costume home and take care of it myself, so you don't have to worry about it." She looked as if she thought a moment. "Oh and it's too bad about that lady, Mrs. Merritt. She was the nicest person. Really, you would've just loved her. Everybody loved her. A good sewer, too."

"I did know her. We were friends from high school."

Edna's painted eyebrows went up. "Oh? Oh, I'm so sorry for your loss!"

"Thank you," said Ruth, trying not to tear up.

Ruth saw Willy poke at Amy and make a face. Then the two started out of the dressing room together, but Ruth held up her hand and they stopped.

"Okay, girls." Ruth was trying to bring some order out of the chaos that was the women's dressing room. "I'm going to hang all the principals' costumes on these three screens over here." She indicated the screens against the far wall. "I'll label them 'Julie,' 'Carrie,' and 'Aunt Nettie.' You all need to hang your costumes up after you wear them. We need to keep this room more organized, Okay?" She gestured at the pile of costumes that were covering the chairs and the makeup table. "So, I need you to tell me which is which?" Then she gasped and said, "Oh, my gosh! Where is your 'Aunt Nettie?' She should be here by now!"

"Ha! Lotsa luck with that one!" Edna laughed ruefully, her large overbite causing her to spit slightly. "She usually comes waltzing in here at the last minute—a regular prima donna. But at least she takes care of her own costumes, like I do. You don't need a sign for hers. She'll take them home with her. She don't trust no one with 'em. I don't, neither! So forget about us, just do the others." Edna looked at the screens. "We keep our own costumes in big baskets we take with us."

As if on cue, the door slammed open and a tall, thin, gray-haired woman dressed in a long calico "Mother Hubbard" and carrying a big basket, did indeed "waltz" into the room, singing *This is a real nice clam ... bake! I'm mighty glad I'm here!*" She looked a bit unsteady in her scuffed brown-leather clogging shoes, and Ruth hurried to take her basket and help her into an empty chair at the makeup table. Ruth could smell alcohol on her breath.

"Geeze-Louise, she's been at the sauce again," Edna muttered, rolling her eyes.

"I'm Gloria! Gloria! *One keg of beer for the four a' ya!*" the woman sang out, giving Ruth a snarky grin and flashing her rheumy eyes. *"And it's glory be to God that there ain't no more of ya! 'cause the four of us can drink it all alone!"* She slumped over in the chair, holding her head in her hands. "Oh God," she moaned.

Ruth immediately went over to the woman. She wasn't sure what the smell was.

Maybe whiskey?

"I'm Ruth Mays, and I'm helping with costumes," she told her gently, getting another whiff of the woman's breath. *Definitely whiskey!* Ruth moved back.

Edna Fuerling immediately took over. "You two girls"—she pointed to Amy and Willy—"go do your warm-ups. And *you!*"—she looked at Gloria, then poured some black coffee from a red and silver thermos into a white Styrofoam cup and handed it to the woman—"You drink this down right now before Pastor Paul gets a whiff of you!" Edna turned her face away from the woman's breath and added, "Before *anyone* gets a whiff of you!"

Ruth, hoping to engage Gloria and find out if she was indeed ready to go on stage, asked her, "Is that your costume for Act One? What you're wearing?"

"Right-e-o, girl-e-o!" Gloria looked up and giggled. She burped and said, "Oops! 'Scuse me!" and laughed as Ruth took her other costume out of her basket to hang it up.

Edna tried to roll the woman's unkempt gray hair into a bun, as she watched her dab powder on her face and try to apply some rouge. "I think this should look pretty good," Gloria told her friend, who was now turning her head this way and that, in order to critique her hairdo.

I wish she'd hold her head still, Ruth thought, looking at the two women. *It's hard to pin up a moving target.*

"I'm s'posed to look like an old biddy," Gloria rasped. "I guess it's type-casting." She began to sniffle again. *"Gawd!* And to think I used to play the leading ladies!" A tear rolled down her cheek. "And just look at me now." She blubbered, "I'm old, and I'm all alone!" She picked up a soiled Kleenex and started weeping into it.

"Listen here, Gloria Simms, you old souse!" Edna shook her by her thin shoulders. "You damn well better stop your crying jag and pull yourself together and get your butt up on that stage for Act One. We *need* you!" Then Edna put her arm around the woman's thin shoulders and whispered to her, "Come on, Gloria, for God's sake don't do this right now. I promise you, I'll take you home with me after tonight's show and we'll send Norm off to bed. You and me will have a nice glass of wine and a good, long talk. Just you and me, okay? It'll be just like old times, remember? You can even stay overnight in my guest room, if you want."

Gloria looked pleadingly into Edna's eyes and seemed to calm down. Ruth watched as Edna took Gloria's hand and pulled her up out of the chair. Then Edna blotted Gloria's face with a fresh Kleenex. "There now," she said. "C'mon girl, we got a show to do!"

Just then Ruth heard someone call out, "Five minutes!"

Everyone started for the door. Edna was last in line, and as she left she turned to Ruth and said quietly, "Don't mind Gloria. She's had a pretty hard life, but she's a trouper. Once she gets on stage, she'll be fine."

Ruth nodded, not certain what to say. To herself she thought, *Hmmn, those two seem to have a history. I wonder what it is?*

She hung up all the costumes she saw lying around and tidied the makeup table, throwing away all the soiled tissues that had been left behind. Then she sighed and hurried into the long, dark hallway that led to the steps and the 'auditorium.' She walked quickly past a small dark room that was serving as a storeroom for props and sets, shuddering as she remembered the incident at the Como Pavilion the previous summer, when Don Olson had tried to strangle her from behind a rack of costumes.

But I'm safe up here. He's gone, and I don't know anyone in Grand Marais. Nobody who would want me dead. And who would hurt an old lady and her granddaughter just helping out?

She walked past two bathrooms with hand-printed signs on the doors: *Guys* and *Dolls.* The whole building had a musty odor. *This place has got to be really hard to clean,* she thought, shaking her head as she climbed the creaking wooden stairs that were dark with aged varnish. *At least they have bathrooms close by.*

As Ruth opened the door into the old sanctuary, she was happy to see an almost full house. Someone had placed "Reserved for Costumer" signs over part of the front pew on the right side. She scanned the room but couldn't see Annika.

I hope she gets here soon.

Chapter 13

Aaand It's Show Time!

RUTH TOOK HER SEAT at the pew and looked around. It was a good space for a small community theatre, even if it smelled like old varnish and Lysol. Black heavy curtains lined the sanctuary walls, cutting off any light from the stained glass windows. There were also black curtains covering the altar area. In front of those, a makeshift set had been placed.

It's sort of claustrophobic, but I guess it works, she thought. She noticed the built-up stage, which had access from both the right and left sides. She could hear murmuring from behind the stage curtains.

Ruth's seat had easy access to the back stage area ... what there was of it. The door to those basement stairs was right next to her. Turning around and watching the front entrance for Annika, she was relieved to see the girl finally enter and come down the center aisle toward her. Behind her walked a beaming Emmy Eklund, carrying all her books and looking so happy it made Ruth feel even more sorry for her.

Annika sat next to Ruth. Emmy sat next to Annika.

"What a wonderful little girl!" Emmy gushed over Annika's head to Ruth. "I wish she were mine!"

Ruth smiled back and nodded her head, not knowing how to respond to such a compliment coming from a stranger, and a woman who so obviously needed a child of her own. To Annika she said, "Well, sweetie, is your tummy better?"

"I'm fine, Gram." Annika leaned into her a little, as if by touching her grandma, things would somehow be okay. Ruth looked at Emmy, who was busy stacking children's books on the seat beside her. The woman was smiling to herself.

Ruth sensed something wrong. "You okay, honey?" she whispered in her granddaughter's ear.

Annika just nodded *yes,* but her body language said the opposite.

Ruth put her arm around Annika's shoulders and hugged her.

Emmy excused herself and, leaving her sweater and purse on the pew, started walking up the aisle to the back of the church, where some of the actors were getting ready to go on stage. "I'll be right back," she had said.

After Emmy left, Annika leaned close and whispered, "She's weird, Gram."

"How so?"

"Well, for one thing, she wants to read me 'baby books.' I'm ten years old and I read much harder books than what she brought. And I can read for myself; I don't need someone to read to me!"

Ruth whispered back, "Well, honey, cut the poor woman some slack. She never had kids, you know, and she doesn't know about age-appropriate reading material."

"I thought Pastor Paul said she was a teacher. Uh oh, she's coming back."

Emmy returned and sat next to Annika, patting the girl's hand and saying, "I just wished Paul *good luck!*"

Annika quickly pulled her hand away and leaned closer to Ruth. She put her head on Ruth's arm.

"You're supposed to say, 'Break a leg,'" Annika said quietly, looking at the stage area.

Just then the "orchestra"—five musicians clustered together in a corner at the foot of the stage—started the overture. Norm Fuerling—Edna's husband—was a lanky, gray-haired and somewhat balding man with a slight pot belly. He looked nervous and attentive as his long fingers played the Carousel Waltz on the piano. He played very well, continually nodding his head to keep the orchestra with him. Ruth noticed the long gray hairs he combed over his balding spot flipping aside as he did so.

She also noticed that the musicians were all dressed in black except the drummer, who wore faded jeans and a Rolling Stones tee-shirt. (Well, it was a *black* tee-shirt, so maybe that counted.) He had long brown hair in a messy pony-tail, and wore dark glasses. Ruth thought he looked like he should have been in a 'sixties rock band.

The violinist was tall and attractive, with thick auburn hair piled high on her head in a stylish bun. She wore a long, flowing black dress, and looked like she was in her fifties. Obviously a good musician, she had her eyes on Norm, smiling and nodding her head in time with his.

Next to her was a flautist—a small, pretty girl—with long, dark curly hair. She was perhaps high school or college-aged, and wore a dressy black skirt and matching jacket.

Last was the cellist, a small blond boy who couldn't have been much older than eleven or twelve. He was wearing a black dress shirt and pants, and could barely see Norm over his music.

An odd collection of musicians, Ruth thought, *but the music sounds pretty decent.*

Scene One commenced, as Arvid Haakala, the 'star keeper,' and the man playing Billy Bigelow, came on stage. "Billy" had a rotund stomach and gray hair that looked too old for the part.

Well ... this is community theatre. You get what you get.

Just then the man playing Billy pocketed a star, as if he intended to steal it.

After that brief scene, supposedly in Heaven, revealing that the entire play was to be a flash-back of Billy's life, the carnival scene began. The whole cast gathered on-stage.

As the Carousel Waltz started up again, and the players assembled, Ruth thought, *The singing and dancing are pretty good. Someone worked really hard with these folks.* She remembered Fritz Gerhardt's direction in the Como Park musicals, and how stern a taskmaster Fritz always was with his cast of amateurs.

I don't think anyone in this show is a professional, yet they work really well together.

"Paul does wonders, doesn't he?" Emmy leaned over and whispered, as if she had been reading Ruth's thoughts.

"Indeed he does," Ruth whispered back, not wanting to talk during the performance. She looked away from the woman and toward the stage again, in order to quell any further conversation. As she did so, she noticed Annika—out of the corner of her eye—slumped down in her seat, looking bored.

Oh dear, this does not bode well.

As Julie and Carrie played their feisty scene with Mrs. Mullin, the owner of the carousel, and Billy Bigelow made his appearance, Annika perked up a bit.

During the first love scene between Julie and Billy, singing "If I Loved You," however, Ruth saw her granddaughter roll her eyes and shake her head.

She probably thinks he's way too old for Julie, and he certainly is, Ruth thought, smiling to herself. They sang so well together, however, with such good voices, that after a while she stopped noticing the age gap.

The man playing Enoch Snow was also much older than Carrie, and much shorter, but he was an impressively commanding tenor. Willy was a decent soprano, and her acting was superb. "When I Marry Mr. Snow" was so much fun to watch, with Willy's flirtatious mannerisms both funny and dear. "When the Children are Asleep" made Ruth's heart ache for Del.

Tomorrow, he'll be up here!

"Billy's Soliloquy" was as powerful as Ruth had ever heard, even if the actor was too old. He captivated his audience and got a thundering ovation from the crowd at the end of his song.

During the intermission, Ruth needed to go backstage and help with costumes. She looked at Annika and asked, "Do you want to come backstage and help me?"

"I have to go to the bathroom," the girl told her. "And I smell popcorn."

Emmy smiled at Annika. "Come on, honey, I'll show you where the bathroom is. And then I'll get you some popcorn. I'll get you a Coke too, if you want one … I mean … that is … if it's okay with you, Ruth. They have the refreshments set up in the narthex."

Emmy was obviously eager to keep taking care of the girl. She looked so heartbreakingly happy to be with Annika, Ruth didn't have the heart to interfere.

"Sure, that's fine," Ruth told her, scanning the theatre. *At least I don't see Mr. Guston anywhere,* she thought. "I need to help with costumes right now, but just be back here by the start of Act Two."

"Don't you worry!" said Emmy, flashing a bright smile. "We'll see you back here in ten minutes. Do you want me to get you anything?"

"Oh … no, thanks. Well … maybe a Diet Coke if they have any?"

"You got it! We'll see you in ten minutes with a Diet Coke!"

As Emmy and Annika hurried up the aisle, Annika looked back at her grandmother and gave her a little wave.

Backstage was not as bad as Ruth thought it might be. The men didn't change much, so there wasn't anything for her to do in their dressing room. And, due to a sense of propriety, Paul had taken over most of it anyway. He stood at the door and instructed Ruth, "Please, just take care of the ladies, for now. And after everyone is gone, maybe you can check on the men's dressing room?"

The women's dressing room was bustling, but it seemed more organized now. Ruth told both Amy and Willy what a good job they were doing. Then she smiled at Edna and Gloria, giving them each a *thumbs up.*

"Hanging the costumes on the screens sure helps," Edna told her. "And thank you for labeling them. You've done this before, I can tell." The woman smiled at Ruth.

Before Ruth could respond, Amy came up to her, holding out her green dress and looking flushed and upset.

"My second-act costume has got stitches coming out!" She showed Ruth where the bodice had split. "I tried getting into it and it just ripped."

"Oh my gosh!" Ruth exclaimed. "I thought I'd fixed it. Put it on, and I'll fix it again."

Ruth grabbed her sewing things while Amy shrugged into the garment.

"Hold still, sweetie," Ruth said, "this will only take a minute. I'll just fix it right now, and then I'll sew it better before tomorrow night." She laughed. "I feel like Mammy Yocum from *Li'l Abner*. She would sew the pants right on Pappy Yocum. Did you ever read *Li'l Abner?*"

"No, but I bet it was funny."

"It was." Ruth chuckled. "Hold still, I don't want to poke you with this needle!"

"You're so nice to me, I wish you were my mom," Amy said quietly.

"Oh, sweetheart ..." Ruth's eyes got misty. "Everything will be all right, you'll see."

"I sure hope so," said the girl, as Ruth finished her sewing.

Ruth hugged her and said, "It will, I just know it will." *I hope and pray I'm right*, she thought.

"Wish me luck in Act Two."

"In the theatre we never say, 'Good luck.' We say, 'Break a leg!'" Ruth patted her shoulder.

"That's a pretty strange thing to say," said the girl.

Chapter 14

Never Say "Good Luck"

RUTH RETURNED TO HER pew for the beginning of Act Two, and scanned the sanctuary for Annika and Emmy. Her pulse quickened when she didn't see them.

But then she finally saw them walking down the aisle toward the front, hands full with popcorn and drinks. She breathed a deep sigh of relief. As they took their seats, Annika was happily eating popcorn and drinking pop and talking about her best friend, Serena.

"... and then her dog tore it to shreds!" Annika was giggling.

"You're kidding!" Emmy laughed too. "Did her teacher accept it that way?"

"No, of course she didn't. Serena had to redo the whole assignment, and was she ever mad!"

They both laughed.

I'm happy to see them getting along so well, Ruth thought, smiling at them as she took her seat and accepted a Diet Coke from a beaming Emmy.

"Thank you, you're a life-saver!" she whispered as she held up the can in a salute.

Then actors came back on stage.

Act Two went smoothly. "A Real Nice Clambake" was rousing, getting cheers from the audience as the actors finished singing it, Ruth included.

Tommy Sherman, as "Jigger," was excellent, and absolutely convincing as a thug.

Mostly because he probably is *a thug,* thought Ruth.

Amy's rendition of "What's the Use of Wond'rin'" was as poignant as Ruth had ever heard it. Ruth was wiping her eyes at the end of the song.

When Gloria belted out "You'll Never Walk Alone," Ruth noticed many of the women in the audience were wiping their eyes, and some of the men, too.

The "Snow children" were full of mischief, and stole the scene every time they were on.

Emmy whispered to Ruth that the young girl playing "Louise" was in real life their older cousin. She didn't even seem to be acting when she was supposed to be angry at them!

Ruth smiled to herself and thought, *I'll bet that girl baby-sat those rascals more than once!*

While the children were acting up and running around, Ruth noticed Emmy's rapt attention and the longing in her eyes.

Good Lord, I hope that woman has a family soon!

And there wasn't a dry eye in the house when the whole cast finally sang "You'll Never Walk Alone." Ruth had to take a Kleenex out of her purse and blow her nose.

When the show was over and the standing ovation ended, Ruth turned to Emmy and said, "That was really wonderful!"

"Yes, yes, it was."

"Would you mind taking Annika back to the hotel? And would you please see that she gets ready for bed? I'm going backstage to straighten the dressing rooms."

"I would love to!" Emmy gushed. "I'll stay in your room until you get there." The woman looked so happy, Ruth didn't feel at all as if she were imposing.

But Annika insisted "I'm not a baby. I can stay by myself!"

"No, of course you're not," Emmy laughed. "But I need someone to make sure *I'm* okay. You can take good care of me."

Ruth said, "Thanks, I'll be down as soon as I finish." To Annika she said, "You could get ready for bed and watch some TV with Emmy. I'll be down soon to tuck you in."

"Oh … okay," Annika grumped.

And, although Ruth had not seen Sam Guston at the show, she felt she should warn Emmy about him.

"A man named Sam Guston was talking to Annika on the boat. I felt … well, something was *off* about him, and I don't want him anywhere near her, okay?" She told Emmy quietly.

Emmy looked at her, then said, "Sam Guston and his nephew go to our church. He's really against this little theatre. I don't know why. I don't like Sam Guston, either, so don't worry. I'll watch out for him." Emmy put a protective arm around Annika's shoulder as they walked off, and as they reached the door, she turned and gave Ruth a *thumbs-up* sign.

Ruth finished cleaning up the women's dressing room, sweeping it out and organizing, as best she could, all of the cosmetics and props. She hung up the costumes that had been dropped helter-skelter on the chairs and sofa. She told herself that she'd have a little talk with the ladies before the next performance.

"This simply will not do!" she muttered.

After that she knocked quietly on the men's dressing room door. There was no answer, so she opened it slightly and peeked in. Although it was mostly dark inside, what she saw from the hallway made her shut the door again. Quickly! A couple was "romantically busy" on the old cot at the side of the room! Ruth did not see who the woman was, but she recognized Tommy Sherman by his balding blond head in the dim light.

Ruth shut the door, gasping for breath.

I hope that's not Amy with him! She shook her head. *Now what'll I do?* Exasperated, she knocked on the door again, and said in a loud voice, "Everybody decent in there? I need to come in right now and clean up this dressing room!"

She heard rustling and whispering from inside. Tommy's voice called out, "Everything's okay in here!" She heard more rustling and the door opened. The light was on now and Tommy held the door only partly open, and filled the space so she could not see in. "I'll clean up the room," he said, smiling widely at her. "You can go on home. I got it covered." Then he closed the door in her face before she could respond.

Dumbfounded, Ruth got her purse and sweater and went out to her car.

Should I tell Pastor Paul what I saw? she wondered angrily. *Maybe someone needs to confront that guy!* And then she thought better of it. *I've only got four more nights of this. I should probably stay out of it.* She shuddered. *He might come after me ... or worse, after Annika! I'd better leave it alone. God, I wish Del was here. I need his advice.*

Ruth drove back to the East Bay.

Maybe I should tell someone. Maybe Emmy? Although I don't know what Emmy could do about it ...

She drove slowly down the hill toward the hotel.

When she got to her room Ruth had developed a splitting headache. She smiled wanly at Annika and Emmy, sitting on Annika's bed. They were looking at some comics Annika had brought from home.

"You don't look so hot, Gram," Annika told her. "Are you okay?"

"I'm ... fine, honey," she sighed. "Just a little tired. It's been a very long day."

"I got you a cup of tea," said Emmy. "It's on your bedside table. It's got a cover on it so I'm sure it's still hot."

"Thank you, but I can't have caffeine this late in the day." Ruth smiled at her and added, "But that was very thoughtful of you."

"It's herbal," the woman assured her. "It's supposed to help you sleep."

"I don't think I'll need anything to help me sleep tonight. But I'll give it a try, thank you." She took the cover off of the cup and sipped the tea. "Mmmm, it's lemony. I like it. Thanks so much, Emmy."

Emmy looked very pleased, then explained how she always carried tea bags in a plastic baggie in her purse.

"You never know when you'll need 'em. I don't like coffee, and that's all the ladies at church serve!"

"Well, they are Lutheran," Ruth laughed, as she dug in her purse and found a bottle of aspirin. "Actually, I prefer tea to coffee myself. I always see to it that we have a pot of hot water and some tea bags at my church at home."

"Where is that?"

"Lake Elmo. Christ Lutheran." Ruth took two aspirin with her tea. "It's not too far from St. Paul, but far enough to be out in the country. Del and I have a little cottage on the lake."

"It sounds so nice," Emmy sighed. "I suppose you're both retired?" She started gathering up her children's books and her purse.

"Well, I am. I was an art teacher in the public schools. Del is an opera singer. He still works. In fact, he was in Boston yesterday, singing a part in *Candide.*

"Does he have a large part?" Emmy sat back on the bed.

Ruth thought, *She wants to talk.* "I guess it is," Ruth told her. "He's singing the part of Dr. Pangloss."

Ruth noticed that Annika had curled up in the bed and had fallen asleep.

"Not that I'd know anything about that," said Emmy, sighing again. "I don't get to see many operas up here in Grand Marais. Just Paul's musicals." And then Emmy seemed to actually see Ruth. "Oh, Ruth, I'm so sorry! You look really tired, and here I am, talking up a storm! I should be going. Look at Annika, she's out like a light." As she rose she said, "Ruth, I know I was acting upset on the boat, and I'm *so* glad you got to see another side of me tonight."

"I ... I didn't feel it was any of my business—what happened today on the boat," Ruth said quietly.

"Paul had just told me about Amy's pregnancy."

Ruth nodded and said, "I talked to Amy about it, tonight, while I was fixing her costumes. It's why they all had to be re-sewn. She's not married, and the baby's father is dead."

"I know, and I've been trying to have a baby for the past six years. And then she just ... well, it's not her fault I'm upset." Then Emmy started crying. "And it's not Paul's fault, either."

Ruth reached over to her and patted her arm. "This has got to be so hard for you."

"It really is," she sniffed, "and it's not anyone's fault. It wasn't fair to take it out on Paul, but when he told me ... on the way to the boat, well ... I ... I just lost it ..."

"Thanks for the popcorn and pop," Annika murmured, rousing a bit.

"You're most welcome, sweetheart." Emmy recovered, trying to wipe her tears away. "We'll get some more tomorrow night." She smiled through her tears at Ruth. "I'd better go, and let you both get some rest. Thanks for not judging me too harshly. I just loved being with you and Annika this evening. She's such a wonderful little girl! And you're such a wonderful grandma!"

Ruth reached out for her and hugged her. "She is that."

"And thank you for being so understanding. I'd better go now."

Ruth walked with Emmy a little ways down the hallway. When they were some distance from the room, Ruth paused and put a hand on Emmy's arm.

"Um ... about the baby's father ..." she whispered.

"You mean Joey-Frank Jurak?"

"Yes, him."

Emmy blinked at her and said, "What about him?"

"Well ... you know he died, right? They found his body yesterday ... actually *I* found his body ... and, well ..."

When Emmy didn't respond, Ruth cleared her throat and continued.

"I mean ... does anyone know anything? Have they found out anything ... yet?"

"About ... ?"

"Who killed him? And why?"

Emmy blinked again and said, "I'm afraid I really didn't know Joey-Frank Jurak. But from what I've heard, Amy is better off without him."

And with that, Emmy turned and exited the hotel, making a beeline across the parking lot to her car. Ruth stood alone in the hotel corridor, mouth open, as Emmy's car started and drove away.

I ... well ... she's a little strange.

Ruth shook her head and returned to her room.

As she put the chains on the door, she said to Annika, "You two seemed to be getting along better."

"Yeah, I guess she's not so bad." Annika yawned. "I told her those books were too babyish for me, and she didn't get mad or anything, so I guess she's okay." Annika, who didn't miss much, looked at Ruth and said, "She really wants a little girl of her own, you know. I wonder why she doesn't have one?"

"Maybe she can't have children. Not everyone can, you know."

"I know, but she could adopt a little girl. Or a boy, even." Annika sat up in bed. "My friend Krista and her brother Max are adopted. Their parents are really nice, too."

"Maybe she could." Ruth grabbed her nightie, asking, "Have you brushed your teeth?"

"Yeah, Emmy made me."

Ruth went over to her and tucked her in, and kissed her goodnight. "It's been a really, really long day," she told her.

"That's for sure!" Annika yawned again. "Emmy said my parents are lucky."

"They are!" said Ruth as she headed for the bathroom.

That poor woman!

A little while later she got into her bed and tried to fall asleep. But as tired as she was, Ruth lay awake, thinking.

I'm glad I said something to Emmy about Mr. Guston. I probably should have said something about Tommy Sherman, but not in front of Annika. I wonder who was in the dressing room with him. God, I hope it wasn't Amy. Please, God, don't let it be Amy.

Then she thought about Gloria.

I guess older women in small towns aren't always happy. I wonder what kind of "tough life" she's had? Poor thing ...

Finally Ruth decided to just concentrate on the sound of the waves again, coming in ... going out ... coming in ... going out ... until she fell asleep.

No Rest for the Wicked, and No Service for Joey-Frank

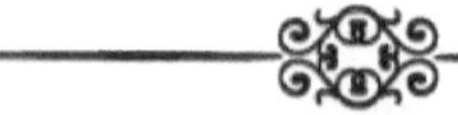

THE NEXT MORNING, WHILE Ruth and Annika waited for their breakfast in the hotel restaurant, Loris Biederman came over to their table.

"How was your night?" she asked. "Did you sleep well?"

"Oh, yes," said Ruth, looking up at her and smiling. "The sound of the waves coming off Lake Superior are so soothing, that I—"

"I saw that Emmy Eklund brought your granddaughter back last night. And she stayed a while? And talked, I suppose?"

"Um ... yes." Ruth was taken off-guard by Loris' abruptness.

"So, what did she talk about?"

Ruth frowned and said, "Not much. I ... don't really remember, I suppose. I ..."

"Did she say anything about Joey-Frank Jurak?" Loris asked pointedly.

"Well, no. Why do you ask?"

"No reason. I'm just curious. Sally Merritt's funeral will be on Tuesday. Do you want to go with me? It's at Pastor Paul's church, at eleven o'clock. We could go up there together?"

"I want to. Sally was a friend of mine from high school. But let me talk to Del first. And speaking of funerals, what about that young man? Is Joey-Frank having a funeral?"

Loris made a distasteful face, pursing her lips, then said, "I guess his sister had him cremated. But Mr. O'Donnel at the funeral home never mentioned any plans for a service. I don't think the Juraks belonged to a church or anything, and the sister doesn't have much money. There's probably nothing at all planned."

"That seems sad," Ruth mused. "He's so young ... and then not to even mark his passing ..."

"Nobody here will miss him. Except maybe his sister. Maybe. Probably not even her." Loris looked like she was sucking on a lemon. "Joey-Frank caused a lot of trouble in this town"—she lowered her voice—"drugs, burgeries, assault ... *rape.*"

"Oh!" Ruth shook her head, horrified. She looked meaningfully at Loris and then at Annika, who was pretending to be interested in her scrambled eggs, but Ruth knew was *all ears.*

"I'm sorry." Loris put up her hands. "That just came out." She looked embarrassed. "Well, I better get back to the desk. We'll have to have a cup of tea later, and talk."

"Yes, we'll have to do that," Ruth assured the woman.

After Loris walked away, and a waitress brought their breakfasts, Ruth glanced over at Annika, who whispered, "I know what rape is, Gram. I see the TV news."

"Let's talk about something else. Okay? Let's just eat our breakfast."

"We're going out to Artist's Point today, right, Gram? Is that a better subject?"

"Much better." She took a sip of her tea." Yes, I promised you we'd go out there, and it looks nice out today. So, as soon as we're finished here, we'll pack up our art supplies and go. That's the plan." Ruth was indeed happy to change the subject.

"Good!" The girl ate some scrambled eggs, and bit into a piece of toast with strawberry jam. "I can't wait to paint my first Lake Superior painting! Also, these are really, really good eggs.

Ruth was startled to see Sam Guston enter the dining room ... especially when he walked straight toward Ruth.

She whispered to Annika, "Take my key and run back to the room, and lock it!" She tilted her head in the direction of the man coming toward her.

Annika nodded, took the key, and made a hasty exit.

"Well, well, Mrs. Mays!" Sam Guston said, approaching. "We meet again." He pulled up a chair and sat down at her table, without even asking her if it was okay.

"You can have this table if you'd like; I was just leaving," Ruth said tersely.

"Not on my account, I hope," Sam said heartily.

"Of course not." Ruth finished her tea and put her cup down.

As she rose to leave, Sam Guston held out something to her. It was a business card. She took it, frowning, and questioned him, "What is this?"

"It's to advertise my new restaurant and event center. *Guston's!* I'm having a grand opening, and you and your granddaughter are cordially invited."

"Thank you, but I really have to go. My granddaughter and I are going out painting today." *God! Why did I tell him that?* Ruth thought, wanting to kick herself.

"You're an artist?" Sam sounded excited. "I'll need some art for my new place! Maybe we can do a little business?" He looked hopeful.

"I … seldom have enough work to sell. Please excuse me, I have to go now." Ruth turned to leave. She quickly walked away.

"We'll talk again!" Sam called to her loudly.

I hope not.

As Ruth passed through the lobby, Loris looked up and pointed to the coffee carafe on her desk.

"Want any coffee?" she asked. "It's complimentary. And I'm really sorry I mentioned rape in front of your granddaughter."

"Oh, um …" *Yeah, what the heck was that all about?*

"It just slipped out. It's just that I really couldn't stand Joey-Frank."

"Seems he wasn't too popular around here," said Ruth.

"He has hurt a lot of women. He has hurt … people close to me. Can I pour you a cup of coffee?"

"No thanks, I'm a … a tea drinker." Ruth held her hand up. "And don't worry about Annika. She already knows about … stuff. Hears about it on the TV news, I guess." Ruth grimaced. "I'm sorry, but I really need to go. I promised Annika we'd paint today. And morning light is best."

"Just hear me out," Loris said in a low voice, coming around the desk and taking Ruth by the arm. "Joey-Frank was dating Arvid's daughter, Vicky. And I guess one thing led to another"—Loris cleared her throat—"and Vicky said 'No' and he wasn't having it." She put her hand over her mouth. "God, it was awful! She came running to me that night, instead of to Arvid. I guess she was afraid of what he'd do. She was bruised and bleeding and hysterical. I drove her right to the clinic. The Norstrands know all about it, because we told them. But Joey-Frank lied and said he was somewhere else that night, and we couldn't prove anything. It ended up being a *he-said-she-said* situation."

"That's awful!" said Ruth, astonished.

"Who knows how many other girls have suffered at that monster's hands?"

"Do you think maybe Arvid killed him?" Ruth whispered. She was feeling sick to her stomach.

"Nah, that Finn wouldn't hurt a fly." Loris' forehead furrowed. "He's a good man, and he's been through a lot. His wife died of cancer when Vicky was twelve. He's all that poor kid has. *Shhh,* here he comes." Loris pasted a smile on her face as Arvid came through the front door. She called out to him, "Hey! I hear you were great as the star-keeper and town doctor last night!"

"*Vell,* at least I didn't have to sing," he told both women, keeping his head down.

"How's room 102 coming?"

"Almost finished," he called out as he turned and walked down the hall toward room 102.

"Whew! That was close," Loris whispered to Ruth. "So, your hubby wants 102, right?"

"Yes, if it's available. He should be here by supper-time." She thought for a moment. "He might be too tired from all that driving to go to the show tonight. Maybe he and Annika can stay and watch television and relax?"

"Sounds like a plan." Loris wrote Del's name in her ledger, then looked up as Annika approached. "Well, here's your painting partner."

Ruth smiled at her granddaughter as she took back the room key. "Come on back with me to the room for a minute, will you, honey?" Ruth said. "I'm just going to go to our room to use the bathroom."

Annika nodded.

Loris held up her hand. "Before you go, I want to tell you something. You know Tommy Sherman, the guy playing "Jigger" in the musical?" Loris took a long sip of her coffee. "Watch out for him. He and Joey-Frank were thick as thieves. And *thieves* is an apt description. Keep your purse with you at all times, when you're there."

"Thanks for the heads-up," Ruth said as she turned to go. *I already know he's a bad one,* she thought. *Maybe I should mention what I saw to Pastor Paul? I'll ask Del what he thinks.*

Just then Arvid returned to the desk. "Excuse me, Loris, but I gotta get over to the hardware store. I'm outta finishing nails ... and I seem to have misplaced my hammer. I can't find it anywhere."

"Did you look in the supply closet?" asked Loris.

"Ya, I looked everywhere. I can't imagine where it could've gone! It was a good one, too." He nodded to Ruth. "Excuse me, Mrs. Mays." He looked down at his hands. "I guess I have to buy another hammer. It sure was a good one."

"Buy anything you need," Loris told him heartily, "and put it on Arnie's account. And would you pick me up a fly-swatter, while you're there? Mine is giving up the ghost. Thanks, Arvid."

"You really did do a good job in the musical," Ruth told him. "I enjoyed your performance."

"*Vell,* I guess I'm glad it wasn't too horrible. But my half-brother, he's the one with all the talent in the family."

"Your half-brother?" Ruth asked.

"Howard Kirkdorff. He's *Billy Bigelow.* "

Ruth was surprised. They didn't look at all alike.

Loris asserted, "You have talent too, Arvid. And you're the best darn carpenter in Grand Marais!"

Arvid lowered his head and muttered, "Gotta go now." He hurried out the door.

"You embarrassed him," said Ruth, shaking her head at Loris.

"Yeah, he embarrasses easily."

Annika pulled on Ruth's sleeve. "Gram, I sure would like to go and paint now. Can we please?"

"We sure can, in just one minute!" They hurried back to their room, so Ruth could use the bathroom and get her hat and her bag of art supplies. But she felt saddened and ... well, *off* ... about the town not giving Joey-Frank any kind of funeral.

Even bad kids deserve to be prayed over ... especially bad kids. They need our prayers more than anyone!

She threw Sam Guston's card in the bathroom waste basket.

As if I'd ever go to his restaurant, or sell him any of my art! she thought grimly.

Chapter 16

Artist's Point—Crashing Waves and Crashing Fists

RUTH AND ANNIKA WALKED along Broadway Avenue toward Artist's Point—past World's Best Donuts, past another little hotel, a few scattered businesses, and over a sprawling parking lot that led to the Coast Guard station. They crossed a stretch of beach and down a stony little path, toward the old stone-and-concrete eastern harbor breakwater. On each side of the path were wild raspberry bushes, with most of the berries pulled off.

"If you can find a raspberry," Ruth told Annika, "It's okay to eat it."

"There's some down at the very bottom of the bush," Annika informed Ruth, "but I wouldn't eat them unless I washed them really well."

"Why is that? I'm sure they're perfectly okay."

"What if a dog peed on them?" Annika asked her.

"Well, okay ... I guess that could happen. In that case let's just get some at the hotel."

I'm glad she's careful, Ruth thought, as they came to the breakwater that separated Artist's Point from the rest of the beach. *She's just like her mom.* Ruth smiled as she remembered Hannah as a child, washing a pear an elderly artist friend had given her from a still life he was painting. The artist had thought it was strange, but Ruth knew her daughter's proclivity for cleanliness, especially since the artist's house did not look all that clean or orderly.

"Oh Hannah's just like a little racoon," Ruth had told the old man. *"She washes everything."*

Ruth was glad Annika was careful like her mom.

They navigated the steps and stones up to the flat stretch of concrete, where visitors could walk out to the lighthouse. Waves lapped at the steep sides. Gulls cried overhead.

Ruth had some difficulty getting up onto the breakwater, because of her arthritic knee. "Watch your step," she warned Annika.

The waves of Lake Superior were crashing today, splashing both rocks and concrete. To their right was a long walk on the wall to the lighthouse station. To their left was the rugged, rocky, Artist's Point. Behind the rocks was a forest of scrubby sea-hardy trees.

"Well, this is it." Ruth pointed at the steep rise of exposed Lake Superior cliff rock. "Artist's Point. What do you think?"

"It's awesome, but I want to learn how to paint the splashing waves!" The girl was staring, mesmerized, at the water.

Ruth breathed in the bracing Lake Superior air. *What a beautiful place!* She thought. *It never ever changes. These rocks are some of the oldest in the world.*

"Be careful now," Ruth told her granddaughter. "I know you're not a *baby*, but these rocks can be very slippery if there's water on them ... and it looks like there is. Let's walk on the path that goes by the trees." She headed to the left where the path wound through scrub pine and undergrowth. "I usually go this way anyway. It's a lot easier." She stopped to button up her sweater. The wind off the lake was chilly.

"Gram, did you know these are some of the oldest rocks in the world?" Annika was pointing. "Mom told me."

"Yes, I do. Your Grandpa Tom and I went to a lecture once when we were up here. They are over two billion years old." She looked out at the lake. "And Lake Superior is about ten thousand years old. It was formed by one of the ice-age glaciers melting."

"And it *never gives up it's dead.*" Annika obviously relished that old phrase.

"Well, according to that lecture we attended," Ruth informed her, "the bodies that don't surface are the ones whose shipwrecks were in very deep water. The deeper water is so cold that it prevents the bacteria growth that makes bodies bloat and come to the surface. So yes, those bodies stay down there."

Annika shivered and murmured, "I wonder how many are down there?"

"Why don't we just paint now?" Ruth asked. "Forget about bodies, and let's just think about how beautiful it is?"

Ruth and Annika painted for over two hours. Ruth had to slip into the woods after an hour and hide behind a bunch of trees to "go potty," as she told Annika. "You keep a look out for me, okay?" she asked the girl, who rolled her eyes.

Annika's painting was so much like her mom's at that age, Ruth smiled when she saw it. "Your mom and dad will just love that!" she told the girl.

"I hope so, because I'm done. This is harder than I thought it would be." Annika stretched and yawned and said, "I have a couple books I need to start on. I have to get them read before school starts. Do you mind if I walk back to the hotel and stay in our room until lunch?"

"I'll go with you," Ruth said. "I'm pretty much done for today." She got out her camera and took a couple of photos of the rocks and trees. Then she packed up her brushes and tubes of Liquitex acrylics. "I'll finish this later, maybe even at home. Besides, all this fresh air is making me a little sleepy, and we have another performance tonight!"

"Can I skip this one?" Annika asked. "I've seen it already, and I can stay in our room."

"I don't feel comfortable leaving you ..." Then Ruth remembered, "You can stay with Grandpa Del of course, but what about your drama badge? Don't you want to earn that?"

"Yeah, I suppose," the girl answered. "I wonder how much I have to do to get it."

"Folding programs, helping put the costumes on hangers, sweeping the floor? You know, helping out backstage."

"I probably can do that," said Annika.

As they were walking back and were just getting through the bushes, Ruth thought she saw a member of the cast on the beach. It looked like she arguing with someone.

"Look over there!" Ruth squinted as she pointed out the couple. She couldn't see the man's face; his sweatshirt hood was covering it. "Can you see who that is? Are they from the show?"

"It looks like the woman who has nine kids—Mr. Snow's wife, Carrie?" Annika was staring now. "Whoah! Did you see *that?*" Her eyes got wide. "That guy hit her! She fell down!"

"Let's go," Ruth said. "We've got to help her!" They hurried down the path and over toward the beach.

Walking was difficult, especially for Ruth. The stones on the beach made a very unstable surface over which to maneuver, and Ruth had to be careful not to fall.

"Maybe she just tripped," she said, hoping this wasn't a fight, or worse—an assault.

Annika snorted and said, "I don't think so. I saw him. He punched her!"

In her hurry and being nervous at coming upon this scene, Ruth tried to remember the young woman's name. She only remembered that she played Carrie Pipperidge Snow.

"Hey! Do you need help?"

What is her real name? Willy?... Willy Guerin!

The man who had been with her left. Ruth saw him skirt around one of the buildings that housed the Coast Guard.

"Willy!" Ruth called out. "Willy, wait up!"

The girl got up off the ground, looked startled, and started running away from Ruth. She was almost across the parking lot.

Ruth and Annika hurried to catch up with her, with Ruth calling out, "Willy! Willy, it's Ruth, the costumer ... remember me?"

But Willy, who didn't even look back when Ruth called her, was hurrying as fast as she could, away from them.

Out of breath, Ruth and Annika saw the girl run around one of the houses near the beach.

"We'll never catch up with her, Gram!" Annika was out of breath. "If she'd wanted our help, she would have waited, don't you think?" The girl shaded her eyes, trying to catch sight of Willie.

"I guess so," said Ruth, who was also out of breath. "I'll ask her tonight if she's all right."

"Maybe it wasn't her? Maybe it was someone else?" Annika adjusted the strap on her bag that held her art supplies.

"I'm pretty sure it was Willy. Her hair was so light. I haven't seen anyone else in town with hair like that."

"Is she's an albino?" Annika asked.

"An *albino?* Where do you come up with stuff like that?" Ruth was almost laughing.

"We learned about it in science class in school. "She didn't have pink eyes though, so maybe not."

"Maybe she wears blue contacts?" Ruth said, making a silly face.

"Maybe, but I sure don't like some guy punching her!" Annika frowned.

"I don't either. So, we'll get to the bottom of it tonight. But let me be the one who talks to her, okay?"

"Okay," said Annika. "But can I be there when you do? *Please?*"

"Let me think about that ... right now I need a bite to eat and then a little nap."

Ruth and Annika returned to the East Bay Inn, each keeping an eye out for the elusive Willy, and neither of them seeing her. Ruth was secretly glad. She really didn't feel like confronting anyone right now. Annika, however, looked like she would love a confrontation!

Chapter 17

Bad News Travels Fast Up Here

As Ruth and Annika walked past the front desk, Loris said "Pssst!" to call Ruth over.

Ruth said to Annika, "Go and get us a table, will you, sweetie? I'll just be a moment."

After Annika disappeared into the dining room, Ruth stepped closer to the front desk.

Loris Biederman had a disgusted look on her face as she said, "That Sam Guston! You know what he did this morning after you left? He asked me for your telephone number and home address."

"What?" Ruth was horrified. "You didn't give it to him, did you?"

"Of course not," Loris said, shaking her head. "I told him, in no uncertain terms, to leave my customers alone." She looked pointedly at Ruth. "Watch out for him. He's known around town as a ladies' man."

"Oh, I really don't think he wants anything like that," Ruth laughed. "Not from me. He wants paintings for his restaurant."

"Oh, well ... do you want to sell paintings to him?"

"No! Never! And thank you for not giving out my information. I just want to forget about him as soon as we leave Grand Marais, and I want him to forget about us."

"Got it." Loris nodded. "Anyway, you can always hang your art here."

Ruth laughed ruefully. "As soon as I get twenty paintings done—oh, in about five or ten years, I'll look you up." She smiled at Loris before walking away to join Annika in the dining room.

Annika and Ruth ate a quick lunch at the hotel. Annika had a tuna sandwich and chips, and Ruth had a bowl of chili and some crackers. When they left the dining room, Loris Biederman motioned for them to come back to the desk again.

"Bad News," she said. "Your hubby just called. He has the flu."

"Oh, no!" said Ruth.

"He's at home and wants you to call him."

"I'll go to my room and do it right away. Thank you, Loris."

Poor Del. He probably caught something on the plane. That happens to a lot of people, breathing all that stale air.

She and Annika hurried to their room.

Ruth put her art bag on her bed, and picked up the phone. She hurriedly dialed their home number in Lake Elmo. The phone rang and rang. She was about to hang up when Del finally picked up.

"Hello?" he croaked.

"Oh, sweetheart, you sound just terrible!" Ruth said.

"Oh, Ruth, it's you! I'm so sorry; I was in the bathroom with a bad stomach ache. It's probably food poisoning. I thought that fish on the plane tasted funny." He groaned. "Sorry, excuse me," he said, and put down the phone. Ruth could hear him running to the bathroom.

She waited for him to return. When he did, she said, "Oh, Del, my poor love. Maybe I should just come home."

At this, Annika, who was listening, looked up at her grandmother with despair in her eyes.

"You can't do that," Del told her. "What about Annika?" He coughed. "I'm sure it's just one of those twenty-four-hour things. I'll rest all tomorrow and drive up on Sunday."

"But only if you feel well enough," said Ruth. "I wish I were there to take care of you."

"Angie and George came over to feed the cats. When they saw me on the couch, practically passed out, Angie covered me up with a comforter and made me some chicken soup." He laughed and coughed some more. "They're coming back tonight with my dinner. Really, don't worry, Angie and George'll take good care of me." He coughed again. "They won't let me die, although last night I wished they had."

"Oh, my poor sweet baby," Ruth whispered into the phone. "Get better, okay? She looked at Annika, who motioned that she wanted to talk too. "Annika wants to say 'hi.'"

"Hi, Grandpa Del." Annika sounded subdued. "I'm so sorry you're sick." She didn't seem to know what to say. "I love you lots, get better soon."

"I love you, too, my favorite granddaughter."

"I'm your *only* granddaughter," She said, rolling her eyes. "Here's Grandma."

Ruth took the phone. "I don't want you driving up here on Sunday if you're still sick. Promise me you'll stay home if you don't feel well?"

"I promise," he said, and coughed again. He sounded tired. "I'm going to take a nap now."

"Me too. Annika and I have been out on Artist's Point all morning, painting. I'm just about done for." She sighed.

"Later, my love," he rasped. "You can call me after the play tonight. I'll put the phone by our bed."

"It might be too late to call."

"It won't matter. I'll sleep all day anyway. Good bye for now, my love."

"Good-bye." Ruth kissed into the phone.

Just then there was a soft knock on their door. It was Loris. Again.

"Trouble up at the theatre," she said grimly. "Tommy Sherman—the guy playing Jigger—up and quit the show. Pastor Paul wanted me to tell you."

"*Quit?*" cried Ruth. "But they've only had one performance! How can he do that to the cast? What happened?"

Loris shook her head. "I don't really know. He's always been a trou-bled kid. And a *troublesome* kid, too, if you ask me. Even in school, he was absent most of the time. He worked for us one summer, and half the time he didn't show up." She shrugged. "Don't worry, though. Pastor Paul says he's already found a teenager in his church who will fill in. But"—she looked at Ruth—"the problem is, Tommy was short and built, and this teenager is tall and skinny. The costumes will have to be re-made before tonight. I'm so sorry to be bothering you with all this."

Ruth was relieved that it wasn't something worse. *Like, they found another body.*

She waved a hand and said, "Jigger's costume won't be hard. I can handle it." Then she wondered to herself, *What did he wear? A striped shirt, dark pants, and a beret?* To Loris she said, "It won't be a problem. He only needs one costume. Not like the women." *And thank God it isn't another murder.*

"Oh, and ... the teenager's name is Jack Guston. He's uh ... Sam Guston's nephew. Thought I'd better warn ya."

Ruth stammered, "Ah ... *oh.* Well ... now that's all I need!"

"He's a lot nicer than his uncle," Loris assured her. "He's a good kid, lives with his mom. She's nice too."

"Whew. Glad to hear that."

After Loris left, Annika, who had heard everything, asked, "Gram, does this mean that weird guy from the boat will be at the play tonight?"

"Probably."

"How will the new guy learn all his lines in time?"

Ruth answered her with hand motions. "He'll use little pieces of paper in his pockets and up his sleeves, probably." Then she added, "Anyway, Jigger doesn't have too many lines. He'll be fine."

Annika settled down with her books. Ruth crawled into bed, fully dressed, and napped until her granddaughter woke her for supper.

Later, as they drove up to the old church, Ruth thought, *Only four more performances to go. I'll sure be glad when these are over. Why did I ever get involved in this? Oh yes, the women's shelter. I keep forgetting.*

When they arrived, Emmy was waiting for them at the door.

She said, "I suppose you heard Paul got rid of Tommy Sherman?"

"I ..." Ruth blinked at her. "Mrs. Biederman told me that Tommy quit."

"*Humph!* Quit, huh? Well, that's one way of putting it." Emmy pursed her lips. "We can't have that sort of thing going on in the cast. I told Paul right from the beginning, that guy was trouble!"

"What happened?" Ruth was glad Annika had gone to talk with some of the "Snow children," and couldn't hear them.

"Last night, Willy—the girl playing 'Carrie Snow'—came to our house. She complained to Paul that Tommy tried to force her to ... well, you know. And Willy said, 'If Tommy Sherman stays in the show, then I'm out!' And we need her! She has a big solo part!"

"Oh dear," Ruth said. "I think I interrupted them last night when I tried to tidy up the men's dressing room. Tommy shut the door in my face."

Emmy looked startled and said, "Ruth, you should have said something."

"Yes, I probably should have. I'm so sorry. But I thought it was ... I thought what I was seeing was consensual. And I was just so embarrassed. To tell the truth, I didn't know what to do." Ruth felt instantly guilty about not helping the girl and added, "I think Annika and I saw her today, though, down near Artist's Point. At least we saw a girl who looked a lot like Willy, and I didn't actually see it happen, but Annika said some guy hit her, and she fell down on the rocks at the beach." Ruth grimaced. "I yelled, and Annika and I both tried to help her, but she got up and ran away from us! I thought it was Willy because she had the same light hair."

"Who was the guy?" Emmy asked. "Did you recognize him?"

"No. He was smallish and wiry ... but we were focusing on trying to help the girl. Who do you think he was?"

"Who knows? Could've been one of Willy's ... well ... let's just say, she runs with a rough crowd."

Just then Annika returned. Her eyes were wide. She whispered, "Gram, I saw that girl—the one from the beach!" She nodded toward the backstage. "And she's got a really big bruise on the side of her face! I saw her trying to cover it up with makeup."

Ruth said, "Oh dear! I'd better go back to the dressing room and see how I can help."

Emmy shook her head. "I'll bet it was Tommy Sherman who hit her. I'm glad Paul kicked him out!" Then she turned to Ruth and said, "Please, if you see anything improper, please be sure to tell us? Paul is trying so hard to keep this going."

"I promise, I will after this."

Emmy looked hopefully at Annika and asked, "Are you hungry for popcorn yet?"

"Not yet. I want to see Gram talk to Willy!" She started following Ruth.

"Oh, honey." Ruth turned toward her granddaughter. "Why don't you go with Emmy and get some popcorn and pop?" She reached into her purse and pulled out a five-dollar bill. "My treat tonight!"

"But Gram, I want to be there when you talk to her!" The girl stood her ground.

Emmy intervened at this point.

"No, honey, your grandma needs to make sure Willy is all right to go on stage tonight. And Willy might be embarrassed if too many people want to talk to her, okay?"

"Oh, okay ... I suppose." Annika looked crestfallen. "But you gotta promise to tell me what she says." She looked pointedly at her grandmother.

Ruth said, "I will, every word! Thanks, Emmy, for everything." She smiled gratefully at the woman as she hurried away with Annika. *That Emmy is a really good soul, I'm so glad she's here to help me with Annika. Especially now, when Del can't be here ...*

Chapter 18

Never Wash Out the Blood

I DON'T KNOW WHAT *I'm going to say to Willy*, Ruth thought. *I guess I'll just play it by ear.*

The women's dressing room was its usual bedlam before a performance. The girls and women were lined up at the long mirror over the makeup table.

Ruth saw Willy right away, and she really didn't notice anything amiss. *If she covered the bruise with makeup, she sure did a good job,"* she thought.

"All right! Who stole my friggin' Kleenex! Again!" a raucous voice called out.

Edna Fuerling shrieked louder than anyone else in the small room. Ruth cringed as she heard its rasping sound, and she looked around frantically for any Kleenex box to give the woman to quiet her. She saw a box over by Willy. "Excuse me, honey," she said to the girl, "I need to give this to Edna."

"What*ever,"* said Willy quietly. The girl was checking her makeup in the mirror.

Ruth gave a fistful of tissues to Edna, who was trying vainly to tame her bushy red hair.

"Mucho thanks," rasped the woman. She then gave up on her hair and started powdering her ample bosom, which was exposed much more than Ruth thought necessary.

At her age, she should cover up a bit more, Ruth thought. And then she relented, *Oh well, she is playing a carnival woman, and a hussy at that. I guess she looks perfect for the part.*

There was an empty chair next to Willy, so Ruth sat down and put her hand on the girl's arm. "Sweetie," she said quietly, "I need to ask you something ..."

"Yeah?" Willy gazed at her blue-eyed reflection in the mirror, not meeting Ruth's eyes.

"I saw you today," Ruth began, "down by the beach ... ?" Ruth cleared her throat. "I just want to say, if there's anything I can do to help you, I hope you know you can talk to me any time."

"I'm okay," said Willy. "Anyway, it's all over now." She looked away.

"Well," Ruth went on, "sometimes just talking it over with somebody, older ... you know, helps you figure things out?"

Seeing Amy arrive, she added, "Or talk with a friend about it?"

Amy came right over to her and asked, "What's wrong?"

"Nothing." Willy apparently didn't want to talk.

Amy turned, shaking her head, and walked toward where her costumes were hung.

The two girls pretended to ignore each other and made themselves busy getting dressed for the first act.

Good actresses, thought Ruth.

A loud knock on the door of the women's dressing room made everybody start.

"Just a moment!" Ruth called out as she hurried to answer it.

She opened the door and stepped out. Pastor Paul was standing there, looking harassed. Next to him stood a tall, thin, fresh-faced youth, whose short brown hair was plastered to his head with sweat. His eyes looked downright terrified, and he had a death grip on what looked like a script.

"Ruth, this is Jack. Jack Guston. He's taking over the part of Jigger. Can you find him an appropriate costume? I'd stay to help, but ... the lighting people are having difficulties." Pastor Paul ran a hand through his hair in a nervous gesture. "I hope Arvid is dressed and ready, I need his expertise." He left the boy with Ruth and went down the hall, calling for Arvid.

Ruth looked at the teenager and smiled. "Jack, is it? It's good to meet you. Why don't we go over to the men's dressing room and see if we can find your costume in there." *He looks scared out of his wits,* she thought. *But at least he's wearing dark pants. They'll be fine as long as we find a shirt.*

Ruth paused at the door to the men's dressing room, knocking.

"Costume lady!" she called out. "Are you all decent in there? I need to come in for just a minute!"

Howard Kirkdorff, dressed as Billy Bigelow, came to the door. "Mrs. Mays," he said as he opened it wider. "Yes, do come in, we're all in costume, everyone's decent." He smiled at Jack. "So, is this our new *Jigger?*"

"He is," she told the man. "And we need to find him a shirt." She ushered the gangly youth into the dressing room.

"Hey, Perry!" Howard called out to Lester Perry, who was playing Mr. Snow. "Did Sherman leave his stage shirt and beret behind when he left?" He sniffed. "You know, that black beret and that striped shirt?"

Lester stopped applying his stage makeup, and picked up a beret from the table. "Here's his hat," he said, handing it to Ruth. Then he looked toward the long cot leaning against the wall. "I think his shirt's over there somewhere, probably on the floor." He indicated the cot with a nod of his head. "Tommy Sherman never hung anything up."

Ruth went to the cot, and, not finding any shirts, asked some of the men in the chorus, "Has anyone seen Jigger's shirt? Could it be anywhere else?"

"Try the closet," said Howard, indicating the closet at the far end of the room. "I'd help you look, but I have to do warm-ups ... and gargle ... I do lots of singing ... sorry."

Ruth noticed Howard had dyed his hair black. *He looks a bit younger now. More like Billy Bigelow and less like Billy Bigelow's uncle. That's good.*

As a couple of the men from the chorus were looking around, Lester Perry finished combing his greying hair and mustache. Putting on his dark blue vest, he got up from the dressing table, went over to the cot, and rummaged underneath it.

He said, "I don't think it's in the closet. I was sure I saw it over ... oh, here it is!" Lester held up a wrinkled black and red striped shirt. "I knew I'd seen it near the cot." He was about to hand it to Ruth, when he looked more closely at it and said, "What the hell? Sorry, Mrs. Mays." He showed her the front of the shirt and asked, "Does that look like blood to you?"

"It sure does," said Ruth, taking the shirt from him. She could see a large reddish-brown stain on the front. "Was Tommy okay when he left here?"

Lester snorted and said, "What he was, was madder than a wet hen. Pastor Paul told him in no uncertain terms that his behavior was not acceptable. That young man is headed for big trouble if he doesn't change his ways."

"I'd better clean this before you put it on," Ruth said to Jack Guston, who was looking slightly queasy. Ruth took the shirt over to the sink in the corner of the room, and after generously dousing it with soap, she scrubbed and washed it with cold water. "Are there any other shirts Jack could wear just for tonight?" she asked, hanging the dripping shirt up on a plastic hanger. Then she told the boy, "Don't worry, dear, we'll find you something."

"Here"—Lester reached for the wet shirt—"There's a tree, right outside the door. I can hang this up to dry. And *here*"—he handed a wrinkled army-green shirt to Jack—"This is an old one of mine, but you can use it for now." He laughed. "Jigger wasn't exactly a fashion-plate!"

Ruth left Jack to get ready and asked Lester to oversee the young man's makeup. The rest of the ensemble was pretty much on their own.

She went back to the women's dressing room to see what she could do there. Amy's dress seemed to be holding up, and Willy was doing better. She heard a commotion out in the hall and went to see what was the matter.

Arvid was talking to Pastor Paul. "*Vell,* I did what I could with the lights," he told him, "but I think before next week, maybe some of us guys in the show should take a long hard look at your stage lighting. I think it's on its last legs!"

"Oh no," Paul told him. "We don't have the funds right now to get anything new." He looked crestfallen. "I have to go see to the tickets, can you guys handle it?"

Arvid nodded affirmatively. "Sure, Pastor."

"Thanks," Paul said as he left.

Lester Perry came out to talk with Arvid. "What, the lights again? I can come Monday afternoon and help you look'em over, say ... around one or so?" He saw Howard and called to him. "Hey, Howie, how about it? Can you come over on Monday and look at the lights with us? We need to re-vamp the lighting, so it'll keep working for next week's three shows. How about one o'clock Monday afternoon? Can you be here too?"

"Sure," Howard told him. "What do you need?"

"An electrician," Lester laughed.

"Well, been there, done that," Howard told him.

"Good," Lester Perry said to Arvid. "I'll bring pretzels, you bring some beer?"

Arvid smiled and nodded affirmatively.

Before she left, Ruth told Jack, "Break a leg tonight." And he favored her with a weak smile.

How can he be so nice, when his uncle's such a scumbag? She wondered. *And where did that blood on Jigger's shirt come from?* Ruth started toward the women's dressing room. As she opened the door, Edna was busy lining up the women in the cast to get ready to go on stage. Ruth noticed that even Gloria Simms seemed alert tonight, and was lined up with the others.

"Break a leg!" she told everyone. *Ready or not, second show, here we come!*

Willy and Amy were arguing about something as they walked several paces behind the others.

"That was a rotten thing to do," Amy told Willy. "Ya know, you gotta stop lying about people. It makes *you* look like a lying slut."

"Oh, shut up!" Willy snapped back.

Amy just shrugged.

When both girls saw Ruth, they clammed up, pretending nothing was wrong.

What now? wondered Ruth.

Once More ... With Feeling

As Ruth sat down next to Annika, who was happily munching her popcorn and drinking her Coke, she looked over her head at Emmy and said, "We've got a new Jigger tonight."

Emmy, who was looking so delighted to be mothering the girl, handed Ruth a Diet Coke and said, "This Jigger will be so much better. For everybody." She nodded her head and added, "The old Jigger was nothing but trouble, although with this one ... well ... his uncle is, ah, not the best person ..." She got very quiet all of a sudden.

"I heard his uncle is Sam Guston. What can you tell me about him?"

"Lots of rumors," Emmy whispered to Ruth.

"Let's talk later."

Emmy nodded. Annika was busy with her popcorn and pop while watching some actors backstage.

Ruth said, "Oh, and thanks for the Diet Coke. It'll keep me awake." She opened the can and took a generous swig of the cold liquid. "Well, this Jigger is scared, but I'm sure he'll do fine."

When the orchestra started the overture, Ruth sighed and thought, *Once this performance is over, there's only three more to go! I'm sure nothing else can go wrong. And I do hope Del is feeling better.*

As Willy and Amy got on stage, Ruth wondered, *What were they fighting about? And what was Willy lying about? Maybe that business between her and Tommy was consensual after all? I wish this was over! I never should have taken this on! Lord, I wish Del was here, so I could talk to him about it all.*

Ruth noticed that Willy's rendition of "You're a Queer One, Julie Jordan," wasn't quite as good as the previous night. However, as she sang, "When I Marry Mr. Snow," she picked up more energy.

The young recover so fast.

Jack Guston was doing a passable job as Jigger, even though Tommy Sherman had made a more convincing "bad apple."

That was great type-casting, thought Ruth. *Too bad Tommy couldn't have been a better, more dependable, person. And Jack's uncle is Sam Guston! Oh Lord! I suppose I'll see him here.* She shook her head. *Del, please, please hurry and get well!*

During intermission, Ruth was surprised to see Janet Foley, sitting toward the back, with Andrea and Norman. Since Emmy had taken Annika out to the concession stand for more treats, Ruth took the time to go over and express her condolences.

"Hi, Janet. Hi, Andrea ... Norman." Ruth smiled warmly. "You know your grandma made most of the costumes for this show. I'm only re-fitting some of them. They are quite wonderful! She did such a good job, and I'm so sorry about everything."

Andrea smiled. Janet, wiping her eyes, said, "Mom just loved this theatre group. She sewed costumes for several of their shows. I can't think of a better way to honor her, than to take my kids and go to see her handiwork."

"That's a wonderful thing to do." Ruth patted her shoulder. "I'm so very sorry about what happened to Sally. I understand that her service is Tuesday?"

"Actually, we're going to put it off until a couple of weeks after this show is over," Janet told Ruth. "Pastor Paul has enough to do right now, and I need more time to plan."

"Did your husband have to drive to Duluth again?"

Janet leaned back in her chair and looked at the ceiling. "Yes," she said resignedly. "The corporate office is in Duluth, and Roy gets so busy when he's outfitting new restaurants. We don't see him for days at a time."

"That's got to be difficult."

"You're telling me. I didn't even get a phone call from him tonight!"

"... Oh?" Ruth felt a strange shiver, like a prickling on her arms. "Does he usually call you at night, when he's on the road?"

"Always! And we waited and waited, but finally decided to just come to the play. But that's why we were a little late. I'm sorry I missed the first couple scenes."

"Oh, well, I'm sure there'll be a call for you when you get back. I'm sorry he has to be gone so much. Especially now."

Janet smiled wanly at Ruth. "In a way it's easier. I can just focus on the kids and their needs. And I don't have to cook as much. I just make sandwiches and soup for the kids, and that's pretty much it." She smiled as she whispered, "You know, sometimes with Roy, it's like having one more kid."

Ruth smiled back, and then, as the lights dimmed, said, "It's nice to see you, but I'd better get back to my seat."

What a brave woman, she thought. *I sure hope that husband of hers remembers to call tonight!* And then Ruth had an idea. *I've got my camera in my purse. Maybe I could take some photos of the actors in those costumes and give them to Janet?*

As Ruth walked back to her seat, she also noticed Loris Biederman and her husband, Arnie, who was sitting next to her, rubbing his right knee. She nodded to them and waved. They waved back. *I wonder who's watching the hotel? I guess their daughter Pam must be in charge.* She looked around the theatre, trying to see if Sam Guston was anywhere in the audience, but didn't see the man. Breathing a sigh of relief, she noticed Annika was telling Emmy something about her school, and the woman was listening intently.

Good practice for being a mom, she thought.

The lights dimmed and Ruth whispered, "Sorry, I didn't mean to be gone so long, but I ran into Janet Foley and her kids. I think I'm going to take some photos of the costumes for her to have." She sat down and looked at Emmy. "Did you know she was putting off her mom's funeral until a few weeks after the musical is over?"

"*What?* But I've already got the kitchen help all organized for Tuesday!"

"Paul didn't tell you?" Ruth whispered back.

"No! Excuse me, both of you, I ... I've got to go over to the church office and make some calls!" She picked up her purse and said, "I'll be back ... but that darn Paul, all he can think about is ..." Shaking her head, Emmy walked away hurriedly.

Annika had been watching and listening. She leaned close to Ruth and whispered, "Pastor Paul's in trouble again, isn't he, Gram?" Then she added, "Why don't you let me take the pictures of people in their costumes? It can be part of my drama badge."

"Good idea," Ruth whispered back. She dug out the camera and handed it to Annika. "Go for it."

As the orchestra played "A Real Nice Clambake," Annika took the whole role of film. Then she put the camera under her seat.

Pastor Paul sure is in trouble, Ruth thought. *That man needs to confide in his wife more.*

Emmy returned after about twenty minutes, just as the cast was singing, "There's Nothin' So Bad For a Woman." Plopping down into her seat with a sigh, she looked over at Ruth, rolled her eyes and whispered, "Men!"

Ruth nodded at her.

But Pastor Paul does have a lot on his mind.

All in all, the second night's performance went smoothly. *It's pretty good,* Ruth thought, *considering one of the main actors had never done it before.* Ruth could see Jack Guston looking down at his palm a few times, before speaking his lines; but he did it surreptitiously and spoke out his lines clearly. *He's doing pretty well. And he's sure a good sport.*

When the show was over, Ruth cleaned up the women's dressing room, while Emmy drove Annika down to the hotel.

When I get back, I'll tell her not to be so hard on Paul. Ruth smiled as she hung up dresses. *With the show and the bad lighting and everything, he does have a lot on his plate.*

As she was walking up to the men's dressing room door, it flung open and Tommy Sherman burst out of it, nearly knocking Ruth over. His eyes looked wild.

"Where's my shirt?" he barked at her. "I need my shirt!" He was turning his head this way and that, before he grabbed Ruth's arm. "You're the costume lady! You must know where it is! My shirt? The striped one? My *shirt?*"

"Ow!" Ruth pulled her arm out of Tommy's grasp. "What on earth is wrong with you!"

Just then, Amy came down the hall. "Leave her alone, Tommy! She has nothing to do with any of your stuff!"

"Who asked you?" Tommy shouted back.

Amy's eyes grew wide and dark, and she fell silent. She stepped back from him, and her hands went protectively over her swelling belly.

Ruth turned to the young man and told him, "Tommy, I washed your shirt. It had some blood on it. We hung it on that tree outside, to dry."

"Washed it?" He stared at her. "Blood? What blood? I don't know anything about any blood." Then he blurted out, "Thanks, lady. I gotta go!" and ran from the room.

Ruth stared back at him, as he ran off. Turning to Amy, she asked, "What was that all about?"

"I-I don't know," Amy replied quietly, "but I don't want any part of it ... or any part of him!" Amy turned and walked away.

Ruth finished putting the men's dressing room into some kind of order. She looked down at her arm where Tommy had grabbed it. Bruises were starting to bloom on her fair skin. She flexed it a little and thought ruefully, *Ohhh, I'm going to be sore tomorrow!*

Driving back to the hotel, she thought about Del.

I hope he's better and he can drive up tomorrow. I have so much to talk over with him.

Then her mind wandered to all of the evening's dramas. She shook her head. *What was Paul thinking? Not telling Emmy about the change in Sally Merritt's funeral? And what was all that fuss about the shirt?* She rubbed her arm, which was really sore now. *Tommy seemed relieved when I said I'd washed it. I wonder whose blood was on it? His? Someone else's? Oh, I wish I'd never agreed to do this!*

Chapter 20

Off the Cliff and Into the Lake!

As Ruth reached the hotel, she was met by Odie, who was sitting on the outside front step. His tail wagged when he saw her.

"Hello, boy." She scratched behind his ears and he leaned into her. "Who's a good boy?" she said to the dog as she walked into the lobby, Odie at her side.

"You've made a friend for life," laughed Loris. "I think he remembers you from when you were up here with your hubby and kids. He was a pup then."

"That was"—Ruth mused—"about ten years ago?" She looked at Odie again. "How old *is* he?"

"Going on thirteen," Loris sighed. "I don't know how much longer we'll have him."

Ruth patted Odie's head and asked, "Are Emmy and Annika back yet?"

"Yah, they're in your room. She ordered some herbal tea and a couple blueberry muffins." Loris grinned. "But I'd hurry if I were you. Your granddaughter ate hers on the way from the dining room, and I'll bet she was eyeing yours!"

"Okay," Ruth laughed, "although you know I'd let her have it if she wanted it."

"I know," Loris said wistfully, looking toward the corner of the room. "We'd do anything for our kids, wouldn't we?" She sighed again and looked down at her desk. "And our grandkids. Lord willing, I'll live long enough to see mine."

Surprised by the ebullient Loris' sudden change of spirit, Ruth turned around and smiled at the woman and said, "I know you will." Loris just looked sad. *What's wrong with her?* wondered Ruth.

When Ruth got to her room, she opened it with her key, entering quietly in case Annika was sleeping. She was surprised to see Annika still dressed, sitting in the easy chair, reading. Emmy was fast asleep on top of Annika's bedspread.

"What's going on?" she asked Annika. "Is she sick?"

"Shhhh!" The girl put her finger to her lips. "Gram, she was so tired she just conked out while we were watching TV. So I turned it off. I thought I'd read until you got home."

Just then, Emmy woke up. "Oh!" she said, and sat up immediately, looking around the room and at Ruth. "I'm so sorry! Here, I was supposed to be babysitting, and Annika was babysitting me! It's so embarrassing."

"That's perfectly all right," Ruth laughed. "When the body needs sleep, it just takes a nap. I do that all the time."

"Me too," said Annika. "The TV was boring. We couldn't get anything but news."

Both Ruth and Emmy laughed at that. "Well," said Ruth, "I watch the news if I want to know what's going on."

"And there sure is something going on," Annika told her grandmother.

"And what would that be?" Ruth asked her, as she sat down on her bed with her cup of tea. "It wouldn't be that there is a blueberry muffin thief residing at the East Bay Inn in Grand Marais, Minnesota, would it?"

"Oh, Gram! Who told you we had blueberry muffins?"

"A little bird," Ruth answered.

"I'm sorry, Gram." Annika looked down and brushed the crumbs off her shirt.

"It's okay, honey." Ruth sipped her tea. "Babysitting is hard work. It makes you very hungry."

Emmy stood up and said, "I should be going. But on my way out I can stop and ask Mrs. Biederman if she could spare another muffin? I'm kind of hungry myself."

"Oh no, it's so late," Ruth told the woman. "I shouldn't eat anything at this hour anyway. Thank you, though."

A knock at the door startled them.

"Who could that be?" Ruth asked.

"It's me, Paul," came the voice on the other side of the door. "Is Emmy still there?"

Ruth unlocked the door to find Paul looking disheveled and upset. Upon seeing Emmy, he looked crestfallen, and said, "Honey, I really screwed up! Mrs. Merritt's funeral on Tuesday? It was postponed. I'm so sorry!" He came into the room shaking his head. "I don't know how that slipped my mind. I looked for your list of ladies who do the funeral lunches, but I couldn't find it."

"Paul ... stop ... stop. It's okay, I've already taken care of it." Emmy smiled as she walked toward him and put her arms around him.

"But, how ... ?" He looked confused.

"I'll tell you on the way home. Let's go and let these good people get some sleep. They've had a long day. We all have."

"Thank you," said Ruth.

"And thank you," said Emmy, smiling a knowing smile at her. She grabbed her purse and led her bewildered husband through the door.

After the Eklunds left, Ruth asked Annika, "What did you see on the news?"

"Oh, yeah." Annika looked up. "Well, it said there was a car accident near Duluth, and Mr. Foley's car almost went off the cliff into the lake."

What? Mr. Foley!"

"He's in the hospital, in Duluth, but they said he's going to be okay. I guess they couldn't find the guy who ran him off the road."

"Someone ran Roy Foley off the road? Oh, my God. No wonder he didn't call Janet tonight." Ruth sat down on her bed. "I ... I should call her. No, it's too late. And she's probably talking to police right now. I'm going to call Grandpa Del, though. I sure hope he's feeling better."

She dialed their home number. Del picked up after the first ring.

"Hello, Ruth?" he said, sounding a lot perkier.

"Hi, it's me," Ruth laughed. "You sound so much better.

"I am, and I'm packing up to drive up there tomorrow," he told her.

"Oh!" She breathed easier. "That's wonderful. Don't forget your fishing pole. And be sure to bring Annika's too."

Annika reached for the phone.

"Hi, Grandpa Del," she chirped. "We can go and fish right off the rocks up here. It's awesome! Do you know they are some of the oldest rocks in the world?"

They talked for about ten minutes. Annika told him all about Artist's Point, and about the play. Ruth could imagine him laughing at her description of the plot. After Annika said her "good-bye," and went into the bathroom to get ready for bed, Ruth took the phone again. "It's me," she smiled.

"I miss you, my love," he told her. "I hope we can get some alone time up there?"

"Of course. You have the room right next to ours."

"Good, you can come and visit me," he said, his voice getting huskier.

"You must feel a *lot* better," she laughed, kidding him.

"Do I ever!" Then he sighed. "And while I was away, I made some important decisions about my work."

"And?" Ruth held her breath.

"And I decided that I am going to be in semi-retirement. I won't take any more parts in any productions unless you can go with me." He cleared his throat. "I am not going to be sitting in any more hotel rooms, missing you. Life is too short for that." He chuckled. "And that's final."

"Oh, I think that's a wonderful plan," she told him. "As long as Angie will care for our cats."

"Oh, I almost forgot," he said, "Angie and George have set a date."

"They have? Oh my gosh! Really? Are you singing for their wedding?"

"Of course. And they're even going to let me pick the songs."

"When is this happy occasion taking place?" Ruth asked him.

"October thirtieth. It was the only time they could get the Lake Elmo Inn for their party."

"That's pretty close to Halloween," said Ruth.

"Well, you know Angie. She'll probably use it to her advantage. Wear a witch costume. Serve drinks out of a cauldron."

Ruth laughed at that, and then yawned and said, "Well, my dear, I've had a long day. I need some sleep. We'll see you tomorrow night? For supper?"

"I'll be there." He kissed into the phone. "Sleep tight, my love. I'm counting the hours."

"Me too. Drive carefully. I love you," she said. She heard, "Love you too," before she hung up the phone.

As Annika crawled into her bed, she told Ruth, "Emmy is more fun than she was at first."

"That's good," said Ruth. "I'm so glad you like her."

They said their "good nights," and Ruth kissed her granddaughter's forehead. Then she got into her nightgown, washed up, brushed her teeth, and crawled into bed. As she turned off her light, Ruth thought about Del and the decision he'd made. She sighed a happy sigh.

I'm so lucky. He'll be here for Sunday night supper. I can talk to him about everything, and he'll help me watch over Annika!

She continued to process the day's events. *I hope Roy Foley will be all right. Janet has enough to deal with. Hmmm, I wonder who was in that other car?* While she was pondering these things, she thought, *Only three more shows, and this will be over. Thank God!* Finally the sound of waves, and warm thoughts of Del, lulled her to sleep.

Chapter 21

A Celebrity at the East Bay

SUNDAY MORNING, RUTH AND Annika waved to Loris Biederman on their way to breakfast. The woman motioned for Ruth to come over to the front desk.

Ruth turned to Annika, and the girl said, "I know, I know. I'll go and get a table for us. And I'll tell the waitress to bring you the cheese omelette and rye toast."

"Thank you, Annika."

Annika nodded and went ahead to the dining room.

Loris wasted no time, as Ruth came near. She whispered, "Did you hear what happened to Roy Foley?"

"Annika heard something on the news about him being in an accident near Duluth. But they said he'll be okay?"

"Supposedly. I don't know how you can be okay, after getting pushed off a cliff." Loris glanced around as if to make sure they were alone. Then she leaned closer. "But I know who was driving the other car."

"You ... you *do?* But the news said they couldn't find the other driver."

Loris paused dramatically and whispered, "I'm sure it was Tommy Sherman!"

Ruth's eyes grew wide. "How do you know that, when the police don't even know?"

"I have my ways," Loris answered, pursing her lips.

"But why would Tommy Sherman try to run Roy Foley off the road? In Duluth?"

"Because he's a no-good thug, that's why!"

"He would chase him all the way to Duluth? Do they even know each other?" Ruth was incredulous.

"How should I know? But I wouldn't put it past him!" Loris slammed her hand down on the desk. "He's a no-good thug, and I hope he leaves this town! In fact, I think it would be better if he left this earth. Permanently!"

Ruth just stared at Loris, not knowing what to say to such venom. She took a deep breath, and finally asked, "Have you heard how Roy Foley is doing? Is he really going to be okay?"

Just then, the Norstrands came into the hotel. The elder Norstrand nodded to Loris and Ruth. "Mornin,'" he said.

"Your coffee's hot and ready," said Loris with a smile. "You guys off to Duluth this morning?"

"Is anything a secret in this town?" said Roberta Norstrand, holding her hands out, palms up, and rolling her eyes. "Yes, we are. We're driving Janet down to see her hubby, and we're going to have a talk with him as well."

"What about their kids?" Ruth asked.

"Oh, yeah ..." Roberta shook her head. "That pastor's wife—Emmy Eklund—she's looking after them. That woman is a saint! That boy's gotta be a handful."

"Emmy's good with kids, though," Loris Biederman asserted. "Every year she runs the Christmas pageant at church. I hope she has some of her own sometime soon."

Just then, Annika came from the dining room and said, "Gram, your breakfast is on the table."

"Oh, okay," said Ruth. "I'd better go eat."

Annika, who seldom missed anything, looked at Ruth as she sat down. "Do you want to tell me what's going on, Gram?" She stuffed a good-sized piece of French toast in her mouth as she eyed her grandmother.

"Well ... do you remember Tommy Sherman?"

"The guy who played Jigger in the show? The one they got rid of?" She kept eating. "Yeah."

"Well, Mrs. Biederman thinks he was driving the other car, when Andrea and Norman's dad had the accident."

"So, he got away?" Annika picked up her orange juice with one hand, and grabbed a piece of bacon with the other. "The news said the other car pushed Mr. Foley's car off the road."

"I'm afraid so." Ruth took a sip of tea. *The young don't miss much,* she thought.

"What about Mr. Foley?" asked Annika, who paused over her breakfast. "Will he be all right?"

"He's hurt, but he's going to be okay."

"I hope so," she said, attacking another piece of French toast. "Andrea and Norman need a dad."

The rest of Sunday went relatively smoothly. Ruth felt a bit guilty for not taking Annika and going up to attend a church service, but she had promised her granddaughter that they would visit the lighthouse out by the rocks.

I can only manage one thing today.

The lighthouse was opposite Artist's Point. To get there, you had to walk on a very narrow breakwater with only a thin cable railing, with which to steady yourself.

That afternoon, as they walked out to the breakwater, Ruth warned Annika, "Honey, please be careful out here. Please don't run on this wall. If you fall in, I can't help you." *I wish Del was here right now,* she thought.

"Yeah, Gram, I get it. Geez! Even *I* don't think this looks safe." The two of them picked their way along on the concrete barrier, careful to hold on to the steel-cable railing when they were there. The waves were like giant hands, their huge fingers clutching the rocks by the concrete wall. Both Ruth and Annika had wet shoes when they finally returned to shore.

The two had planned on making some sketches of the lighthouse in their respective sketchbooks, but it was so windy, they decided to leave the books in their backpacks and purchase some post cards with pictures of the landmark at the Ben Franklin store, and sketch from those. Annika also wanted to buy more comic books and snacks. Ruth was very happy to get in a late afternoon nap while Annika read her comics, looked at her postcards, and munched on the cheesy snacks she got at the store.

By suppertime, Ruth and Annika were sitting on the front porch of the hotel, looking out the front door for Del's car.

I was hoping he would come in and wake me up from my nap, Ruth thought. *I wanted him to kiss me awake, like Sleeping Beauty.* She smiled at her silliness.

They sat outside in the porch for a while. Annika was petting Odie and scratching his ears, to the old dog's delight. Ruth worked at the puzzle of a boat house, which was still incomplete. She kept looking down the main street, hoping to see Del's white Lexus. No such luck.

Finally, Annika said, "Can we go and eat, Gram? I'm getting really hungry." She stood up from the white wicker table. "Maybe Grandpa Del got a late start?"

Ruth and Annika sat in the dining room—Ruth enjoying a cube steak grilled to perfection, a fully loaded baked potato, and coleslaw. Annika had ordered a hamburger, fries and Coke. Ruth looked up from her meal and saw Del, escorted by Loris Biederman.

"Del!" Ruth cried, waving from her seat. "You're here!"

Loris Biederman was in her glory. She clapped for everyone's attention, then made Del, who was trying vainly to get out of her clutches, wait with her.

"Guests of East Bay Inn, it is my extreme pleasure to introduce to you, one of opera's biggest stars!"

At this, Del looked down and tried even harder to get away, but Loris' grip was too firm.

"Delancy Mays!" Loris threw her arms out in a tribute, letting go of Del. He hurried and sat down next to Ruth.

Several people clapped, and one man stood and yelled a loud "Bravo! Bravo!"

"That looks good," said Del, eyeing her plate, then whispering, "And you do, too!" He reached for Ruth and enfolded her in a hug. She had tears in her eyes.

"Oh, my love!" He held her briefly, but Ruth could see he was embarrassed by all the commotion.

As the room quieted down and people started eating again, he reached over and tweaked one of Annika's braids. "Hey, fishing partner, how're ya doin'?"

Before the grinning girl could answer, a waitress hurried up to their table. She took Del's order and rushed off again.

The man who had stood up, yelling *Bravo!* came over with a pad of paper and a pen. "Mr. Mays, I saw you in Chicago, in *Othello.* You were just marvelous!" He stuck the paper and pen practically under Del's nose. "May I have your autograph, please? For my daughter?"

"Certainly," Del said kindly. "What's her name? I'll write something just for her."

"Ah, well ..." The man stammered. "Actually, it's for me." He looked sheepish.

"No problem," Del chuckled, "I get lots of these. What's *your* name?"

"Darwin," the man said.

Del wrote a generous note to "Darwin" and handed it to the man.

"I will keep this forever, thank you!" The man took the pad and shook Del's hand. "Thank you so much! I'm gonna *frame* it!"

Del nodded and smiled. "You're quite welcome."

Chapter 22

Deep Lake, Dark Secrets

DEL LOOKED AT RUTH. "Sorry about all that." He looked uncomfortable.

Ruth laughed. "It's okay. It goes with the territory." She reached over to him and squeezed his hand. "By the way, you'll need to sign a photo I have of you, for Loris. She wants to hang it in here."

"Sure," he said. "You have it with you?" He seemed embarrassed.

"Yeah, of course, Grandpa Del, you're a celebrity," Annika told him. "I never knew a celebrity before you." She started eating again.

Ruth was so happy, she just smiled at Del and forgot to eat.

"Don't wait for me," Del said to her. "It will get cold."

"I'm just so happy to have you up here." There were tears in her eyes. "I've got lots to fill you in on."

Ruth began to tell him about the production, leaving out the murders in front of Annika.

Annika piped up, "It's a really dorky story, if you ask me." She commented on *Carousel,* stuffing fries in her mouth. "I guess the music's okay, though."

"I'm sure Rodgers and Hammerstein would be happy you approve," Del said to her, laughing.

The girl finished her supper before Del even got his. She stood up and asked Ruth, "Grandma, may I please be excused and have your keys, and go back to the room?" She looked restless. "You guys can sit and eat and talk. I'm gonna lay on my bed and read my comics."

"Of course, honey," said Ruth. "But stay in the room and lock the door, okay?" And then she thought better of it. "You know, sweetie, I'm just going to walk you back there, and see that the door's locked and you're tucked in safe and sound, okay?" She turned to Del. "Excuse me, my love, I'll explain later."

Del gave Ruth a puzzled look. But just at that moment his food arrived.

"Gram," Annika said, as they walked down the hall to their room, "can we go and get ice cream later? For dessert?"

"Sounds great. We can go to Dairy Queen."

As soon as Ruth returned to the dining room, the waitress served their coffee.

Ruth waited until the waitress was gone. Then she looked at Del and said, "I didn't want to tell you over the phone, but there's some things going on here, that I don't like."

"I know," said Del. "I could tell by your voice. You sounded strained. Okay, fill me in. Why are you so anxious about Annika's safety, that she can't even walk back to the room by herself?"

As Del was eating, Ruth told him as much as she knew. She was quiet about it, because they were in a public place. But she told him about the two murders and the car incident, and even about how venomous Loris

Biederman had been, when talking about Tommy Sherman. And after she told him, in a lowered voice, about the incident with Sam Guston and Annika, on the boat, Del looked worried.

Ruth said, "I am so glad you're here to help me with Annika. I'm worried about that man, Mr. Guston." She whispered, looking around. "I'm not sure he believed that Annika didn't see him throw his gun overboard. I can hardly think about it, but if Annika is in danger … I don't know … I'm just glad you're here to help me keep an eye on her."

"Please don't tell me it's going to be like last summer." He wiped his mouth with his napkin. "Because if it is, I say we all just pack up and go home." He looked intently at her. "We could just take Annika home right now." He whispered urgently, "We can just get in our cars and drive back home, where she'll be safe and sound. We all will." He sounded hopeful.

"We can't do that," said Ruth, shaking her head. "I promised that little theatre group I'd help them. They're making money for a women's shelter in town. It's a really good cause. And I don't think the cast is in any danger, so it's not like last year." She went on, "And now that you're here, you can help me keep an eye on her. She's so excited about being up here, I would hate to go home early. She'd be so disappointed."

"I think we should get back to the room," said Del. "I'll just pay the bill and we'll get out of here."

Ruth agreed. "But don't pay for me or for Annika," she said with a smile. "We get our meals free for helping up at the theatre." Del grinned and got out his credit card.

As they walked down the hallway, Ruth whispered to him, "It seems to me that there is a 'bad element' here in town. And they're doing something"—she paused—"I don't know what? But it seems to me that something ... illegal is going on in Grand Marais!"

"What about the costumer who got killed?" said Del. "Wasn't she an old friend of yours?" He looked intently at Ruth and he asked, "Why do you think she was killed?"

"I really don't know much about Sally, or her part in this. I just don't know." Ruth didn't want to mention Sally Merritt's *proclivities.* "But according to Loris Biederman"—she lowered her voice—"I guess maybe she had some romantic things going on with at least a couple of men in the town, maybe more. Loris thinks one of them might have ..." She shook her head.

Del made a face. "Another Blanche Voorhees?" he asked her, referring to another opera star whose promiscuity was legendary.

Ruth chuckled. "I don't think there could be 'another Blanche.'"

"And thank God for that," Del quipped. "But speaking of Blanche"—he frowned—"she did hear from some blabby cast member that I was coming up here to meet you. She even asked me about it." He made a face and a helpless gesture. "I can't lie very well. But I hope to God she doesn't show up here."

"Oh, Del. Me too. I don't think our marriage made a bit of difference in her pursuit of you."

"Well, she's one of the reasons I want you with me for the rest of my career," he told her.

"Uncle Tony keeps a sharp eye on her, but I'm not going to take any chances. That woman is positively nuts!"

"Nuts about you. At least she has good taste!" Ruth nudged him and laughed.

"Lord help me!" Del looked at her with a horrified expression.

"And, not to change the subject—"

"Please do!" said Del, grabbing her hand and holding it to his heart.

"Did you understand what I was telling you before? When you paid for your meal?"

"Yes. You are helping the theatre, so you eat here free?"

"That's right," Ruth said. "Annika and I get all our meals here, free of charge!"

"What about me?"

"You have to pay."

"Well, okay, that seems fair." He grinned.

"So, how is Uncle Tony?" Ruth asked him.

"Oh, that's the best part," Del told her. "Uncle Tony came to Boston. He keeps really good tabs on Blanche. He's at every rehearsal, and every performance. I don't think Blanche can even go to the bathroom without Uncle Tony waiting outside the door." He laughed.

"He seems to know her pretty well." Ruth nodded, remembering the opera star's romantic antics from the previous summer.

"Uncle Tony's no fool," said Del, shaking his head.

When Ruth and Del finally got back to the room, Annika was watching television, her comics and sketchbook lying on her bed. "It's ice cream time!" She jumped up.

"We've got plenty of time." Ruth looked at her watch. "The Dairy Queen is open until nine." She rubbed her stomach. "It's only seven-fifteen. Why don't we let our food digest a bit, and let Grandpa Del unpack, and just rest up a while. Let's walk up there around eight or so?"

"Okay, but I want a banana split," Annika told her grandmother.

"Ah, the young!" Ruth laughed, looking over at Del.

"Here"—Ruth took the photo of Del out of her suitcase. "Please sign this 'to Loris and Arnie,' and we'll give it to Loris tomorrow."

Del signed the photo, handing it back to Ruth. "Annika, how about you and Grandma come over to my room and help me unpack?" He grinned. "I think there's something for you in my suitcase."

The girl jumped off the bed and hurried toward the door. "Oh, Grandpa Del, what is it?"

"Well, you'll see ... and you too," he motioned to Ruth.

When they were in Del's room together, Ruth and Annika watched while he put his suitcase on the bed. "I spent an afternoon at the famous Fanueil Hall Marketplace in Boston," he told them. "The next time I have to be in Boston, I want you two with me."

Annika was jumping up and down. Ruth was smiling.

He dug around in his suitcase. "Here," he said as he handed a ten-inch-high bronze statue of the "Revolutionary Minute-Man" to Annika. "Something for 'show and tell' at school."

"Good grief!" Ruth exclaimed. "How on earth did you get that through the airport? It looks like it could be a deadly weapon!"

"I carried it openly and showed it to the guards. They love the Minute-Men. It is Boston, after all."

"It's awesome, Grandpa Del! I love it! Thanks!" Annika turned it over and over in her hands. "I could really conk someone over the head with this." She grinned.

"Annika!" Ruth chided her. "Don't even think about stuff like that."

"Kidding, Gram," the girl hastily said.

"Have you studied about the Revolutionary War, yet? In school?" Del asked her.

"I think we have it next year," Annika said. "And I will have this!" She held the statue up high.

"And for *Madame* ..." Del looked through his bag again.

"You didn't need to bring me any—" Ruth started to say. "Ohhhhh ... !" she breathed, as Del held up a bracelet, silver, and obviously artisan-crafted. "I love it!" she exclaimed as he fastened it around her wrist.

It was indeed beautiful, with ten slightly different-shaped cobalt blue stones, surrounded by hammered silver. It felt wonderful around Ruth's wrist, and looked even better. "Oh, Del! It's just stunning! Thank you so much!"

"I saw it and just thought it was *you,*" he told her. "And now I can see that it is."

"Oh, my love!" Ruth just looked, transfixed, at the piece. "Do you know the name of the artist who made it? It looks hand-made."

"Oh no!" he exclaimed, "I think I threw that away in Boston, when I packed it. I wanted to limit the space it took up in my suitcase, so I threw away the paper bag and probably the artist's name, and rolled the bracelet up in one of my socks to protect it."

"That's all right," she said and hugged him. "I love it, no matter who made it. Thank you!"

Chapter 23

Let's All Go to the Dairy Queen!

AROUND EIGHT O'CLOCK, RUTH, Del and Annika got their sweaters and went out of the hotel and into the cool night air. Sunday night in Grand Marais was fairly quiet. Because it was the tourist season, however, most of the restaurants were still open, and groups of people were out walking. The Dairy Queen was open too.

As the three walked up to the building, they saw the Fuerlings. Edna looked a little surprised to see Del, but she recovered quickly.

"Hey, Mrs. Mays," she called out. "It's a good night for ice cream." She smiled. "Who's this handsome fella with ya?"

Norm Fuerling spoke up quickly. "I know who he is." He held out his hand to shake Del's. "Mr. Mays, I'm very honored to meet you." He smiled, bowing. "Good news travels fast up here, and I heard you were in town. Welcome to Grand Marais! I've never been lucky enough to see one of your operas, but I have two of your CDs, and I've read plenty about you, in the papers and in music magazines." He looked at Edna and said, "Mrs. Mays is married to Delancy Mays, a famous opera singer."

"Well, my stars," said Edna, smiling. "Famous, huh?"

Del looked down, embarrassed by the conversation.

Ruth piped up, "He's on vacation. And even famous opera singers have to eat. Are you in line?"

"Yeah," Edna motioned to just behind her. "Come on, get over here. That young-un looks mighty hungry."

They got in line behind Edna and Norm, and ordered and got their ice cream. The Fuerlings had saved them seats nearby.

Del whispered, "I'd just like to take my cone and walk," but then he noticed Annika and her banana split. "Okay, we'd better sit for a while."

"Have you seen our little show yet?" Norm Fuerling asked Del, as he sat down.

"I'm sorry, no. I just got into town this evening. I will see it on Thursday, though. I'm really looking forward to it."

"Well, we're not the Lyric Opera, but we do our best to give the folks a good show." Norm was obviously proud. Just then he noticed his wife frowning. "And my Edna here does a great job as Mrs. Mullin." Edna smirked. "A great job," he repeated, patting her hand.

Edna said, "That was very good of you, Mrs. Mays, to help us with the costumes and such."

Ruth smiled. "Please call me Ruth. And it's my pleasure. I'm enjoying the show."

"Yeah, once we got a new Jigger," said Edna, "things looked a lot better. Didn't they, Norm?"

Norm Fuerling looked startled. "Um ... yes ... that whole thing was, um ... unfortunate." He shook his head, looking down. Then he looked back up and added, "We were lucky to get Jack Guston to take over the part."

Edna continued. "The guy who was playing Jigger before, had a criminal past. I don't even know why Paul let him into our theatre to begin with! We're better off without—" Edna stopped when Norm put his hand on her arm to quiet her.

"Sorry," he said to Del, after giving an exasperated glance at his wife. "You don't want to hear all our small town gossip."

"I came from a small town too," Del assured him. "I know all about small town gossip. It's pretty much the same, everywhere."

Norm Fuerling looked relieved to not be talking about the negative things happening in Grand Marais. As they continued eating and making small talk, however, Edna was unusually quiet.

Finally, Norm stood up, taking Edna with him. "It was very nice to meet you, Mr. Mays, and we'll see you all next Thursday." Edna merely nodded and they went out the door.

Del looked at Ruth and asked, "Is she usually that quiet?"

"No," said Ruth. "In fact she's just the opposite. I would call her garrulous."

"He didn't want her talking, that's for sure. And what's all this about criminals in their theatre? Are the actors that badly behaved?"

"I'll tell you later."

They had a nice walk back to the East Bay. Ruth promised that tomorrow they would drive farther up north and see the famous Naniboujou Lodge. When they got back to their room Annika was excited to show the flyers to Del.

"We can have tea there," she explained. "It's just like lunch, only later in the afternoon. And we can all eat a bigger breakfast so we can wait and have our tea at three. It's traditional to have your tea at three."

"So I've heard," said Del, smiling. "I can't wait!"

After Del had gone to his room and Annika was finally asleep, Ruth put a dressing gown over her nightgown, slipped on her slippers and quietly locked room 101. She stepped into the hall and knocked softly on the door to 102.

Del opened it quickly, embracing her and pulling her into the room. "Is Annika asleep?" he asked Ruth quietly.

"Finally," she whispered. "And you look tired." She rubbed her hand down the side of his face.

"I'm not that tired." He took hold of her hand and kissed the inside of it, making her shiver. "It's a very nice room, but there's only two single beds."

"We'll manage," Ruth giggled. "First, I need to tell you—"

"You bet we'll manage," Del whispered, slipping off Ruth's dressing gown and rubbing his hands down her arms. He looked at the beds. "We can just lie down here and ... Oh, God, I've missed you so much!" He kissed her neck and started kissing her breasts.

"There's not much room," Ruth whispered. "Let's push the beds together. Against the wall, that'll be better." She lay down on the nearest bed, and Del settled beside her.

They made love, carefully and quietly. For the most part, the beds stayed together. Del did get up once to push them together again, against the wall.

After about an hour, Ruth leaned into Del, kissing his cheek. "I should get back to Annika."

"No, stay," he moaned.

"She's alone," she reminded him. "What if she wakes up and I'm not there?"

Del sighed. "This is going to be a long week."

"But you're going fishing tomorrow morning," she whispered as she kissed him again.

"You're right," he answered, brightening considerably. "This might be a good week after all." He reached for her. "Just one more cuddle?"

"Men and their fishing." Ruth grinned and moved closer to him, leaning her head on his chest.

Del lifted her face up and kissed her, nibbling first on her bottom lip and then on one of her earlobes.

"You're still hungry?" Ruth smiled, shivering with delight.

"For you, always," he whispered.

They lay entwined for a long while. But finally, Ruth could hear Del snoring. She got up to quietly let herself out. Then she thought, *He needs to have the door locked while he's sleeping.*

Going back to the bed, she shook Del gently.

"You going?" he said sleepily.

"You need to get up and lock the door after I leave."

He just turned over in the bed.

"Del, honey, please get up and lock the door after me?"

He continued snoring, deep in sleep.

Ruth finally took his key and went out the door, locking it as she left.

As she let herself into her room, she saw that Annika was still sleeping soundly. She sighed a happy sigh as she quietly got ready for bed.

I'm such a lucky woman.

Ruth felt better than she had since Del had left for Boston. Looking at herself in the bathroom mirror, she noticed her flushed face and shining eyes. *That man makes me look beautiful,* she thought, smiling at her reflection.

If This Old Church Had Ears

MONDAY MORNING, DURING A bigger than usual breakfast for all of them, Ruth noticed Del looked very rested. And she was feeling better than fine.

"By the way, here's your room key." She grinned at him. "You might want to lock your room before you and Annika go fishing."

Del took her hand and held it longer than usual.

"Thanks," he told her, and she could see it was for more than just giving him his key.

"Grandpa Del, you are just going to love the lake!" Annika exclaimed.

"I love it already," he told her, smiling at Ruth.

After breakfast Del and Annika gathered up their fishing gear for a day at the lake. Ruth had decided she would paint the lighthouse from the photos on the postcards they bought. "I'm just going to stay in the room and work on a painting," she told them as they headed out. "You two have fun."

After Del and Annika left, Ruth painted for a while, then decided to read. She took her book club book out of her suitcase and lay down on the bed. It was a historical novel—something of more interest to Del than to her. Within minutes, she was fast asleep.

Around noon she woke up refreshed and feeling like a walk. *I'll bring my camera out to the rocks and take some pictures of Del and Annika fishing,* she thought. But looking through her suitcase, she couldn't find her art bag. She remembered having it with her during the previous performance of *Carousel.*

"Oh darn!" she said out loud. "I must have forgotten it after Annika took photos of the actors in their costumes. I'd better get up there and find it. It's probably still under my seat."

Ruth hurriedly got her purse and car keys. *I sure hope no one has taken it,* she thought as she drove.

Parking next to the old church, Ruth went up the front steps and opened the door. *I'm surprised it's not locked,* she thought, stepping inside. She paused in the tiny narthex when she heard men's voices coming from further back in the sanctuary. It sounded like there were at least four men, all talking together. And one of them was Arnie Biederman; Ruth recognized his voice.

"... and after Pam told her about the whole deal, Loris went straight to him and ... well, you know what happened. I've never seen her so mad in my life!"

"I sure wouldn't want Loris Biederman mad at me. Sometimes she overreacts, you know."

"Overreacts? It was a rotten thing he did."

"And he was a rotten guy!"

"Well, that's for sure. And I'm not a bit sorry that he got—"

"Shh! Someone's here!"

Ruth backed up against the wall, her heart beating hard. She heard sudden whispering, followed by rustling sounds, like the noise of a ladder being moved.

Then Arnie Biederman yelled out, "Who's there?"

Ruth took a deep breath and answered, "I-It's Mrs. Mays, the costume-lady!" She tried to sound as if she'd just arrived (and hadn't heard anything). *What were they talking about?*

"Oh, Mrs. Mays! C'mon in!" called Arnie. "We're in the light booth, just ... trying to fix this mess!"

Ruth acted innocent as she walked into the sanctuary. She smiled and waved at Arnie. "I forgot you guys were meeting to fix the lights." She walked down the center aisle to the front and started peeking around under her reserved seat. "I left my art bag with my camera inside, and I ... I need it. To take some family pictures. Out by the rocks."

"Oh, that's *your* camera," Arnie said brightly. "Ya, we uh, we hoped you would come back for it."

"Ya," agreed Arvid Haakala, standing behind him in a work shirt and overalls.

"Glad you found it!" piped up one of the other men, whom Ruth now recognized (out of costume) as Howard Kirkdorff.

"It's right there, in that bag under your pew!" added Lester Perry.

Ruth laughed shakily and said, "Oh, there it is! Honestly, I'd lose my head if it wasn't attached."

"Well, we ... wouldn't want *that* to happen!"

"No, haha!" She grabbed her art bag and hurried back up the aisle, frantic to get out. "Bye, now!" she shouted over her shoulder, trying to sound cheerful. "And good luck with those lights!" Not waiting for an answer, she ran outside and got quickly into her car.

Oh Lord, what was that all about? I sure hope to God they don't realize how much I overheard. And Loris Biederman ... what have you done?

Ruth calmed herself as she drove away from the church. She felt safer in her car. She drove past the East Bay Inn, past the art gallery and the donut shop, past the little town museum with its New England ambience. She didn't breathe more easily until she could see Del and Annika, walking with their poles, back from Artist's Point.

Parking her car and rolling down the window, Ruth called out, "Hey you guys, where's all the fish you caught?"

Annika ran up to the car first and answered, "No fish today, Gram. They were all too small, and we had to let 'em go."

"The only fish I'm going to have will be off a menu," Del said dispiritedly. "And those lake trout looked tasty, even if they were too small."

Ruth said, "Let me get a couple photos, then you can put your gear in the trunk. I'll drive us all back to the hotel. You can clean up and rest a bit before we drive up to Naniboujou."

She took a couple of cute photos, then everyone got into the car.

"You okay?" Del asked her from the passenger seat.

"I'm fine." Ruth tried not to purse her lips.

"You're gonna just love Naniboujou, Grandpa Del," Annika announced from the back seat. "My mom told me all about it, and showed me pictures. There are paintings all over the place!"

"Yes," agreed Ruth. "It's pretty amazing—a mix of Native American and Art Deco design, with big, colorful geometric paintings covering the walls and ceiling. It was built in the 1920s as a private club for the wealthy."

Annika got a pained look for a moment and said, "You're not going to give us an art history lesson, are you?"

Ruth laughed. "It doesn't hurt to know a little about what we're going to see."

Luckily there were brochures featuring the Naniboujou Lodge in the hotel. Ruth took a couple as they were going to their room.

"Here," she said as she handed them to her granddaughter. "You can look at the pictures, and read up on its history. If you decide to write a paper about Naniboujou in school this fall, you'll have some visual aides."

Annika took the brochures. "Wow! This looks awesome!"

"Wait 'til you see it in person!"

"Gram"—the girl held up the pamphlets—"is it okay if I keep these?"

"You do that," Ruth said. "We can even mount them on some tagboard so you can show them to your class. "I'll ask Loris if I can take extras."

"I think I need a short nap," Del told them. "Annika, do you mind if Grandma Ruth comes into my room for a nap?"

"Nah," said the girl. "I'm going to change into something nice, and then I'm gonna read these in our room." She waved the brochures as she went into room 101.

"Lock your door," Ruth told her.

"I always do, Gram," was her pert answer.

When they entered room 102, Ruth and Del found a double bed—all made up—against the far wall. A handwritten note on the pillow said,

"I thought this might be more comfy for you than two singles." And it was signed, "Love, Loris."

"What a thoughtful woman," Del commented, as he put his fishing gear behind an easy chair.

Ruth just stood there, saying nothing.

"Come here," said Del as he sat down on the "new" bed and patted the space next to him.

Ruth told him what she had overheard, carefully recreating the men's conversation back at the church.

"Huh," said Del when she finished. "They were talking about that nice lady who works at the front desk? I wouldn't have guessed that about her."

"Loris Biederman has always been such a kind soul. I've been coming up here since my kids were in elementary school. I cannot imagine her even telling anyone off. But she seemed to really hate that Joey-Frank—the guy whose body I found. I've never heard her talk about anyone like she talks about him." Ruth cleared her throat. "She had so much venom in her voice. And I still have to wonder ... how *did* he die? I haven't heard any news about it."

"Ruth, dear, it's not our business. Mrs. Biederman must have had her reasons for not liking him. And bad-mouthing him doesn't mean she killed him. That's quite a jump to make."

"You're right," Ruth agreed. "I'm really making a leap here."

"Just leap right into my arms," Del laughed as he put his arms around her.

They lay down on the bed together; and as Ruth nestled in his arms. she felt safe. She fell sound asleep. So did Del.

Chapter 25

A Private Club Named for a Trickster

Annika knocked on Del's door after about forty minutes. "Gram? Grandpa Del? Are you awake?"

She knocked again.

Ruth got up and opened the door. "I'm sorry, honey, I guess we fell asleep."

"I did too. All that fresh air this morning made me sleepy." Annika handed Ruth's sweater to her. "Can we go up to Naniboujou now?"

"Thank you, honey, sure. I just need to freshen up a bit." Ruth smiled at the girl, then glanced at her watch. "It's two-thirty now, and we'll get there just in time for tea." She looked back at Del, who was getting off the bed. "Can you be ready to go in a few minutes?" she asked him.

"Give me five," he said.

Ruth gave him a thumbs up sign. She took Annika back to their room.

Soon they were all in Del's white Lexus, driving north, past the little church on the edge of town.

"Hey Gram, isn't that the same church they have a painting of? In the hotel? It sure looks like it."

"Yes, I believe it is," said Ruth from the passenger seat, craning her neck for a better look.

"This is a wonderful place for artists," Del commented. "All this natural beauty? I might just try to paint something myself."

"You can use any of my paints and brushes," said Ruth.

"Mine too!" added Annika from the back seat. "Grandpa Del, I didn't know you were an artist."

"I have many hidden talents," he told her.

Ruth just grinned, nudging him.

They continued driving north, past rocky beaches, past an old fishing shack that had seen better days, past "Five-Mile Rock," which looked a lot closer to the shore than it actually was.

Finally, they came to the driveway of Naniboujou, the famous Art Deco restaurant and hotel.

"I didn't know it was a hotel too," Del commented. "Why didn't you just stay up here? It's lovely here!"

"Oh, it is, and I'll bet the prices are lovely too," Ruth laughed. "I guess I've been going to the 'East Bay' for as long as I've been coming up here. Loris and Arnie Biederman seem like family." She shrugged. "And I like being in town. There's so much to do and see. I'd feel too isolated up here, I guess."

"It's pretty," said Annika, picking up a rock and putting it in her pocket.

"Wait 'til you see the inside!" Ruth told the girl.

As they walked into the main room of the lodge, Del whistled softly. Annika said, "Wow!" as she looked around. "Who painted all this, Gram?"

Before Ruth could answer, a young hostess came and welcomed them and brought them over to a table by a window overlooking Lake Superior. They couldn't see the lake very well because there was a sun-porch between them and the lake, but it didn't matter. The main dining room was splendidly decorated with the bright red, blue, orange and yellow geometric Art Deco designs the building was so famous for.

Ruth took a piece of paper from her purse. "I looked this up for you," she told Annika. "In case you want to write a paper on it. The artist who painted this was named Antione Gouffee. He designed it with a mixture of Art Deco and Cree Indian designs. He painted it in the late 1920s. Naniboujou opened in 1929. It was used as a private club for wealthy businessmen. It was named for Nanabozho, who was a trickster spirit, and a hero in Cree mythology."

"Oh! Just like Loki!" Annika cried. "I guess everybody has a *trickster!*"

Just then, a young man came up with menus and a pad of paper to take their orders. They ordered tea and little sandwiches and cakes.

As they were waiting for their food, Del turned to Annika and asked, "How did you learn about Loki?"

"Before we went to Sweden," she told him, "Mom made me read all this stuff on Scandinavia, so I would know what people were talking about. But nobody there ever talked about Loki ... except this one lady we met, who named her dog Loki." She sat up straighter and laughed. "I think I impressed her when I asked if he did tricks."

"I'll bet you did," said Ruth, looking proudly at her granddaughter. "Ok, another fact: See the fireplace over there?" She indicated the stone fireplace at the far end of the room. "Supposedly, that's the biggest fireplace in the state of Minnesota."

"Awesome!" Annika said.

Very soon their tea came, with lemonade for Annika. The small sandwiches were egg-salad, ham-salad, and tuna-salad. The bread had the crusts removed, and were cut with an oval cookie cutter. Each one had a design of an olive and some parsley leaves on top. The cakes were small squares, frosted on all sides, decorated with small buttercream rosettes.

"Pretty fancy," Del commented. "Mama Wilda would love this." He laughed as he thought of his late wife's mom, who was still alive, and who *heartily approved* of Ruth. "That woman loves anything fancy."

"Let's take her up here," said Ruth. "Has she ever been this far north?"

"Don't know. We'll have to ask her."

"Mama Wilda said she would teach me how to knit," Annika told them.

Ruth smiled at her granddaughter. "I've got plenty of yarn and needles," she told the girl. "You can look through my knitting stuff when we get home."

They had their tea, paid for it, and afterwards they walked outside around the grounds.

"This is so beautiful," said Ruth as she looked at the lake. "Maybe next time we come up here, we should stay here."

"I'm stuffed!" said Del, rubbing his stomach. "I think I could just as well skip supper tonight." They walked toward the parking lot and their car.

"That's fine with me, but Annika might want a little something."

"My dad says I have a 'hollow leg,'" the girl told them. "Mom says I'm just a growing kid."

Just then they heard, "Del! Ruthie!"

That voice! thought Ruth, turning to see who it was. *It couldn't be ... what is she doing here?*

It was Blanche Voorhees—the soprano who had been chasing (and harassing) Del all last summer! She came hurrying around the side of the building, screeching at them, "What a *mar*velous sur*prise* to see you here!" Blanche was walking in satin high heels on the sand and rocks, teetering a bit, holding on to "Uncle" Tony Ancino for balance. Her frosted-blonde updo was looking tousled from the mid-afternoon wind.

Chapter 26

The Diva at Naniboujou

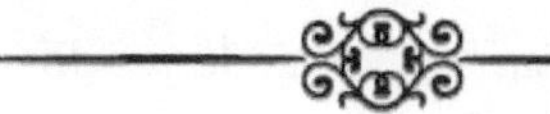

DEL WHISPERED, "OH MY God, no," and he looked toward the lake as if frantically seeking a way out.

"It's *her!*" Ruth whispered back. "She actually followed you up here!"

"And I see she has dyed her hair again. She's back to being blonde."

Ruth quickly took over the situation, and turned back toward the couple. "How lovely to see you two," she lied. "What, ah ... brings you up to Naniboujou?"

"Oh, you know," Blanche simpered. "We had time off, and I just felt I needed a place that was quiet and, well you know, quiet and beautiful ..."

"What Blanche wants ... Blanche ... gets," muttered Uncle Tony, who was huffing and puffing, as though the walk was too much for him..

She shook back her frosted blonde hair, wet her lips and graced Del with a smoldering smile. "It seemed like the perfect place!"

"I hope you enjoy your stay," Ruth said politely. "We were just leaving." They continued walking toward Del's car.

"And who's this little one?" Blanche followed them and motioned toward Annika.

"I'm not little," Annika told her in no uncertain terms. "I'm ten."

"This is our granddaughter," Ruth said, emphasizing *our*. She put her arm around Annika's shoulders and gave her a little squeeze, hoping to quiet her. "We came up here to paint the scenery."

"And Del," Blanche said archly, "what do *you* do while Ruth and her granddaughter are out painting scenery? Maybe you have time to have a little *drinkeepoo* with us?"

"I'm painting with them," he said. "Sorry. No time for *drinkeepoos*." He sounded curt, but then winked at Ruth and added, "Unless they're with my wife."

"How very ... loving." Blanche was smiling but sounded angry.

"I guess I'm just a loving married man." Del clicked his key and opened the car door for Ruth.

"So nice to see you two *together*," Ruth told them as Del ushered her into the front seat and Annika got in the back.

Del started the car and they drove out of the parking lot, leaving Blanche and Uncle Tony standing there, looking after them.

"Augh!" Del said as he drove quickly out of the driveway onto the highway.

"Who's that lady?" Annika piped up. "And why don't you like her, Grandpa Del?"

"It's a long story, and we'll talk about it another time," he told her tersely.

"Huh!" Annika snorted. "Well then, I don't like her either. And I'm not little!" She looked at Ruth. "Who is she, Gram?"

Ruth looked at Del and smiled and shook her head. "You take this one," she whispered to him.

"Okay, here goes," Del pronounced. "Blanche Voorhees is an opera singer who frequently sings in the same productions that I'm in. *Unfortunately.*"

"So, you don't like her?" Annika had picked up on his meaning.

"Nope." Del kept his eyes on the road.

"But she likes you, huh?" Annika was grinning. Ruth just kept quiet.

"I guess ..." Del answered back with a resigned shrug.

"I get it," Annika said wisely, "she's a *nudge.*"

"A nudge," Del repeated.

"Yup." Annika went on, "My friend Rachel has this boy in our science class who really likes her, but she doesn't like him. He's just dumb, and he bothers her all the time. She calls him a 'nudge.' I think it's a Jewish word, and it means someone who pesters and bothers you all the time. It looks to me like that Blanche lady is a nudge."

Ruth started giggling and Del laughed out loud.

"Out of the mouths of babes," Del said, when he was done laughing.

"I'm not little and I'm not a baby!" Annika piped up from the back seat.

"No, you're a very smart and extremely perceptive young lady!" Del told her.

"That she is," Ruth replied. "A nudge." She laughed.

Tuesday and Wednesday seemed to go by too fast. On Tuesday, all three of them went back out to Artist's Point. Ruth and Annika did some more painting while Del walked carefully out on the rocks.

On Wednesday, they went shopping in Joynes Ben Franklin. Annika bought some Marvel comics she hadn't read yet, along with another bag of Cheetos. Ruth and Del found beautiful matching Scandinavian sweaters for each of them.

Annika wanted a Grand Marais sweatshirt instead. "I have enough sweaters from Sweden," she told them. They also went to the Lake Superior Trading Post, and bought two wool shirts, for Annika's dad and for Uncle Robbie, and some Norwegian earrings for her mom.

"She'll love these!" the girl told them. "She has a bracelet with this very same design!" While looking through the toys, Ruth noticed that Annika kept picking up, and putting down, a small stuffed fox. It had the same bright blue eyes that her granddaughter had.

"Would you like that little fox?" Ruth whispered to her.

"I'm not a baby, Gram," Annika responded, then grinned and said, "But yeah."

As they finished shopping, Ruth added a small hand-blown cobalt-blue bowl for her good friend, Angie. They walked up to the clerk to check out. As Annika held the fox up to be scanned, she told her, "I'm calling him 'Loki.'"

"That's a nice name," the clerk said without much inflection.

On the way back to the hotel, the girl sniffed. "I don't think she even knew what the name meant."

"Probably not," Del said. "Not everybody's up on their Scandinavian lore."

They carefully placed all their purchases (except for 'Loki,' who stayed in Annika's arms) in the trunk of Del's car.

Ruth asked him, "Would you please drive us down by the old fishing shacks? That was the first painting I ever sold, and Robbie wants a copy of it. But I need a photo. Way back then I painted it *plein air*. I never took any photos."

"I am at your service." He opened the passenger door for her while Annika climbed into the back seat.

Annika piped up, "Do you know what '*plein air*' means, Grandpa Del?"

Del thought a moment and then told her, "I think it's French for 'open air.' So, I imagine it means painting in the open air?"

"You're pretty smart, Grandpa Del."

"I married your grandma, didn't I?"

Ruth squeezed his arm and instructed him to drive past the bear cub statue, and then over a block and down the small hill that ended near the shacks.

He looked around. "Are you sure it's okay if I park here? This seems like private property."

"I'm sure it's okay," said Ruth. "It's pretty isolated right now, and we're only going to be here a few minutes. If you want, you can wait in the car while I go and snap a few photos. Then, if someone comes you can explain what I'm doing and that we're leaving right away."

"But Loki and I want to see the fishing shacks," Annika said, getting out of the car with the little stuffed fox clutched in her hands.

"I'll just wait here for you two," Del told them. "But please hurry."

Just then, a police car came down the hill and parked right next to Del. It was the Norstrands. Ruth went over to them.

"Hello," she said. "Sergeant Norstrand and …" She paused, not knowing what Roberta Norstrand's official title was.

"Roberta," the young woman said, smiling at Ruth.

"And Roberta." Ruth smiled back and motioned for Del to get out of the car. "I'd like to introduce my husband, Delancy Mays." She nodded at him. "Del, these are the Norstrands, who keep Grand Marais safe for tourists like us."

"Nice to meet you," the elder Norstrand said, and shook Del's hand. "My late wife loved the opera, and we saw you in Minneapolis one time. I don't remember the name of the opera … *Rigg* something?"

Del smiled. *"Rigoletto?"*

"Yup, that was it. I remember you were mighty good." The elder Norstrand nodded affirmatively.

"Thank you, sir." Del bowed slightly. "I'm glad you enjoyed it."

Roberta Norstrand was looking around. "Are you going to stay here long?"

She looked worried. She pursed her lips and narrowed her eyes, and craned her neck as if she was looking for something or someone.

"No, we weren't," Ruth explained. "I'm just taking a couple of photos to paint from, and then we're going back to the hotel."

"Good. Because we got a call that Tommy Sherman was back in town and that he might be hiding around here. He's a 'person of interest' in Sally Merritt's death."

Oh no! Ruth thought. She had been careful to hide the bruise on her arm from Del. She felt if he saw it he would want to confront the boy, or insist that they return home immediately. She surreptitiously rubbed her arm. *It's almost gone anyway*, she thought. "If you two can wait a minute, I'll just take a couple of quick photos, and then we'll be off."

"Sure, we can do that," Roberta told her. "Dad and I are going to look around, though."

Ruth had just finished her photo-taking when she saw Annika pointing toward the woods that were south of the shacks. She heard her yell, "I see someone!"

Then Ruth heard the elder Norstrand holler, "It's him! There he is!"

"Annika! Get back here!" Ruth yelled. The girl had started to go out on the dock. Ruth ran and grabbed her in a hug, pulling her back to the car.

"I saw him, Gram, he was running in the woods! I helped the police!" She thought a moment and added, "I wonder if I can get a Girl Scout badge for helping the police?"

"I wonder if you can get a Girl Scout badge for giving your grandma a heart attack!" Ruth told the girl. "Get in the car! Hurry!"

After a few minutes, the two Norstrands walked back to their police car, minus Tommy Sherman.

Roberta shook her head in disgust. "He got away. He was too fast for us. But at least now we know he's around town. We'll find him. He won't get far."

"And don't worry," said Sergeant Norstrand. "I don't think he killed Sally Merritt. He was always more of a 'follower' than a killer. We just need to ask him some questions."

"And please don't let this ruin Grand Marais for you." Roberta looked at Del and Ruth. "Usually we are the most peaceful, beautiful place in Minnesota."

"I'll keep that in mind," said Del, looking at her skeptically.

As Del started the car, Ruth said, "Del, please stop for a moment. I need to tell them something about Tommy." Rolling down the window, she motioned for Roberta to come over.

"Is there something I can help you with?" asked Roberta.

"You know Tommy Sherman used to play Jigger in the musical at the old church?"

"I knew he was involved in the musical."

"Well, when he left, I was getting his costume ready for the new boy playing Jigger. There was a big blood stain on the shirt. He seemed very relieved when he came back for it and I told him that I had washed it." She cleared her throat. "He even thanked me, and then he ran off."

"Y-you ... Washed. The. Shirt." Roberta shook her head as if she couldn't believe what she was hearing. "Why did you do that? Didn't you think it might have been evidence?"

"Evidence for what? I thought maybe he had had an accident or something. I was washing it so the new boy could wear it. He couldn't wear a shirt with a big blood stain." Ruth defended her actions.

"Well, I guess I can see why you did that. Dad and I will follow you up to the old church and we'll pick up the shirt. We still might be able to get something from it."

Del said to Ruth, "You'll need to tell me where this church is."

Ruth gave Del directions as they drove up the hill to the church.

Annika was excited. "I'm sure glad Loki has good eyesight." She held up her little fox. "He saw Tommy first."

"He's one smart fox, that's for sure," Ruth told her.

"The fox is Loki's animal spirit," Annika informed them.

They drove to the old church and Ruth found the shirt and gave it to Roberta, but she had done too good a job, washing it.

"Well, this won't help us any," Roberta told Ruth. "You're too good at cleaning. Thanks anyway. And remember, this is usually a peaceful, quiet little town."

Del just nodded. "Peaceful and quiet ... from her mouth to God's ear," he whispered to Ruth.

Chapter 27

Third Time's a Charm?

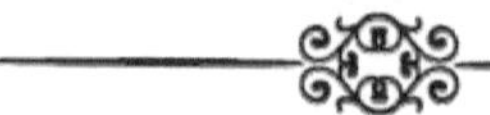

THURSDAY NIGHT, RUTH WAS excited for Del to finally see the show. If Pastor Paul was surprised at Del's being Black, he handled it with aplomb.

"How nice to meet you." He extended his hand. "I hear you're a famous opera star."

"Only in my own mind," Del laughed.

Pastor Paul handed Annika a bunch of programs to fold. "Here you go. Just put them on the table by the door when you're done. Thanks, sweetheart."

"Always the pastor," Paul said to Del. "I hear you folks are leaving early Sunday morning. I sure wish you were staying. I'd have you sing our offertory!"

"Next time we're up here, maybe then?" said Del.

"Let me know ahead of time, and I'll pack the church." Paul grinned. "Sorry, I've got to run, trouble backstage!"

"What now?" Ruth asked him.

"Nothing you have to worry about. It's just some minor disagreement between the actors. I'll handle it." Paul smiled, but appeared to be nervous.

"I have to go backstage for a bit myself," Ruth told Del. "Annika, will you please stay with Grandpa Del tonight? Do not leave his side for one minute." She gave her a look. As she stood there she thought, *I suppose, with Jack Guston playing Jigger, his uncle will be here.* She shivered at the thought of him being in the audience, so near to Annika.

Del smiled at Ruth. "We'll be fine. You go and help out. I'll just keep this girl scout company, folding programs."

Annika nodded affirmatively. "I'm earning my drama badge."

After a while, Del smelled popcorn. "Boy, that smells good. Do you want some popcorn?" he asked Annika. Then he took out his wallet and handed his granddaughter five dollars. "My treat. But hurry, it's only five minutes before the show starts."

"Something to drink too?" Annika asked.

"A bottle of water if they have it," he told her.

Just then, Annika saw Sam Guston come in and take a seat in the back of the theatre. She stopped in her tracks. "Grandpa Del," she whispered, "leave your jacket on our chairs, and come with me?" She handed him the five dollars back. "You know what we promised Grandma Ruth. I'm supposed to stick to you like glue."

Noticing the man in the back of the theatre, Del nodded and got up.

They left their seats and headed for the concessions, walking up the aisle just in time to see Blanche and Uncle Tony taking their seats toward the back, also. Uncle Tony was glowering at Sam Guston. Del could see him whispering to Blanche, who was looking around. When she saw Del she waved and smiled.

"Uh oh, it's the *nudge,*" Annika whispered.

Backstage, Ruth checked on the men first, and was happy to see that Jack Guston had on the striped shirt, and the stain was impossible to see. She was glad to see that the boy seemed more at ease. She saw Howard Kirkdorff pat the boy on the back and exclaim, "You're doing a good job, kid!"

Jack grinned at him. "I spent the week learning my lines. I'm going to try it without slips of paper tonight."

"Good boy!" Howard laughed, "But I always say, if you need 'em, use 'em."

Things in the women's dressing room had quieted down to a "mild roar," as the kids used to say. *Edna Fuerling has her box of Kleenex, and all's right with the world.* Ruth smiled to herself. She saw that the floor was getting dirty, and she quickly got a broom and dustpan and proceeded to sweep it. *I wonder who was disagreeing? And about what?*

As the overture began, and Ruth went back to Annika and Del, she saw that Annika was sharing a large bag of popcorn with Del. Emmy Eklund came hurriedly down the aisle, herding Andrea and Norman Foley before her.

"Sorry I'm late," she whispered as she sat down, urging the Foley children to sit on either side of her. "Getting dinner done and out of the house was a challenge tonight." However, she smiled a radiant smile as she said this, and she put her arm around both kids and hugged them.

Ruth leaned over and whispered, "Emmy, this is my husband, Del. And Del, this is Emmy Eklund, Pastor Paul's wife, and, well ... his good right hand."

"Pleased to meet you." Del reached over Andrea Foley's head and shook Emmy's hand. "And to shake your good right hand." He patted Andrea's head when he was done greeting Emmy. He smiled at Norman, who ignored him and continued rocking back and forth.

Del tried not to look at the rocking boy, but Emmy noticed and whispered, "He has autism." Del just nodded back at her.

"How wonderful for Ruth that you're here!" she whispered. Then she looked at Andrea, who was sitting next to her. "This is going to be so much fun!"

Andrea smiled back at her. Ruth noticed that both kids had popcorn.

Norman didn't eat his, he just held it, rocking back and forth, but at least he was quiet.

Emmy whispered, "I got a phone call from Janet Foley that Roy is doing okay, thank God. But she says he'll need some physical therapy. They're staying in Duluth for now. Roy is still in the hospital. Janet will be here sometime tomorrow." She smiled again. "And in the meantime I get to have these two wonderful kids at my house whenever she's in Duluth." Emmy was looking very content.

Ruth could see Andrea moving closer to Emmy, leaning into her, and holding her popcorn up to share with her. Norman just stared at the stage, but he rocked a bit less.

Ruth smiled as the curtain opened, thinking, *I sure hope she's a mom soon. She'll be such a good one.* As Annika shared her popcorn with Del and Ruth, the actors came out on stage, and the show began.

All through the performance, Ruth couldn't help but think, *Only two more shows, and Del will be here for both of them! I feel as if nothing bad can happen if he's here.* She leaned into him, almost purring, she felt so happy. *I'm going to just forget about Loris Biederman and Tommy Sherman and Sam Guston and everything else bad, tonight. I'm just going to enjoy myself.*

Del put his arm around Ruth's shoulders, squeezing them a bit, as Ruth leaned back into his hug.

Amy and Howard Kirkdorff were so wonderfully expressive in the first act. Del smiled when they sang "If I Loved You," and made a thumbs up sign to Ruth. Willy as Carrie was a bit more brittle than the other performances, but Lester Perry handled it well. He sang as well as ever.

During the second act, in the clambake scene, Norman was rocking harder and making noises—loud enough so that Emmy felt she had to take him out of the theater.

"I'd better get Norman home and put him to bed," she whispered to Ruth. "Sorry."

Ruth nodded and watched as she whispered something to Andrea.

"Do you think Andrea could stay with you, so she can see the rest of the show?" Emmy asked Ruth.

"Of course, we'd love to have her," Ruth whispered.

"There's a cast party tonight," Annika whispered to Emmy. "Can we bring Andrea with us?"

"That sounds wonderful." Emmy smiled at Andrea. "You have a good time, honey; you can always sleep in if it runs late."

Ruth saw Andrea look at Emmy with such love it made her heart ache.

After the performance was over, Del told Ruth, "I am going to help you backstage. *You-know-who* came to the show tonight. Just pretend you don't see her." Ruth saw Blanche and Uncle Tony hurrying down the aisle as they hurried backstage and pretended they didn't hear her *"You-hoo!"*

Ruth and Del, along with Annika and Andrea, straightened up the dressing rooms after the performance.

"Gram, we'd better get over to Sven and Ole's Pizza Place," Annika said. "I heard some of the ladies in the cast talking about the party being there."

"I would love a piece of pizza tonight. We've worked hard for it," Ruth said. "What about it, Grandpa Del?"

"Nothing better than a cast party," Del assured her, making a face, but laughing.

"I know, my love." She patted his shoulder. "But you'll enjoy it. No press at this one."

"Yeah, and no Blanche, if we're lucky," he quipped, hoping Blanche and Uncle Tony had gone back to Naniboujou.

"Yup, I'm your date tonight." Ruth grinned, remembering what he had told her about the ill-fated cast party in New York, where he was set up to be Blanche's escort.

"And for that, my love, I am eternally grateful." He leaned over and kissed her cheek.

As they drove down the hill to Sven and Ole's Pizza, Annika was being her true empathetic self. "Andrea, this party will be so fun for you! It must be so hard to always have to help take care of your brother."

"Yeah, sometimes," the girl said, "but I'm kind of used to it." She sounded resigned. "I don't need to help with Norman when I'm at school, but I don't get to go to many parties. I'm really glad you asked me to this one."

Annika grinned. "You're going to have so much fun tonight."

She's just like her mom, thought Ruth, proudly. *Empathetic to a fault.*

Annika looked at Andrea and rubbed her stomach. "Boy! I just love pizza!"

"I do too!" the girl laughed. "Sometimes my mom makes frozen pizza for us, but I hardly ever get real pizza, like, from a restaurant."

That poor kid, Ruth thought, *I'll bet they don't go out much with Norman the way he is. I wonder if Janet gets any help with Norman? I know there must be schools for kids with those kinds of problems.*

Chapter 28

Cast Party and Confrontation at Sven and Ole's

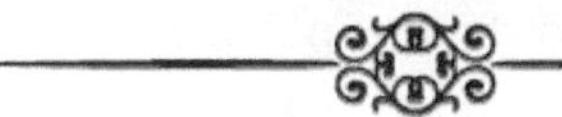

SVEN AND OLE'S PIZZA Place was the hub of night life for the young people of Grand Marais. The street was lined with cars, and Del had to park about a block and a half away. They could hear the loud music and raucous laughter as they walked up to the building.

The restaurant portion of the establishment was a simple large room—pine-paneled and full of tables placed end to end. There were plenty of chairs so the customers could eat "family style." There were also blue booths lining the north wall of the place, but tonight, the actors were all at the tables.

Ruth saw Paul standing at the counter, where people could order their pizzas and drinks, pay for it all, and then sit down at the tables until the pizzas were ready and names were called.

"What kind would you like?" Ruth asked the girls, who were looking over the menu on the wall behind the counter.

"I want a vegetarian one, with olives, green peppers, and tomatoes, but no mushrooms," Annika said, "and a large Coke."

"Oh, sweetie, it's a little late for that much caffeine. Why don't you just get 7-Up?"

"Okay," the girl replied. "Andrea, what do you want?"

"I'll get the same as you." The girl beamed. "That sounds really good."

Ruth took Del's arm and asked him, "What do you feel like?"

"Let's see ..." Del scanned the menu. "Why don't we split a small pepperoni-and-veggie pizza? And I would love a beer."

"That sounds good. But I'll stick with a diet 7-Up."

They ordered their pizza and drinks, and Del paid for them. The drinks were given to them right away. Carrying their drinks, they went into the main room to look for a place to sit, and wait for the pizza.

"Over here, Ruth and Del!" cried Edna Fuerling in her loudest voice. "I got three places. I was savin' 'em, just for you!" Then she saw Andrea and added, "Oops, move over guys, we got one more kiddo here." Everyone moved down one, and Edna waved them over.

Ruth made introductions all around. First, she introduced Del and Andrea to everyone (they already knew Annika). She could see smiles and nods for Del from the adults. The kids were pretty interested in their pizza when she introduced Andrea, but a couple of the adults whispered to each other and looked sad.

They must know about her grandmother, Ruth thought. *Poor kid, it's sure a lot for an eight-year-old to deal with.*

Edna was the most forthright, as usual. "I'm really glad to see ya again, Del. I'll bet Ruth is happy you're here." She grinned at Ruth. To Andrea she said, "Gee, kiddo, I'm really sorry about your grandma, that's a real shame." She shook her head. "She was a real nice lady, and she made some great costumes for us over the years."

Andrea just smiled wanly at her, taking a sip of her drink.

"Norm!" Edna Fuerling screamed to her husband, who was sitting a couple of chairs down from her and talking quietly with Howard Kirkdorff. "Pass us a couple pieces of that pizza in front of you, will ya?" She pointed at the pizza. "These guys need some!"

"Oh no," Ruth said to her. "We just ordered. Ours should be here any minute."

Annika, however, looked hungrily at the pizza in question, as Norm Fuerling put four delicious-looking slices on four large paper napkins and passed it down to them.

"But we've got ours coming ..." Ruth insisted.

"Nahhh!" Edna boomed, "Don't worry about it, it's the guys' treat tonight." She indicated Norm, Howard, Arvid, Lester Perry and his partner, Tim Stoltz, with a sweep of her arm. "The women in the cast put on the final shindig on Saturday, so the men-folk pay for tonight's party."

"Oh," said Ruth. "Should we be planning to bring something for the final cast party?"

"Nope," Edna assured her, "Loris Biederman usually puts it on, in her dining room ... but I guess Sam Guston beat her to the draw. We're having the final cast party at *Guston's*. It's just finished; and because his nephew is in the show, he gave it to us free of charge. He's even catering it, free of charge!"

"Oh dear! How did Loris take that?"

Edna lowered her voice to a whisper. "I'm not sure. I haven't talked to her recently, but I don't think she liked it much."

Ruth, who had to lean across the table to hear her, asked, "Who made that decision?"

"I'm not sure. I know Sam and Jack go to Paul's church, so I think maybe Paul?"

Just then, their name was called, and Del got up to retrieve their pizzas from the counter. As soon as he got it to the table, Annika, who had already finished her cheese pizza, dug right in.

"Thanks, Grampa Del, this is so good!" she said over a mouthful.

Andrea, her mouth still full of the cheese pizza, nodded in agreement.

Ruth laughed at Annika. "Swallow first, then talk," she told the girl.

The next half-hour was small talk about the show. Ruth heard the guys tell about the disagreement that evening. It was over the knife that Billy Bigelow had to carry. Howard, who was playing Billy, thought it should be more real-looking. But Lester and Arvid agreed with Pastor Paul, that they should use the plastic one he had provided. Jack, the 'new Jigger,' wisely kept out of it.

His uncle was there, sitting quietly in the corner, eating a slice of pizza and drinking a beer, while staring at Ruth and Annika. Annika didn't seem to notice, but it made Ruth uneasy.

Howard's wife, Jeanine, was there. She was the attractive red headed violinist in the show's orchestra. At Howard's begging, she gave an impromptu violin concert for the entire restaurant, playing "What's the Use of Wond'rin," after which were loud cheers and *Bravas* from the crowd.

Then Gloria Simms, who played Aunt Nettie, sang "You'll Never Walk Alone," with Janine Kirkdorff's violin accompaniment.

She's in better form tonight, thought Ruth.

"Good girl, Gloria!" yelled Edna at the end of the song. "You're still a star!"

Gloria gave Edna a 'thumbs up' sign and smiled as she sat back down.

"I'm glad she's in a better mood this week," Edna said. She shook her head. "She has a drinkin' problem, see? And the least little thing sets her off. Why I remember one show—*Fiddler*, I think it was—when she almost fell off the stage, and then she ..."

Ruth was not overly interested in hearing all of Edna's backstage gossip, so she put her napkin down and smiled and interrupted the woman. "Edna, I've been meaning to ask you, where do you store all the costumes when the show is over?"

"They have a closet at the real church," Edna told Ruth. "We just put 'em in big plastic garbage bags and pile 'em up in there."

"You don't hang them up anywhere?" Ruth was surprised.

"Nah," said Edna, shaking her head. "We wash and dry 'em, and then fold 'em, and put them in the bags." She shrugged. "We've been doin' that for years. Works just fine. When we need to use 'em again, everyone irons their own."

"Well, it certainly sounds easy enough. When do you want to wash them?"

"Always the week after," said Edna. "It takes that long to collect all of them."

"But I won't be here. We're leaving for the cities on Sunday morning."

"It don't matter." Edna laughed. "What else have I got to do?"

Norm Fuerling came up to Del and put his arm on Del's back. "Hey, Del, how 'bout another beer?"

"I would, but we have to get the girls home." Del looked at Ruth.

"No worries," Norm responded. "They can get home by themselves, and you can just walk home. Your hotel is just down the block."

Ruth rolled her eyes and smiled. "Go ahead," she laughed, "have some guy time. I'll drive Andrea home, and Annika and I will see you back at the hotel later. To tell the truth, I am getting a little tired."

"Gram," Annika said, "I need to use the ladies' room." And finally noticing Sam Guston, she told Ruth, "I'll take Andrea with me, so don't worry, Gram."

After the girls left, as if on cue Blanche Voorhees and Uncle Tony made their grand entrance. Blanche came right over to their table while Uncle Tony ordered their pizza and drinks.

Plopping down in Annika's seat Blanche shrieked, "Del!" shaking her finger at him. "A cast party?" She laughed. "Since when have I ever missed a *cast party?*"

"But you're not in the cast," Del said.

"Not this time, but I was the lead in one of Fritz Gerhardt's productions of *Carousel!*"

She yelled at Tony, "Tony! Over here, there's an extra seat for you!"

"But that's the girls' seat—" Ruth started to say.

"Tony! Didn't they have any wine?" Blanche yelled again when she saw the 7-Up he was carrying.

"Sorry, babycakes, no wine in this here place, just beer. 'lo Del, 'lo Ruth," Tony Ancino muttered as he sat down in Andrea's place.

Tony could see that there were plates in front of him, with half-eaten pizza. He sighed as Blanche swept them to the side and crossed her arms on the table, owning it. Then he noticed Sam Guston.

Tony's face darkened and he looked daggers at the man. "What the hell. What's *he* doin' here?" he asked Del.

"His nephew is playing Jigger," Del said quietly.

"Do you know Sam Guston?" Ruth asked him.

"Everybody knows Sam Guston," said Tony, curling his lip. "Wish I didn't." He sniffed. "*Sonofabitch* still owes me money. He was a bigshot down in the cities, back in the day, and not in a good way. Had his hand in every dirty deal from White Bear to Wayzata."

Ruth tried to imagine what sort of "dirty deals" had gone down in Wayzata in the 1970s, and drew a blank.

But what do I know?

Tony cleared his throat and continued, "He needed cash from me to get out of town. And like a fool, I lent it to him. I always wondered what became of him ..."

As if he'd been called, Sam Guston got out of his chair and walked over to Uncle Tony. "Hey, Ancino, my ears are burning."

"Yeah, so?" Tony smoothly turned in his chair and looked Sam Guston straight in the eye. "What're you gonna do about it?"

The table got suddenly quiet. Ruth held her breath.

Sam said, "I got somethin' to settle up with you." Everyone gasped and froze as he reached into his sport coat ... and pulled out a fat stack of hundred-dollar bills, which he laid on the table in front of Tony's plate. "I know we've had some bad dealings in the past, but I'm trying to start fresh up here in the North Country." Then he pulled another thick bundle of bills out of his wallet and added it to the pile. "Here's interest."

Tony opened his mouth as if to say something, but no words came out.

Sam honored Blanche with a nod, then continued, "I've been helping to raise my sister's kid. And, uh, he's a great kid, and I wanna do right by him." He glanced over at Jack, who straightened in his chair. "I ... I didn't want him to be an actor. Not at first. But then I saw him tonight, and he's good at it! Isn't he good?" Sam asked the whole table.

Everyone nodded and loudly agreed in exuberant tones. Jack was very very good.

"He's *damn* good! Jack is a fine actor, and I'm going to be there for him!"

"Hear, hear!" shouted Lester Perry.

Ruth just stared, not believing what she was hearing.

Sam walked over and stood behind her chair. "Mizz ah ... lady, I know your granddaughter saw my gun on that boat. I threw it overboard to get rid of it."

Ruth just sat very still, feeling the hairs rise on the back of her neck.

"Ohh?" she said timidly.

"That's right. I got rid of it because I want a start fresh. A fresh start! I don't want anything from my old life around our place."

"Th-that sounds wonderful. And very wise."

"I'm going to be a new man. And Pastor Paul over there"—Sam pointed across the table at a visibly shaken Pastor Paul—"he's going to help me stay on the straight-and-narrow."

Tony muttered, "Well, son-of-a-bitch." Then he grinned at Sam and pushed the bills back at him. "Here. Start a college fund for yer nephew."

"But this is what I owe you, Ancino, and I pay my debts."

"And I want Jack to have it. You can, uh, name the scholarship after me, if ya want."

"You always were a good man, Ancino," Sam said, taking back the bills and tucking them into the inside pocket of his sport coat. "Thanks from my nephew and me!"

About then, Blanche had had enough of being overlooked. "I don't believe I've had the pleasure," she said, extending her hand to Sam Guston.

"Wow! Ancino!" Sam said, kissing her hand. "You're sure comin' up in the world!"

Blanche just beamed.

"This is Blanche Voorhees, my wife-to-be, I hope." Tony put his arm around Blanche's waist. She held out her left hand just then, showing off a huge diamond ring that glittered in the low light from the restaurant.

"Blanche here, is an opera singer," Tony said proudly. "A real star, she is, too!"

By then, Tony's pizza order was called out and he excused himself to retrieve it.

Sam Guston turned to go back to his table, but then turned again to Ruth and said, "I hope we're okay here, so nice to meet you all." He bowed.

"Um ... sure," Ruth stammered. "Good luck with everything." *I hope he's telling the truth,* she thought.

When Annika and Andrea came back from the ladies' room, they noticed their seats were taken by Uncle Tony and Blanche. They stood by Ruth, and Annika took their plates and moved them over by Ruth's.

"It's okay, honey," Ruth told her. "We have to leave soon anyway."

Annika started wrapping the leftover slices of pizza in two napkins, one for her and one for Andrea. "Breakfast," she whispered to Andrea, who nodded, "Yes!"

"Del!" yelled Norm Fuerling. "The guys are going to have an extra beer and some guy talk. You wanna join us?"

Del started to shake his head "no," but Ruth smiled at him and said, "Go ahead, my love. Guy talk will be fun for you."

Blanche fumed, but Uncle Tony took no notice.

As Del nodded his thanks to Ruth and got out of his seat, Blanche looked at Ruth as if she wanted to murder her. And as Ruth and the girls were about to leave, Del kissed her and mussed both the girls' hair, to the delight of each.

He gave Ruth the car keys. "Please excuse me, Tony. Blanche." He looked adoringly at Ruth. "See you in a bit, my love." Then he joined Howard, Norm, Al, Lester and Tim at the "guy's table," which they had commandeered in the corner of the room. Lester and Tim were grinning at Del, and they told him immediately about the several operas they had seen him in.

"We have season tickets at the Lyric," Tim told him proudly.

Ruth said her good-byes to everyone, including Blanche and Tony, and ushered the two girls out of the restaurant. *I'll have to tell Annika what Sam Guston said,* she thought.

While they walked to Del's car, Andrea grinned and said, "Thanks for saving me the pizza. I'll eat mine for breakfast too. And thank you for taking me to the party. I really had fun tonight!"

"We're so happy you could come with us," Ruth assured the girl.

Emmy was looking through the front window of the parsonage as they drove up. She opened the front door immediately. "I'd ask you in," she said to them, "but I just got Norman to sleep." She smiled at Andrea and asked, "Did you have fun, honey?"

"Did I ever!" Andrea replied. "Thank you again," she said to Ruth and Annika.

"She needs to get out with friends more," Emmy chimed in, while Andrea looked adoringly at her. "Thanks so much for tonight."

"Any time," Ruth told the woman. "Annika loves having her with us, don't you, honey?"

Annika hugged the girl. "I sure do!" she told her.

Ruth and Annika said their good-byes, and as they were driving back down the hill to the East Bay, Ruth said to her granddaughter, "Please do not leave that pizza in Grandpa's car tonight, because by tomorrow night it will smell like *dead, dead skunk in the middle of the road!*'"

"Nope, this dead skunk's gonna be in my stomach." Annika laughed, as they got into Del's car and drove down the hill. "Did you notice the *nudge* tonight? She even took our seats!"

"That she did," said Ruth, shaking her head.

"That's what nudges do."

Neither of them had noticed the beat-up dark sedan that was following them from the parsonage to the hotel. It was moving slowly, keeping about a block behind them.

Chapter 29

The Dark Sedan on Wisconsin Street

As they got near the hotel, Ruth had to drive by Sven and Ole's. She could see the "guys' table" through the window. The men all seemed to be having a really good time.

"I think Grandpa Del's found his 'tribe.'" She laughed. She noticed that Uncle Tony and Blanche were gone.

"My dad says that 'guy time' is as important as 'girl time,'" Annika told her.

"I know, honey. They get all the world's problems solved and they come home lots happier. Grandpa Tom had the guys at work. They were so good to him during the time he was sick. Especially that last year. They watched over him and gave me time to get groceries and run errands, and do some things for myself." *And thank God for them,* she thought.

"I'm sorry, Gram. I don't even remember Grandpa Tom much."

"You were so little when he died. But when you were at our house, you were always in his lap while he read to you."

"Oh! I kind of remember that." Annika brightened up. "I remember, he did all the voices when he read me stories. Like *Red Ridinghood*. He did the Wolf, even the Grandma." She laughed. "He was so funny."

"Yes, he was." Ruth smiled at the memory. "And he loved you so much."

As they got out of the car, the dark sedan pulled up behind them. Ruth looked in the rearview mirror and saw Tommy Sherman at the wheel!

"Annika," she whispered, "run into the hotel right now and tell Mrs. Biederman to call the police. Tell them Tommy Sherman is out here, right behind my car. Hurry! Run fast! Do it right now."

As Annika ran into the hotel, Ruth saw Tommy leave his car and come up to her window. She rolled her window down a little.

"Mrs. Mays," Tommy said with a catch in his voice, "please help me! I didn't kill no one. Please help me!"

"You didn't kill *anyone*," Ruth said.

"You believe me?"

"I was correcting your grammar," Ruth explained, exasperated.

Tommy shook his head and went on. "Everybody thinks I killed Joey-Frank, but I didn't! He was my best friend!"

"Nice friend," Ruth said sarcastically.

"I know he wasn't a good person. But he was still my friend ... 'cause I didn't have anybody else. And ... and he was different when we were growing up. And anyway, I didn't kill him!" He started sobbing.

"What about Willy? I saw you two in the men's dressing room that night after the first performance. What were you doing to her?"

"Nothing!"

"Then why did she accuse you?"

"I don't know! I mean, I guess it wasn't nothing. But—" He looked at Ruth with anguish in his eyes. "It's not how it looked! Amy was mad at me, and said she didn't want me around, and Willy just ... she just ... I thought she really liked me, you know? So I ... but then she ... and I know how it looked, but we weren't—" He looked frantic. "Anyway, that was Joey-Frank's thing, not mine. I don't *do* that to girls! I'm not like Joey-Frank. He used to get off on that ... rough stuff. He liked it when they fought him. He was a sicko. But I didn't do anything to her!"

"Oh yeah?" said Ruth, not sure what to believe. "Then who gave her that bruise on her face?"

"That wasn't me, I swear!"

"Then *who?*"

"I don't know! Willy knows a lot of guys. Some of 'em aren't from around here. And some of 'em deal drugs ... which I don't do. Anymore."

"So why did Willy complain about you to Pastor Paul?" She questioned him, not sure if she was ready to believe him. On the other hand, he looked and sounded genuinely earnest. She got out of the car so they could talk together more easily.

"Willy was mad at me."

"I thought you said Amy was mad at you."

"They were both mad at me. I guess Amy had a good reason, but Willy ... I mean ... she was going to ... but I said 'no,' and then she ..."

Ruth sighed. "Just tell me what happened between you and Willy. Why was Willy angry with you?"

Tommy looked at his shoes. "She wanted me to tell Pastor Paul that if he wouldn't give us ten thousand dollars, we would tell people he had sex with her."

"*What?*"

"Willy wanted us to lie about him so we could both go somewhere else and live. She *hates* Grand Marais. I told her *no way*. I'm not doing that! But even if I'm not part of her plan, she'll still try to get money from Paster Paul. She's mean, Mrs. Mays. I don't know if you noticed, but Willy Guerin is *mean.*"

Ruth thought back to that day out on Artist's Point. "My granddaughter and I saw *somebody,* who looked a lot like you, fighting with Willy and knocking her down. That wasn't you?"

"No!"

"Are you telling me the truth?"

"Yes, Mrs. Mays! And I like Pastor Paul. He gave me a chance to be in this show. He even gives me money for groceries, sometimes." Tommy gulped. "He's a good guy. He doesn't deserve what Willy's planning to do to him."

"Hmm. But what about the blood on your shirt?" Ruth rubbed her arm absentmindedly.

Tommy looked at her rubbing her arm. "I'm sorry I grabbed your arm like that."

"Whose blood was it?" she asked, sternly.

Tommy looked down at his feet again. "Mine. I got in a fight with … one of Willy's other guy-friends. He saw my prop-knife, for the musical, and grabbed it away from me. I was worried people would think I killed somebody." He shuddered and looked back up at her. "That's why I was so upset when I couldn't find my shirt. Thanks for washing it out, by the way."

"You're welcome. At least *someone* appreciates what I did."

"And there's something else you should know."

"Oh?" said Ruth.

The young man glanced nervously in the direction of Sally Merritt's house. Then he cleared his throat and said, "I, uh, know who killed our first costume lady."

Ruth gasped.

"It was Joey-Frank."

"Are you certain about that?" Ruth asked quietly.

"Yeah. Yeah, I am. See, he called me up right after he shot her, and told me to help him move her body. But I said no. And then, uh, he uh … well, he threatened to shoot me next. 'Cause I told him no."

"He was going to kill you too? I can't believe it!"

"Mrs. Mays, I told you Joey-Frank wasn't a good person. And he wasn't a very good friend, either, I guess. Although he was different when we were kids. And Sally Merritt was such a nice lady. She used to feed me whenever I went over there. I don't … always have a place to live, you know? And sometimes I would go in her house and take a shower while she was gone. I even used her towels, but I always put 'em in the wash afterwards!" He laughed a little. "I'm pretty sure she knew all about it. She even left dinners out for me on the kitchen counter."

"So, why did Joey-Frank shoot her?"

"He was trying to rob her house. He used to rent from her last year, and she kicked him out. He didn't know she was home, I guess, and she walked in on him, and he—"

Just then both the Norstrands pulled up in the police car. Roberta was out first.

"Hands up, Tommy," she said.

Tommy put his hands up immediately, but looked pleadingly at Ruth, as Roberta handcuffed him and put him in the back seat of the police car.

The elder Norstrand got out of the driver's side of the car and said, "Thank you. We finally got our man."

"Maybe, maybe not," Ruth said.

"Well, we're not going to do anything with him tonight. We'll put him in a cell for the time being." Sergeant Norstrand looked at Tommy, slumped in the back seat of the police car, head down and sobbing.

"Be sure and feed him something. I don't think that boy has had much to eat," Ruth told him. "I'll be over in the morning to tell you what he told me. It's just too late tonight."

"Don't worry," the elder Norstrand said. "We'll give him a warm place to sleep and some chili that Roberta just made tonight. It's real tasty."

"That sounds like a plan. I think it'll be better if you take care of him tonight. I'll be over in the morning, to talk to both of you." Ruth looked up at Bob. "I'm just too worn out tonight. But I don't think, after what he told me, that you should book him or anything. I think the only thing he's guilty of is taking showers in someone's house without permission. Please just listen to what he has to say."

The elder policeman laughed. "This isn't television. We don't 'book' him." He smiled. "We just need to talk with him. Can you come over to the station after your breakfast tomorrow?"

"How about nine-thirty? Can I say something to him?"

"Sure."

Ruth went over to the police car and leaned down over the back door, which was still open.

"Tommy, nothing's going to happen to you tonight, except a good bed and a warm meal. I'll be over in the morning. Okay?"

Tommy looked at her, tears rolling down his cheeks. He quietly said, "Thanks, Mrs. Mays. You're a real good lady."

Scared Kid or Con Man?

Ruth put Annika to bed, after telling her what Tommy had said to her.

"Do you believe him, Gram?" the girl asked, pulling Loki under the comforter, with just his head sticking out.

"I'm not completely sure, honey, but I've been a teacher all my life and I pretty much know when kids are lying, and when they're telling the truth." She tucked the blanket around Annika and Loki. "And I think that maybe Tommy Sherman was telling me the truth."

"So, you don't think he killed that man that you found?"

"No, I don't think he did."

"Who do you think did it, then?"

"I don't know," said Ruth, "but I'm going to find out."

"I hope the killer doesn't find you first!" the girl said in a worried tone.

"They won't. I promise."

While Annika fell asleep, Ruth got into her nightie. She tried to read her book from book club, but her mind was racing with other thoughts.

Del came home about half an hour later. He knocked on her door.

"Who is it?" she asked quietly, going right up to the door so she wouldn't wake Annika.

"Your errant husband."

Ruth opened the door and kissed him. "Annika's asleep, and I need to tell you what happened tonight. Can we talk in your room?" She grabbed her robe from the chair and locked the door to room 101.

"God save me from any more cast parties!" Del said to her once they were in his room. He started searching in his suitcase for his bottle of aspirin. "I'm getting too old for this."

"Too old for *what?*" Ruth kidded him. "I thought you were enjoying all this. Hobnobbing with theatre folk, having beer and pizza with the guys?"

"Well, I was enjoying it, until Blanche and Uncle Tony waltzed into that pizza place!"

Del shook his head

"Poor Uncle Tony!" Ruth said.

"Poor Uncle Tony?" Del retorted. "How about poor *us?*"

"We'll be fine. Only two more performances and we're out of here."

"Yes, I know. And don't get me wrong—these are all very nice people—but I am tired of 'people.' I came up here for some peace and quiet."

"I'm sorry." Ruth stroked the side of his face. "There are two more performances and one more cast party. Can you believe what Sam Guston said tonight?"

"I ... hope we can? I don't know the guy. But I'd like to believe people can change for good." Then he looked more closely at her. "What's going on? Did something else happen here?"

"You can always read me. Sit down, my love. I have to ask your advice about something."

Ruth told Del what had transpired when she and Annika got to the hotel, and how she felt about what Tommy Sherman had told her.

"Somebody killed Joey-Frank, but I don't think it was Tommy Sherman," she said quietly. "I'm going to the police station after breakfast to talk with Bob and Roberta. I'm still wondering about that conversation I overheard up at the old church. You know, when the men didn't know I was in the building? If Loris Biederman hated Joey-Frank Jurak that much, could she possibly be the one who killed him?" She looked at Del. "What do you think? Should I tell the Norstrands what I overheard?"

"God!" Del put his head in his hands. "I wish we could just get in our cars right now and get out of here and drive home!" He stayed that way for a moment, and then he looked up at her. "I know you want to do the right thing."

"Yes, I do. That poor boy doesn't have anyone on his side. I'm pretty much his only chance to redeem himself. Okay, maybe it's the teacher in me, or maybe it's the mom in me, but I have to help him, Del. I couldn't live with myself if I didn't."

Del took her in his arms. They lay down on the double bed and held each other for a while, saying nothing.

After a bit, Ruth spoke. "I know how awful it was last summer, and I don't want any repeat performance of that, but Del, he's so alone ... such a scared kid."

"All I know is what you've told me, and what I've heard from other cast members." He stroked her back. "The guys mentioned him tonight.

They seemed glad to get him out of the cast. One of them—Howard, I think it was—called Tommy a *con man.*"

Ruth sighed. "I think the Norstrands ought to get Willy Guerin in, and talk with her. I don't think that girl is what she seems to be. Is there such a thing as a 'con-woman?'"

"Yes," he sighed. "In my lifetime, I've known at least one."

Ruth laughed quietly and tickled him in the ribs.

After a while, when they had snuggled and Del started falling asleep, Ruth got up.

"Are you going to change into your jammies? And brush your teeth?" she asked him.

"Yes, Mama," he laughed. "I'll be a good boy." He got up and started getting his nightclothes and toothbrush out of his suitcase.

"I'm going back to Annika," she told him. "Lock your door."

"One more kiss?" he asked.

The kiss lasted a few moments. Ruth looked up at him. "I actually cannot wait to get home, and be in our own room," she whispered. Del just nodded his head in agreement.

Ruth kissed him again, and then went quietly to room 101.

Chapter 31

We May Never Solve This One

FRIDAY MORNING AFTER BREAKFAST, Ruth left Annika and Del with their fishing poles. She walked the couple of blocks from the East Bay to the police station and jail. She hoped the walk would clear her mind.

How am I going to tell the Norstrands what I suspect? Loris Biederman is a really fine citizen of this town, a pillar of the community and a friend. And if I'm wrong, I certainly don't want it to go any farther than the two Norstrands. I've known Loris for years. She's a wonderful person. What would she think of me for doing this? Oh God, please let me say the right thing.

As she walked along, looking in shop windows, she didn't notice Sam Guston cautiously following her. When he saw her go into the door of the station, he kept on walking as if he didn't have a care in the world. But his face said otherwise. Ruth was so lost in her own thoughts, she didn't have a clue that he was behind her. She was focusing on what she would say to the police. She just hoped and prayed it would be okay.

As Ruth entered the front office, Sergeant Robert Norstrand got up from his desk. He was not in his usual uniform. He had on a green plaid long-sleeved shirt that made his ruddy complexion seem even ruddier.

"It's the real me," he chuckled, throwing out his arms. "On Fridays, we just sort of relax a bit. I know it's not regulation, but we do 'casual Fridays' here."

"You look nice," Ruth told him.

He ignored the compliment, and offered Ruth a seat in front of his desk. "Please," he said.

"Thank you," said Ruth, sitting down in the metal-backed office chair.

"Now, before you say anything else, I want you to know that Tommy Sherman is going to stay here, but not in the jail part of the building. We're giving him a room and bed, until he can find a place to live. We might even hire him as a janitor, until he can find a job somewhere in town."

"That's so good of you," Ruth exclaimed. "I think he's innocent."

"Yeah, after talking to him, I think so too. He's just a kid who's been down on his luck for a long time." Sergeant Norstrand sat back down, then took his glasses off and cleaned them with the corner of his shirt. "And he has had a bad choice of friends. He says Joey-Frank shot Sally Merritt. Joey-Frank was renting from her, and I guess she found drugs in his room and told him to get out."

"Tommy said Joey was robbing her house."

"Uh-huh. That was after she had kicked him out."

"And did he explain about his bloody shirt? The one I, uh, washed?"

"Tommy says the blood on his shirt was his own. He was cut by someone he owed money to."

"Ahh. He just told me there was a fight."

"Apparently Tommy's been sleeping in his car in the alley behind Sally's house. And sometimes Joey-Frank would let him in to take a shower when Sally wasn't home."

"He told me something like that," said Ruth.

"And that night he was woken up by a telephone call. Joey-Frank called him and asked him to help move her body. But Tommy was too upset to help. Joey-Frank apparently threatened him, so Tommy got into his car and drove out of town. There's apparently some cabin north of here that he knows about. And he didn't tell the police because he was afraid Jurak would kill him. So ..."

Ruth leaned forward in her chair and echoed, "So ... ?"

"I don't think Tommy would be considered an accessory to murder. He's just a witness."

"Do you think Joey-Frank meant to murder Sally?" asked Ruth. "Or was he just startled?"

Robert Norstrand looked down and shook his head. "I wish Sally would have called me to get Jurak out of there." He wiped his eyes. "None of this had to happen."

"I'm so sorry," Ruth whispered.

Robert took a moment to compose himself. He said, "I've been at this job long enough to know when someone isn't telling me everything." He leaned back in his chair and folded his hands. "So, how about it, Mrs. Mays? Do *you* have something else you want to tell me?"

Ruth straightened in her chair and sighed. "I'm almost afraid to." She looked in her lap and shook her head. "I don't want to hurt good people."

"How about you start at the beginning?" Sergeant Norstrand said gently. "There's no one here but us."

"Well, you know I've been working with the theatre group?" She sighed again.

"I know you have. I think it's commendable that you're helping the women's shelter."

"Well ... I drove up to the old church on Monday. I'd left my camera up there, and I wanted to take pictures of Del and Annika fishing." She blew out a *"Whoooo"* through her mouth. "Anyway, I overheard the guys in the show, talking. They were up in the light booth and they didn't know I was there. They were talking about how much Loris Biederman hated Joey-Frank, and then I heard them say ..." Ruth repeated the overheard conversation as well as she could remember, then sighed again. "How did Joey-Frank Jurak die?" She looked at Sergeant Norstrand, hoping he wasn't going to say anything about a hammer.

"The coroner said he was bludgeoned to death, and he thought it could have been a large rock or maybe even a hammer of some sort." The sergeant took his glasses off and held his hands over his eyes as if he had a headache. "I know how this sounds, but Joey-Frank Jurak was a drug dealer for years. He had lots of enemies all over Cook County. Any one of them could have killed him." He looked pointedly at her. "We may never solve this one."

"Maybe I just heard them wrong?" Ruth looked at him hopefully.

"Perhaps you did. Who knows what they were talking about? But let's just leave this here, okay?"

"I'm fine with that," Ruth told him feeling relieved. "I've been coming up here for over twenty years, and in all that time, Loris has been nothing but wonderful to us." She grimaced. "I didn't even want to tell you this, but ... I don't know ... I just thought I should."

"It's okay, Mrs. Mays. If more people would share even little things with the police, our job would be a hell of a lot easier, pardon my French."

"Did they find out who ran Roy Foley off the road?"

"That's another case we may never solve."

"I mean, he outfits restaurants, for crying out loud. Who would want to kill a man who sells equipment to new restaurants?"

"Mrs. Mays," said Sergeant Norstrand in a warning tone-of-voice.

"I'm sorry, I'm sorry. I should just leave it alone, right?"

"Right." He stood up, signifying that the conversation was over.

Just then, Roberta came into the front office. She was in a tee shirt and jeans, and looked considerably younger than she had in her uniform.

"Dad, Tommy's had a shower, and I found him some clean clothes. I'm also going to give him a haircut. He agreed that he needs one." She looked at Ruth. "Oh, hi, Mrs. Mays. I'm sorry, I didn't mean to interrupt."

Ruth smiled at her. "It's okay, I was just leaving. It sounds as if you have everything in hand."

"We try," Roberta said, grinning.

Ruth thanked the Norstrands and said her good-byes. She walked out of the police station, feeling lighter than she'd felt in days. She returned to the hotel with a spring in her step. There was no one at the desk.

Good, she thought, *I don't really want to face Loris right now.* When she got to her room, it was empty. She knocked on Del's door and there was no answer.

Ruth went back out to the lobby to find Pam at the desk. Pam Biederman was dressed in a pant suit instead of her waitress uniform. She looked troubled.

"Hi, Mrs. Mays," she said. "Your hubby and your granddaughter went fishing." Her smile looked forced, and didn't quite reach her eyes. "They'll be back for lunch. Oh, and there's a phone message for you. Angie something. She wants you to call her." She handed Ruth a slip of paper with the message and Angie's number.

"Thanks, Pam." Ruth took the paper, although she knew her neighbor's number by heart. "Is everything all right? Where's your mom?"

"Ah ... she's taking a nap. She needed a little down time."

"Everyone needs that sometimes." Ruth felt instantly guilty for what she'd told Robert Norstrand. "Thanks." She held up the note.

I wonder what Angie wants? I hope there's nothing wrong with the cats. Morrie and Griselda are getting older, after all.

Chapter 32

Surprise Visit From Angie

RUTH HURRIED TO HER room and dialed the phone number of George Sandstrom—her neighbor. Since she and Del had been together, her good friend, Angie Corbello, and her neighbor, George, had also decided to live together. Angie had been divorced for years and George's wife had recently died in memory care. Angie and George were the perfect "odd couple." Angie was bubbly and talkative, with no discernable filter. George was reserved and quiet and absolutely devoted to making Angie happy.

After the difficult life she has had, raising her daughter, Tracey, all by herself ... on all those low-paying jobs ... she deserves someone to pamper her!

The phone rang and rang. Ruth was just about to hang up when Angie answered.

"Hello," Angie said, out of breath, "Sandstrom residence, Angie speaking."

"Hi, sweetie, it's Ruth. You left a note to call? I hope Morrie and Griselda are okay."

"Don't be such a worry wart," Angie laughed. "We were just over there. I think Morrie has adopted George as his 'favorite human,' and you know that Griselda loves anyone who feeds her."

Ruth heard George laughing in the background. *Angie has that effect on everyone*, she thought.

"Anyhoo," Angie went on, "we're driving up there tomorrow."

"To Grand Marais?"

"Yep! George booked us the only double left in the East Bay. We'll be there until next Saturday. And I want to see *Carousel!* Ruth, you didn't tell me they were doing *Carousel* up there! Remember when we were in it?"

"I sure do! Remember Blanche's performance as *Mrs. Mullin?*"

"How could I forget! She was squeezed into that low-cut dress like it was a tube of toothpaste! The old duffers from my building sure liked her, though." Angie cackled over the phone. "Anyway, I heard tomorrow is the last night. Is there a cast party, I hope? Maybe we can go together? Or have you seen it already? Do you think you guys could stay another week? We'd have so much fun! Whatdaya say, Ruthie, huh?" Angie was bubbling over.

Ruth took a deep breath and said, "Okay, Angie, slow down. First of all, I'd love to see you. But as for staying, I have to run this by Del. It all depends on his schedule. Second, if you guys come up here, who will be taking care of Morrie and Griselda?"

"Oh, that's the part I want to tell you about. Tracey and Danny are buying a little house in Lake Elmo. It's not too far from us. But they can't get in it for another week. So, they're staying at our place. They're happy to watch the cats. They'll have the dogs at our house, of course, and you can visit them when you get home." Angie took a deep breath. "So, how about it, huh? Ruthie? Can you guys stay another week up there? We'd have so much fun! Whatdaya say, huh? Just one more week?"

Ruth shook her head and laughed. Angie was so overwhelming, and so dear. "Like I said before, Angie, I'll ask Del and call you back. Annika's up here too, so I'll have to call Hannah. We'll be going to the show tomorrow night because I'm helping with the costumes."

"The costumes! On your vacation? Oh, Ruth, you're too nice."

"That's what Del says."

"He's right. And I can't wait to see you."

"At least we can spend Saturday night together." Then Ruth added, "And there is a cast party. It's at a new restaurant and event center called *Guston's.*"

"Sounds swanky."

"So I've been told," Ruth said with a nervous swallow. "And yes, you are definitely invited."

"Whoo *hoo!*" Angie yelled into the phone. Ruth held it away from her ear. "I'll start packing right away," Angie chirped. "Just call me! Okay?"

After the phone call, Ruth decided she needed a nap!

But first, call Hannah. She dialed her daughter's number, and as always, Hannah answered immediately.

She must be working at her desk.

"Hi, sweetheart. We're having such a wonderful time." *I don't want her to think there's something wrong.* Ruth listened to Hannah's new ideas for the rest of the summer, which included enrolling herself and Annika in a mom-and-daughter art class. Fortunately, it was in two weeks. *Good timing,* Ruth thought.

Ruth listened to her describe the class. Then she piped up, "We've been busy volunteering at a little theatre up here … Annika and Del? They're out on the rocks, fishing right now … Yes … No, we eat the hotel's fish." *Just bite the bullet,* Ruth thought. "What I was wondering, honey, was, would you mind if we stayed one more week? I know … Yes, it is lonely … But Annika's having a wonderful experience with the theatre, and there's so much up here we haven't seen. We haven't even had time to see the Gunflint Trail yet. I know … Yes … lots of memories.

She heard Hannah ask Eric and heard her laugh. They agreed, one more week, Ruth and Del could have Annika.

"I still need to talk to Del about this," Ruth told her daughter. "But I'm pretty certain he will want to stay. He loves it here. So, another week? … Yup, we'll be home a week from Sunday, sometime after supper. Thanks, sweetie." She hung up.

Whew! Now I really need a nap. Ruth lay across the comforter, pulling her long sweater over her, and was soon fast asleep.

Del and Annika arrived about an hour later and saw Ruth sleeping on the bed. It was lunchtime. Del said, "Shhh." He turned Annika toward his room and whispered, "Grandma's had quite a morning, let's let her sleep. I'll leave her a note to meet us in the dining room."

As he was putting the note on the dresser, however, Ruth woke up.

"Did you catch anything?" She smiled at the two of them.

"I caught a small fish," Annika told her, "but Grandpa Del said to throw it back and let it grow up some more." She made a face. "I wanted to keep it, though." She slumped her shoulders.

Over a lunch of grilled, open-faced tuna-salad sandwiches, smothered in cheese, Del grimaced and said, "This is the closest thing we'll have to fish today."

Ruth told him about Angie's call. "She wants to know if we can stay another week. I told her it depends on your schedule, and that I'd call her tonight."

"Who's watching the cats?" was Del's first question.

"I guess Tracey and Danny are going to be our new neighbors." Ruth smiled. "But they can't get into their new house for another week, so they'll be staying at George and Angie's. They've agreed to be on cat duty."

Del smiled and said, "Another week here would be heaven, providing the hotel hasn't rented out our rooms. How 'bout it, fishing partner?" he asked Annika.

"It would be awesome!" Annika answered. "My mom agreed?" She looked at Ruth.

"She misses you, but said it would be okay."

As soon as they finished lunch, they went to ask Pam, who was at the front desk, if their rooms could be available for one more week.

"I'm so sorry," Pam told them, "you'll need to leave your rooms this Sunday morning. We have another two families coming for a family reunion. They've been on our calendar for more than three months now." She shook her head at them. "I'm really sorry, I wish I could accommodate you."

"Well, that's that." Ruth felt dejected. "I'd better call Angie and Hannah. Angie will be so disappointed."

But just as they were entering their rooms, Pam ran up to them and said, "I might have a solution." She was breathless. "We own a cabin up the shore. It's just about a mile north of Naniboujou. It's nothing fancy. We haven't had the time or the money to fix it up, but it has two small bedrooms and a bathroom with a shower. The kitchen isn't much—a stove, a fridge, a sink, and a small table to eat on. It has a fireplace, and there is some wood you can use. And it's right on the lake, with a door that opens onto the beach. I'll rent it to you for what you'd pay here. We can use the money."

"That sounds perfect," said Del, smiling. "I can fish right outside my front door."

Ruth's mood lifted. She said, "Thank you, Pam. It sounds just perfect for us."

"Does it have TV?" Annika asked.

"Yes," Pam told her, "but the reception is terrible. I'd bring lots of books if I were you."

Annika looked down at her feet, saying nothing.

"Does it have a phone?" asked Ruth, who thought about their safety, and about communicating with Angie and George.

"It does," Pam said. "Actually, I've been staying up there, sometimes, trying to fix things up and paint the rooms in my spare time. I've only got the one smaller bedroom done, though." She sighed. "I'll go and clean it up tonight and try to organize my stuff into one closet. I don't usually stay there. I have my rooms next to my parent's rooms here. And I don't usually eat there, either. I usually eat here, at the hotel. You'll need to buy some groceries. You can drive out to see it tomorrow if you'd like. It'll be straightened up by then."

"Thanks so much," said Ruth. "I can't wait to see it."

Del paid their bill, then smiled at Ruth and Annika. "It really does sound perfect."

Pam snorted. "Well, why don't you drive up and see it first? It's pretty rustic." Then she remembered, "By the way, it has a row boat, pulled up on the shore. It's yours to use if you want. It's dad's." She laughed. "It has seen better days, but it has oars and it floats."

"We'll go and see it tomorrow," Ruth told her. "But we trust you, Pam. I'm sure it'll be fine. We'll buy some groceries, and drive up there."

"Okay, here's my extra key." Pam handed it to Del. "I hope you're happy way up there."

"It'll be just fine," Del told her.

Back in their room, Ruth said, *"Ooookay,* I hope we've made the right decision."

"No cable," said Annika, sounding dispirited.

"Oh come on, kiddo," Del said. "It's only for a week."

"I hope you're right. Maybe I can earn my cooking badge."

"I can help with that," offered Ruth.

"It'll be a wonderful adventure!" Del added.

"With no cable." Annika sighed.

Before supper, Ruth called Angie, telling her how glad she was that she and George were driving up to stay at the East Bay. "But after Sunday morning's checkout, our rooms are rented. So Del, Annika and I will be staying at a cabin, about half an hour's drive from the hotel."

"That sounds nice, and we can still do things together," said Angie. "Is it on Lake Superior?"

"Yes!" Ruth told her. "Apparently the only door opens right onto the beach."

"I love it already! I wish George and I were staying there."

"You'd have to do all the cooking." Ruth laughed.

"Forget it, then." Angie sniffed. "George popped for a two-room suite. We have a separate living room and everything."

"Well, okay, Mrs. Van Snoot. Maybe you can keep Annika with you, part of the week. She's all upset because the cabin doesn't have cable television."

"I don't blame her," Angie retorted. "She can stay with us whenever she wants, and watch cable with me."

Ruth told Angie again how happy she was about them coming up. They said their good-bye's. Then Ruth told a very happy Annika that Auntie Angie thought that cable television was pretty darned important, and when she wanted to, she could stay in their rooms.

"Yipee!" shouted the girl, jumping up and down.

It takes a village, thought Ruth.

Chapter 33

Your Money or Your Life!

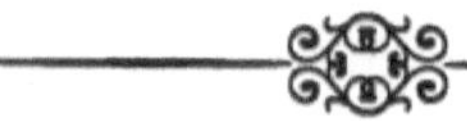

AFTER SUPPER, DEL WANTED to stay home. "Can I miss this performance and just read?" He looked at Ruth hopefully. "Annika can stay here, with me."

"I don't want to stay home, I want to go up to the theatre. After all, I'm earning my drama badge," Annika told him.

Ruth spoke up then. "It's fine, sweetheart," she said to Del. "All that time fishing wears a guy out. Stay home and rest up. There's no cast party tonight, so you won't miss anything."

"God forbid I should miss a cast party." Del looked at the ceiling and held his hands up in supplication.

Ruth burst out laughing. "You sound just like Tevye from *Fiddler on the Roof.*"

"Sometimes I feel just like Tevye."

"Well, Tevye, tonight you have the night off." She laughed. "Read. Go for a walk. Do whatever your little heart desires."

"Woman, you are a gem." He kissed her, and then sang, *"Tradition!"*

Ruth and Annika drove up to the old church. Annika helped with the dressing room, sweeping it and hanging up costumes.

Edna Fuerling complimented the girl. "She's a regular little trouper."

"I'm earning my Girl Scout drama badge," Annika told her.

"Good for you, kid!"

When the orchestra started playing, Ruth and Annika hurriedly took their usual seats. Emmy and the Foley children were not there tonight.

"I wonder where Emmy and the Foley kids are?" Ruth whispered to Annika.

"I bet Norman doesn't like having to sit still so long," Annika whispered back.

"You're probably right."

The show went well. No mishaps or missed lines. *Jack Guston is really into it tonight,* thought Ruth. *He's hitting his stride. That's good. But I wish Tommy hadn't had all that trouble.* She shook her head. *Poor kid.*

She noticed Sam Guston, Blanche Voorhees, and Uncle Tony in the audience, but she avoided them. They were all sitting together. She vowed to keep Annika right by her side.

During the intermission, she and Annika hurried out to get some popcorn and something to drink.

As Ruth was getting her money out of her purse, Sam Guston stepped up behind her and handed the concessions volunteer a twenty-dollar bill. "Let me pay for this good lady," he said, and smiled at Ruth.

She was surprised and shook her head 'no.' But the boy had already put the bill in his cash box, smiling as Sam told him, "Keep the change!"

"You don't need to do that," said Ruth.

"Oh, yes I do." Sam looked at her as if he was the Wolf and she was Little Red Riding-Hood. "Where's your famous friend tonight? And why would he leave someone as attractive as you all alone?"

Ignoring the *line,* Ruth said to him, "Thank you for the popcorn, but we have to go backstage and work now." She turned and gently pushed Annika down the aisle toward the dressing room door. Sam followed them.

"I'm not so bad once you get to know me." He grinned, opening the stage door for her.

"Mr. Guston," Ruth said quietly, "I'm going to work in the women's dressing room now, where men are not allowed."

Just then Paul came down the hallway.

"Sam!" Paul smiled. "Sorry, my friend, no audience allowed back stage!" He ushered Sam Guston back out of the door and toward the seats.

Saved by the bell! thought Ruth.

"I think we have another 'nudge,'" said Annika.

After the show, Ruth and Annika worked hard together to put both of the dressing rooms in some kind of order.

As they were driving toward the hotel, Annika piped up.

"Gram, after all that hard work, I could really use a Dairy Queen blizzard."

Ruth smiled and said, "I think that can be arranged. Should we pick up Grandpa Del?"

"He's probably asleep, and the Dairy Queen closes in ten minutes." The girl was looking at her Mickey Mouse watch.

"Okay then, let's hurry and get you some ice cream." Ruth turned her car toward the Dairy Queen.

She got a strawberry blizzard for Annika, and a small chocolate-covered cone for herself.

They sat in the car, eating their ice cream.

"Brrrr," said Annika. "I'm getting cold."

"Where's your sweater?" Ruth asked the girl, while she turned up the car's heat.

"My sweater? I ... Oh no, Gram, I think I left it at the church."

Ruth finished her cone quickly and said, "Let's go back right now, and get it. You'll probably need it tomorrow."

They returned to the old church building, and Ruth parked her car. She noticed a light on.

"Stay here, honey, lock the doors, and eat your blizzard. I'll be right back. There's a light on inside, so maybe Pastor Paul is probably still there." And then Ruth told her again, "Lock the car doors, okay?"

"What's wrong, Gram?" Annika asked, as if sensing Ruth's uneasy mood.

"Probably nothing. I ... I'll be right back."

Annika did as she was told, and Ruth started quietly for the building.

The sweater should still be on our pew, or under it," she thought, as she quietly opened the door to the back of the box office. She could hear voices as she came in. Stopping in her tracks, Ruth thought maybe she should announce her presence, but something told her not to.

She heard a man say, *"But why? Why would you do that? That would ruin my life!"* His voice sounded desperate. It was Paul! Ruth stood behind the door that led to the seating area. He was talking to someone backstage!

Then a woman's voice laughed. Ruth couldn't tell who it was from the laugh right away, and then it hit her: *Willy is doing exactly what Tommy said she would!*

The girl sounded bitter as she responded, "What about my life? Did you ever think about my life when you decided to screw me?"

"But ... but I never ... we never ..." Paul sounded as if he was choking.

"Maybe not," Willy Guerin retorted, "but I can convince your wife you did."

The man made a strangled sound in his throat as he stammered out, "I-I don't have that kind of money!"

"Then get it. Take it from your stupid church, I don't care! Or I'm going to tell your little *wifey* that you've screwed half the cast! Don't think I won't!"

"Why are you doing this?"

"That's none of your business," Willy said in a smug tone. "And I don't care what happens to your pathetic job, your pathetic life, or your even more pathetic marriage. I don't care what happens to you!"

Ruth could hear perfectly. She saw Annika's sweater on the front seat, and, grabbing it, she walked quietly up toward the stage.

Willy was still talking. "You get me that money within the next three days, or you can kiss your life, your marriage, your job, and this stupid town goodbye! Do you understand me?" Willy's voice hissed, "Who do you think people will believe? I've lived here all my life." She laughed nastily. "You're *new!*"

"But it's … it's all lies!" Paul pleaded. "Why would you do something so terrible?"

"I need the money. I need to start over. And who cares if it's lies?" Willy chuckled. "When I'm done with you, you'll have to leave town! So, if you want to keep your little life here, get me that money! Do you understand me?"

"I understand you perfectly, Willy Guerin!" announced Ruth, stepping forward so she could be seen. "And I know extortion when I hear it!"

"What are *you* doing here?" Willy snarled at Ruth.

"I guess I'm here to witness on behalf of Pastor Paul that you are threatening to spread lies about him in order to extort money from him," Ruth said evenly.

"Mind your own business, you old—"

"The people I care about *are* my business!"

At this, Willy lunged at Ruth, but Paul grabbed her and pulled her back.

"Let me go!" the actress screamed.

Willy broke away from him and ran out of the building, yelling, "You can both go to hell!"

Chapter 34

You Were Lucky, This Time

PAUL LOOKED ASHEN AS he said, "Thank God you came when you did! She asked to meet me here. I thought it was something about the production."

"Paul, I think after this, you need to meet your people in more public places," said Ruth. "What if I hadn't come by?"

"I know. It was stupid of me ... thank God you were here. But why did you come?" He looked at Ruth with a dazed expression.

"Annika forgot her sweater on her seat ... *Annika!*" Ruth gasped. "She's alone out in my car!"

Just then Annika and the two Norstrands came through the front door.

"You were gone too long, Gram, so I went to the neighbors and called for help."

"Does anyone want to tell me what's going on here?" Robert Norstrand asked.

"I interrupted a plot to extort money from Pastor Paul," said Ruth. "Willy Guerin was threatening to spread terrible lies about him if he didn't give her what she wanted."

Roberta Norstrand sighed. "I told you she was trouble," she said to her dad. "Willy was that way in high school too. I knew kids who actually paid her off, just so she wouldn't spread lies about them!"

"She did this back in high school?" The elder Norstrand shook his head.

"Yep. She's exactly the same."

"She threatened Ruth, too," said Paul, looking worried.

"Ok, that's it. I say we pick her up and let her cool her heels a while," Roberta told her dad. "And I want to know what she knows about Joey-Frank. She used to date him, you know, before Amy ..." She made a face.

"Let's not go into that right now," Robert said to his daughter. "These good people need to get home."

Paul turned to Ruth and said, "Thank you so much. You're a life-saver!" To the Norstrands he added, "And thanks for coming so quickly."

"I'll drive you home," Ruth told Paul. "You may need me as back-up when you explain all this to Emmy." She looked at him pointedly. "In fact, I think you should let me explain it to her.

I'll take Annika to the hotel first."

Annika protested, but Ruth held firm. "This is grown-up stuff, honey."

Ruth dropped Annika off at Del's room and told him to expect her back in half an hour.

"Trouble with a cast member," she explained. "I'll tell you everything when I get back. Please tuck Annika in? Make sure she brushes her teeth?" Then Ruth added as an afterthought, "And please keep Annika in your room. We are dealing with ... well ... I don't know how far this person would go to hurt someone, but things are starting to feel too much like last summer."

Del looked puzzled. "What happened?" he asked.

"Willy, the girl playing 'Carrie,' had Pastor Paul cornered, and she ... look, I'll explain everything later."

"Okay, I'll watch out for her. And see you soon?" He kissed her cheek.

"Half an hour," assured Ruth.

By the time Ruth and Paul arrived at the parsonage, the Norstrands were already there.

Sergeant Norstrand said, "I thought we should warn Emmy not to open the door for Willy."

Emmy looked pale. "Paul, what is this all about?" Her hands were shaking. "Why would that girl want to hurt us?"

Paul just walked into his house and collapsed on the sofa.

Ruth, seeing he was in no shape to explain, spoke up for him. "Emmy, Willy Guerin told Paul to meet her in the church. He thought it was about the production. I came in to pick up Annika's sweater, and I overheard the whole thing. Willy told him if he didn't give her money, she would spread lies about him that would get him fired. Or worse."

Emmy looked stricken. "What lies?"

Roberta Norstrand decided to chime in. "Pastor, forgive me for saying so, but you are very naïve to think you could meet some young woman in the theatre at that hour, and alone." To Emmy she said, "Ruth heard

Willy threatening to tell people that your husband was being inappropriate with her and other members of the cast ... if he didn't pay her the money."

Emmy gave Paul a look. "That was dumb," she said to him. "You're lucky Ruth showed up when she did."

"You're right. And I've learned my lesson."

"I hope her understudy can do the last show. Otherwise, I don't think you can continue the musical."

Paul choked back a sob as he turned pleadingly to his wife. "Will you call the understudy and ask her to do the part tomorrow?"

"I'll call her right now." Emmy got up and went to the kitchen phone.

He just shook his head, looking dazed, when Emmy returned after a few minutes.

"She's got strep throat," announced Emmy. "What'll we do now?"

Paul just groaned, then glanced up at Emmy, who went over to him and hugged him.

"We'll figure it out," she told him.

"You are in charge of all the theatre 'talks' after this," he said to her. "I'm stepping down."

At this point, Ruth spoke up. "I don't know whether she'll agree to it, but there is a professional soprano staying at Naniboujou right now. I'll have my husband call her and ask her if she'll fill in for Carrie for the last night." Ruth laughed. "I think she'd do anything for Del. She's infatuated with him. And she was in *Carousel* years ago at Como Park in St. Paul, so she's at least familiar with the score."

After Ruth promised to call Paul in the morning, they went their separate ways. The Norstrands went back into town, and Ruth returned to the hotel.

"All's well that ends well," she told Del and Annika, who were both ready for bed, but still awake.

"Was Willy trying to hurt Pastor Paul?" Annika asked. "She's mean to some of the other girls, I've noticed."

"Yes, she's mean, and she's out of the show. In fact, I'm quite sure she has left town. So now we need to find someone to take her part." Ruth looked pointedly at Del. "I think we know someone up at Naniboujou who would love to sing in this show!"

"Oh no. Oh, nonononono." Del groaned. "Please, not the Diva."

"What's a diva?" Annika asked.

"A royal pain in the butt."

"... who sings," clarified Ruth.

Chapter 35

The Delighted Diva

THE NEXT MORNING DEL called Naniboujou and was immediately transferred to Uncle Tony and Blanche's suite. Del explained to Uncle Tony what they needed. Blanche was in a good mood, and sang to Del a song from *Oliver*.

"I'd do anything, for you dear, anything, for I'd do anything, anything for you!" Blanche was ecstatic!

"Ruth will help you with your costumes, in case they need altering." He handed the phone to Ruth.

"I'll be there two hours early," Blanche promised.

Ruth took the phone receiver and said, "Thank you so much for being such a good sport, Blanche. I think this cast is extremely lucky to have someone of your caliber singing in their show. I'm certain you'll do a beautiful job! We'll pick up a score from Pastor Paul and bring it to you. How about at lunch time? Our treat?"

Ruth looked over at Del, who quietly groaned.

They had picked up the score and were just leaving for Naniboujou when Roberta Norstrand arrived at the East Bay and told Ruth, "Willy has left town. I don't think you have to worry about her. She was trouble, even back in high school."

"You know her, then?" Ruth asked.

"Yeah, I knew her. But this is off the record, okay?"

Ruth could see Annika shift in the back seat of their car, moving closer to the open window, where she would be able to overhear the conversation while pretending to read her comic.

"Little pitchers ..." Ruth whispered to Roberta.

"Heard that, Gram," Annika quipped.

"It's okay," said Roberta. "Everyone in town knows her background. Her parents both died of overdoses when she was in junior high. She moved in with a friend of her mother's, who drank too much and didn't take care of her. Then, as soon as Willy turned eighteen, that friend ran off to Canada with some guy she'd just met, leaving Willy in a broken-down trailer, on her own."

"That poor kid!" Ruth shook her head. "She never had a chance, did she?"

"I guess not. I should be more charitable, I know." Roberta looked down. "But in school she was so nasty to us nerdy kids, it's difficult to think of her as a 'poor kid.' By the way, Dad and I did look for her last night, and again this morning." She shrugged. "She's probably in the cities by now. We contacted all the precincts. There's not much more we can do at this point."

"Well, it's awfully lucky for Pastor Paul that he has someone who can step in and take over."

"It's awfully lucky for Pastor Paul that he had you as a witness."

"I was glad to help him," said Ruth. "I know he means well."

"Yeah, well ... Pastor Paul is a little on the nerdy side too. His wife, though, she knows what's what. Give her enough time, she'll straighten him out." The girl laughed, then said, "I've gotta run. Dad needs me." She got back into her squad car and left.

"I do like Emmy," Annika piped up after Roberta left. "She tells me lots, just like I'm a grown-up!"

"What does she tell you?" Ruth asked her, feeling suddenly wary.

"Oh, just about her three miscarriages, and how much she wants kids."

"What?" Ruth was appalled. "You're a kid! Why on earth would she talk about things like that to you?" Ruth took a deep breath and asked, "Do you even know what a miscarriage is?"

"Gram!" Annika rolled her eyes. "Of course I know about that. My friend Rachel's mom had five miscarriages. That's why she went to the orphanage and got Rachel!"

"What?" Ruth was flabbergasted.

"And I told Emmy about Rachel's mom, and told her that's what she should probably do."

"I never heard of such a thing!" Ruth wiped her brow. "You're only ten, and I'm really uncomfortable with you talking about things like that with an adult."

"It's life, Gram." Annika shrugged her shoulders. "And it's not my fault what my babysitter says to me."

Just then there was a knock on the door.

"It's me!" Del called out.

"I know you can't help what adults tell you, and I know it's not your fault," Ruth told her granddaughter. *"It's open!"* she called through the door.

Del was quieter than usual. "Let's go and get this lunch over with," he said to them.

"Lunch with the *nudge!*" Annika snorted.

"Annika!" Ruth laughed. "She's a famous opera star. This will be exciting for you."

"Yeah, yeah, Gram, but she's still a nudge."

Del ruffled Annika's hair, and they all laughed.

At Naniboujou, they met Blanche and Uncle Tony, and had a rather nice lunch.

Blanche regaled them with stories about the shows at Como Park and other St. Paul theatres, back in the day.

"Fritz Gerhardt absolutely adored me then, and he still adores me now!" she said.

Ruth quietly thought, *Oh no, he doesn't.*

When they were done, Blanche gave Annika a photo of herself. "For show and tell at school. You can tell *all your friends* you had lunch with a famous opera star!"

Annika thanked her politely and even curtsied.

"What a sweet child!" Blanche cooed, before leaving to study the score in the privacy of her hotel room.

"Gram, I'm not going to bring her picture to school," Annika said disgustedly when Blanche was gone.

"That's fine." Ruth took the photo from her. "We'll put it up on the bulletin board at the church so people will know who's singing the part of Carrie." She laughed. "At least Blanche and Mr. Snow are a lot closer in age!"

Del had gone to look at the pamphlets at the main desk. He came back, excited.

"I've got a great idea for some fun this afternoon." He kissed Ruth and then hugged Annika. "We can go see Pam's cabin and then go to a place called "Agate Beach." He grinned. "It's only four more miles north of the cabin."

"Cool idea, Grandpa Del!" Annika cried. "Let's go!"

"That does sound like a good idea," Ruth added. "The cabin, then agates."

On the way to the cabin, Del told them about looking for agates when he was a boy.

"There was a big rock quarry near my grandparent's farm. It was just down the road about a mile or so." He chuckled. "My buddies and I would go there to hunt for agates."

"Did you find any?" Annika asked him.

"Sometimes. Not very often, though."

"Maybe you'll have better luck today," said Ruth, patting his leg.

Del looked at her. "I'm already pretty lucky." He smiled, making a kissing mouth toward Ruth.

Chapter 36

The Mystery Ring and a Trunk Full of Rocks

THEY FOUND PAM'S CABIN and let themselves inside. After peeking into each little room, Ruth said, "Well, it's rustic all right. It's a good thing we're only staying a week."

Del laughed. "I remember cabins like this when I was a kid. This is what we would call a hunting shack. Or ... I guess up here, it's a fishing shack. I didn't expect much, and this certainly meets my expectations." He winced as he looked around the spare main room, with it's tiny kitchenette and threadbare furniture. "Are you sure you want to stay here?"

Ruth surveyed the bare walls, which had cheap plywood panels painted a medium beige. There were worn plaid curtains on the windows. The faded brown sofa faced a small fireplace. She said, "We have to stay here. I don't want to hurt Pam's feelings. Maybe we can go to the store and buy some bright pillows? Maybe we could put up some pictures?" She looked at the worn patterned linoleum on the floors and sighed.

"I think it needs a lot more than pillows and pictures," Del told her. "But hey, it looks clean at least. And look!" He pointed into the smaller bedroom. "She painted this room, and it's not beige!" He laughed. "It's rust-colored. And that looks like a home-made quilt on the bed."

Annika was fiddling with the television. "Ugh! You can only get two channels: wrestling and news."

"I like wrestling and news," Del said with a grin.

"Grandpa Del!" the girl was obviously disgusted.

Trying to be more positive, Ruth looked out the front windows at Lake Superior, in all it's glory. "The view is amazing," She said. "Even better than at Naniboujou!"

"That it is," Del replied, wrapping his arms around her.

"I think I'll stay with Auntie Angie," Annika finally told them.

They were driving up the lake highway once more. Ruth loved it. They rode in relative silence, admiring the scenery and drinking in the serenity of the landscape. Very few cars passed them. A couple of times, Ruth had Del stop the car, so she could take some photos. First, of an abandoned fishing shack, in which part of one wall was collapsed. She could see the lake through it. Then she took some more photos of a stretch of lakeshore with a bunch of birch trees on it.

"I can paint these after I get home," she told Del as she got back in the car. She looked in the back seat. Annika was fast asleep.

"Ah, the young," said Del. "The sleep of the innocents."

"She won't be innocent for long, if Emmy Eklund has anything to say about it," Ruth whispered, so as not to wake her granddaughter.

"What's all this about?" Del whispered back. "I thought you liked her?"

"I do like her. I like her a lot. But she's been talking to Annika about how much she wants children, and even told Annika about her miscarriages!"

"Really?" Del made a face. "That's a bit much to tell a ten-year-old. Are you going to talk to Emmy?" Del kept his eyes on the road, but took Ruth's hand in his.

"No ... I don't think so." Ruth pressed her lips together. "Emmy has enough on her plate. And anyway, we're only here for a another week." She sighed. "I think that poor woman has had so much to deal with. Maybe it's hard for her to find friends. You know, being the pastor's wife? In a small town? It's got to be difficult. Maybe she just needed someone to talk to. And Annika is used to being around adults. And she's very bright." Then Ruth remembered when she first saw the Eklunds. "Emmy was really mad at her husband out on the boat to Isle Royale. Annika and I both saw them. I'm surprised Annika hasn't asked her about that."

"Maybe she has," Del told her.

Ruth put her hands up to her eyes and rubbed them, shaking her head *no. "Uffda!* I sincerely hope not! Anyway, they seem to be getting along pretty well."

"I've been meaning to ask you." Del chuckled. "What does '*uffda*' mean?"

"It's a Scandinavian expression. My mother used it all the time. I think it's a nicer way of saying, 'Oh, shit!'"

"So *that's* it. Scandinavian manners. Well o-*kay* then, you betcha." Del tried to sound very Minnesotan. Ruth just shook her head and laughed. "Oh look!" He slowed the car down. "This looks like a good stretch of beach," he said, indicating the flat, sandy area on his right. "Why don't we get out and search for agates here?"

Annika stirred and mumbled out, "Are we there yet?"

"I'm not sure," Del answered. "I don't really know where Agate Beach is. But this looks like as good a place as any. Let's try our luck here."

"I have to go to the bathroom."

"I wish you'd said something when we were at the cabin," said Ruth as they got out of the car.

"I didn't have to go when we were at the cabin."

"Well"—Ruth looked around—"there's some bushes over there." She pointed toward the shore. "Be careful now." *I hope there are no bodies!* Ruth thought to herself.

After a few minutes, with Ruth keeping an eye out for strangers, Annika came running back along the beach, shouting, "Gram! Look! Look what I found!" The girl's eyes were wide as she happily produced a gold ring set with a large green stone, Celtic designs carved into the band. "Isn't it beautiful? Can I keep it? It was underneath the bushes."

"May I see?" Del held out his hand. "This looks real. I wonder what it's doing way out here."

Ruth said, "I think we should show it to the Norstrands. And if they don't know anything about it, then I guess it's 'finders keepers.'"

Annika tried it on. "It's too big for me," she sighed. "But I'll grow into it," she added hopefully.

"Why don't you put it in your jacket pocket for now, and help me find some agates?" Del had a birch stick and was combing through the rocks.

"I really like the round rocks," said Ruth, putting a few in her purse. "I suppose the lake is like a big rock tumbler." She studied one in her hand. "I could put a bowl of these round ones on our coffee table. My mother used to collect these too. I think I may even have some of hers."

"Annika, since this is your lucky day, do you know what an agate looks like?" Del asked the girl.

"Of course I do," she told him. "I already got a big one at the rock shop." Then, as if reciting from a book she'd read, she said, "An agate is a combination of igneous and sedimentary rock, frequently found on the beaches of oceans or lakes. Sometimes with striations of various reddish colors, often found in the Great Lakes regions."

"She takes after me," Ruth laughed. "Only smarter."

After about forty-five minutes of searching, Del found two small agates, Annika found nothing but the ring, and Ruth's purse was getting very heavy with all the round rocks she was picking up.

Ruth gasped, "I've got to get out of here pretty soon, or I won't be able to lift my purse!"

Del took the purse from her and carried it to the car, putting it on the floor in the back seat. "It weighs a ton!" he told her. "Do you really want to take all those rocks home?"

"Maybe you could dump the rocks in the trunk, so I could have my purse back?" Ruth said hopefully.

"Woman, you know I'd do anything for you. But rocks in my trunk?"

"It's only until we get back to the hotel. Then I'll put them in *my* trunk. They'll be a good memory of this beautiful place."

"Okay," he said, "I give up. Good memories it is." Del took the purse to the back of the Lexus and emptied the rocks into the trunk. "They're going to rattle around back there, but I guess they'll be okay."

"I've got an old blanket in the back of my car," Ruth answered. "I'll put the rocks on that. They'll be fine.

Del just laughed.

They drove the Lexus back to Grand Marais, the rocks making noises every time Del turned the car either right or left. He gave Ruth a "look."

Ruth was giggling. "When you have a wife, sometimes you have to put up with a little noise."

"I'm sure those rocks will look really nice on our coffee table," he told her. "And they'd better!" He laughed.

Annika was quiet on the way back. Ruth could see her turning the ring over and over in her hands.

They finally returned to the East Bay Inn. As they walked in the front door, Odie, the Biederman's aging Labrador, greeted them with a tail thump.

Loris Biederman was manning the desk, as usual, and she greeted them, but without her usual smile. "Lunch is still being served in the dining room, folks," she said, and then went back to whatever she was doing at her desk.

"Thank you," Ruth told her.

Loris ignored her, keeping busy at her desk.

Oh no, thought Ruth, *she knows I went to the Norstrands and told them what I heard.*

The three of them sat down at a small table by the window. They ordered hot tea and muffins for Del and Ruth, and orange juice and muffins for Annika. The waitress was new, someone they didn't recognize, but she made sure they had lemon wedges for their tea, and two muffins per person.

"I'm not that hungry any more," Ruth sighed as she bit into her first muffin.

"Don't you want yours?" Del asked Annika, when he noticed that she wasn't eating, but looking at the ring she'd found.

"Yeah, I do," she told him. "Course I do." She took a huge bite of muffin. "But I sure hope I can keep this ring."

That night, Ruth took Annika to the police station, but the Norstrands didn't recognize the ring, and hadn't any reports of it being lost or stolen.

"You can keep your treasure," Roberta told the delighted Annika. "I don't know whose it is, and you found it miles away. It's yours now."

Ruth wanted to ask if they'd talked to Loris, but she thought better of it. *They probably have*, she thought. *That's why she's so cool to me.*

They stopped at Joynes Ben Franklin right before it closed, and Ruth bought some white bandage tape. She put a little tape around the ring's gold band, so it would fit her granddaughter.

Annika put the ring on her pointer finger. She was gazing at it as she crossed the street, and not watching. Just then, a car full of teenagers whizzed past, nearly hitting her.

"Annika!" Ruth cried as the girl jumped back just in time. Ruth was nearly hysterical. "You can't walk around looking at that ring. You almost got hit by a car!" Ruth hugged the girl and asked, "Are you okay?"

Annika nodded *yes.*

"You can't wear that ring if you can't stop staring at it!"

"I'm sorry, Gram. I'll be more careful. I really will."

"I need to get you home safe and sound to your mom!" Ruth told her.

One more show, Ruth thought. *I'm sure going to be glad when this is over and we're back home. I don't even want to go to that cabin. But I don't want to disappoint Pam. She and her family probably need the money. What a mess!*

Chapter 37

The Diva Saves the Day

SATURDAY NIGHT'S SHOW WAS the last performance of *Carousel*. Angie and George had shown up just before supper, and Ruth was so happy to see a friend. The five of them had supper together, while Ruth brought Angie up to date on the cast.

"Oh no, not her!" Angie cried when Ruth told her about Blanche. "Well, at least we know she can sing!" Angie made a face that made Ruth laugh.

In her usual form, Angie regaled them with tales of when she and Ruth had been in *Carousel* at Como Park.

"Ruth, do you remember that handsome guy who played Billy Bigelow? He started flirting with Vivian, and Fritz got all pissy about it? For God's sake, Vivian was old enough to be his mother! It was only a mercy flirt! Fritz didn't need to worry about him."

"He was crazy about that little gal who played Julie Jordan, though," Ruth added. "You know, the pretty little one with the beautiful voice? Heather something? I think she was from White Bear?"

"I do," Angie answered. "Boy, that little gal had a set of pipes, didn't she? Wow!"

"I remember her mom and sister were in the chorus," Ruth said. "Probably watching over her. She was awfully young, if I remember correctly."

They talked "theatre talk" all through dinner. Ruth finally said, "Annika and I have to leave early for dressing room duty. I have to see that Blanche fits into all her costumes, so we need to get ready." She smiled at Del. "How about we see you three around seven thirty or so? You can get good seats and buy your popcorn." Then she asked Del to please pay Loris Biederman for the cabin for the time they would be there. He gladly agreed.

At least I don't have to deal with her right now, she thought.

As they walked to their rooms. Ruth told Del, "Remember, the cast party is at *Guston's* tonight. I don't know why, but Sam Guston has been hounding me, so please stay close, okay?"

"I will do that, but I'm pretty much up to here with theatre stuff!" Del made a motion with his hand, moving it to the top of his head.

"Me too!" Ruth assured him.

On the way to the church, Ruth thought, *I've dealt with Blanche before. I can be the "grown-up" tonight, and help her with her costumes.*

When Ruth and Annika arrived at the women's dressing room, Blanche was already there, doing vocal warm-ups.

She really does have a beautiful voice, Ruth thought.

Blanche wanted the "Carrie costumes to be much tighter." Ruth obliged, taking them in to her liking. Of course, Blanche pulled the necklines down as far as they could go. The Diva looked in the mirror and added more makeup than Ruth thought was necessary. Blanche was in a jovial mood tonight.

"Is Del here yet?" she asked Ruth.

"No, he'll be here for the curtain, though. No one wants to miss this performance. We are so excited to have you singing with this cast," Ruth told Blanche honestly.

"So, how's the little 'wifey thing' going?" Blanche gayly laughed.

"We are doing just fine," Ruth said as she continued sewing, not looking up.

Annika cocked an eyebrow, but said nothing. Ruth gave her a stern look that said, "Don't get into this conversation!"

"I imagine that Del is a very good husband," Blanche said, before she pursed her lips and added more lipstick.

"That he is." Ruth smiled and nodded.

"He's a good grandpa, too," Annika piped up.

Ruth sighed, but kept sewing. She and Annika had both had just about enough of Blanche!

"I never give up, you know," Blanche said quietly. "Never."

I don't have the energy for this nonsense.

"Would you like to run through your lines? Annika, would you please help Blanche while I finish sewing these costumes?"

Now Annika gave Ruth a "look."

Blanche said to the girl, "Come on, sweetie, let's sit over here on the sofa and you can help your Auntie Blanche run through her lines."

Annika rolled her eyes, but did as "Auntie" Blanche requested.

After a while, the chorus members and others started entering the dressing room. Blanche looked at them as if they were trespassing.

"Who the sam hill are you?" asked Edna Fuerling abruptly, coming in the door and giving Blanche the once-over, after seeing her in Willy Guerin's costume.

Blanche just stiffened and turned her nose up at the woman.

Ruth stepped in. "This is Blanche Voorhees, a very well-known and respected opera singer. She has agreed to take the part of Carrie tonight. Isn't that wonderful?" Ruth was trying to be upbeat.

"What the hell happened to Willy?" Edna looked upset.

"You'll need to talk to Emmy about it," Ruth told her. She didn't want to have Edna bother Paul. "There was some trouble and Willy left the show."

Edna *harumphed* and looked at Blanche again. "You look familiar. Were we in any other shows together?" She was scrutinizing Blanche.

"I hardly think so," Blanche told her in a haughty voice. "I'm going into the hall to do my warm-ups," she informed Ruth. Annika immediately came over to Ruth and sat by her.

At eight o'clock the orchestra started the overture. All seven were in their seats. Angie and George were seated just behind Emmy, Andrea, Annika, Del, and Ruth. Ruth had introduced Angie and George to Emmy and Andrea. Emmy had her arm around Andrea, who was leaning into her.

"Your daughter looks just like you, same eyes and nose," Angie told Emmy.

"Oh!" Emmy laughed. "I *wish* she were my daughter! Her mom is up at the parsonage with her brother. They're taking the night off. Ruth tells me you're a theatre person."

"If there's a musical at Como Park, I'm in it," said Angie proudly. George just beamed at her.

Emmy told Angie she would always be welcome in the Grand Marais shows, too, to which George feigned horror and said, "Sorry, too far to drive!" Emmy immediately made a disappointed face, and they all laughed.

She's such a good person, thought Ruth. *I'm not going to say anything to her about what she said to Annika about her miscarriages.*

It was closing night, and Paul announced to the audience, "The part of Carrie will be played by internationally known opera singer Blanche Voorhees!" People in the audience sat up straighter in their seats and whispered to one another as he said this. The excitement was palpable. Del just looked at Ruth and rolled his eyes.

Uncle Tony was in the fourth row, aisle seat. He was beaming. He was dressed in a suit, and holding an enormous bouquet of red roses. Most people were looking at him as if he were from another planet!

Blanche Voorhees played the part of Carrie to the hilt.

She's really wonderful, even if it's a bit over the top, thought Ruth, giving Del a smile that said, *It's better than okay!* And things really did go better than Ruth thought they would. In fact, the man playing Mr. Snow was closer to Blanche's age, and he played to her as if they had been partners all along.

Amy wasn't feeling all that great during the first act, but Blanche was so stellar in her part, Amy perked up, just being near her. By the second act, Amy was her old self again.

In the audience, Del and Annika were munching their popcorn, along with George and Angie, Emmy and Andrea. Everyone seemed to be thoroughly enjoying the show. Andrea was snuggling up to Emmy, who had never looked so happy.

Andrea's finally getting the attention she needs, thought Ruth. She was pleased things were going well, and she sighed in contentment. There was even a standing ovation, led by some of the older men in the audience. *They probably are just getting up to go home, but its's nice anyway.*

Ruth smiled to herself as Blanche took many, many bows—more than "Julie" and "Billy Bigelow." Ruth didn't care. When Uncle Tony went forward and handed Blanche the bouquet, Ruth thought, *She acts like she's just won an Oscar!* People shouted, "Brava!" and applauded loudly.

I'm just so glad this whole thing is over! Ruth thought, clapping along with everyone.

Del sighed. "It's over, thank God," he said under his breath. "Now we can have our vacation."

When all the noise had subsided, Ruth leaned into Del and said, "Why don't you, Annika and George go back to the hotel? I have to check the dressing rooms." To Angie she said, "Want to come backstage and help me? Then I can get a ride back to the hotel with you?"

Just then, Blanche—dressed in her usual tight satin dress and pumps—came down the aisle, escorted by Uncle Tony and carrying her bouquet of roses like a beauty pageant queen.

Blanche made kissy faces as she sidled up to Del and cooed, "See you at the cast party, Mr. Mays."

Del winced, but nodded and smiled a weak smile as he told her, "Good job, Blanche."

Uncle Tony steered Blanche away from the group and up the aisle.

Just then, Paul came out to talk to Emmy. "Thanks for all your help, and ... you know ... just everything." Paul looked at his wife with love, hugged her, and asked, "Honey, can you and Andrea wait for me a minute? I just need to check the dressing rooms, and then we'll drive to *Guston's* for the cast party."

"We shouldn't stay at the party too long," said Emmy. "Andrea has had a really long day, and her mom is waiting up at our house."

Paul gave her a thumbs up sign. Then he kissed her, and ran off to take care of the dressing rooms.

Emmy sure has a funny grin on her face, Ruth thought. *I wonder what's up?*

Andrea and Annika were busy looking at the gold ring on Annika's finger.

"I found it yesterday on a beach, under some bushes," Annika told her.

"Wow!" Andrea tried on the ring. "That's really neat," she said, handing it back. "Whenever I'm on a beach, all I ever find is driftwood."

Ruth and Angie went backstage, only to find that costumes had been thrown everywhere! Ruth surveyed the mess.

"You can tell it's the final night," she said to her friend. "They don't need these anymore."

"What are these big plastic bags for? Don't tell me they store the costumes in these."

"I'm afraid so." Ruth started folding up dresses and fitting them into the bags. "I guess Edna will take the dresses out and wash them later."

"Quite a system." Angie began stuffing another bag." She sniffed at one and said, "I hope this Edna—whoever she is—does a thorough job washing them." She made a face.

"Edna was the woman playing Mrs. Mullin."

"Oh, *that* one. You know, I keep thinking I've seen her before. I think she was in one of Fritz's shows." She furrowed her brow. "Yeah. Yeah, she was. I remember now. It was during that time when you were out, taking care of Tom."

"That was a while ago." Ruth kept folding clothes, adding them to the bags.

Angie pursed her lips. "Her hair's a different color now, but I remember the eyes and mouth. And speaking of mouth, the woman I knew had a real mouth on her. Does this one?"

"Does she what?" Ruth hadn't been paying attention. She was busy folding and wondering if every costume would fit.

"Does Edna have a mouth on her? You know, swearing and such?"

"Oh, gosh, yes. You could say that." Ruth laughed ruefully.

"Then I'm sure it's her." Angie clapped her hands together. "I'm gonna find out at the party. If I recall, she was involved in stealing some of Fritz's ticket money."

"*What?*" said Ruth, looking up from the costumes to stare at Angie.

"Uh-huh. Quite a lot of it. Both she and her niece were in the show. Fritz thought the niece had stolen it. She'd been 'helping' Vivian with the tickets. The niece stole a lot of money, and this 'Edna' tried to cover it up. Nobody could prove anything, but Fritz told 'em both to *'never darken his door again,'* in so many choice words." Angie shook her head and added, "Fritz never recovered the money, and the two thieves disappeared."

"Angie!" Ruth warned her in hushed tones. "You need to be really careful, and don't accuse her of anything. That could backfire."

"But—"

"No, Angie. Not tonight. Not this cast. Seriously, leave it alone."

Angie blinked, then whispered, "I heard Del say something. Is it like ... like *last summer?* My God, Ruth, what's going on?"

"Shh! We can't talk about it here. Anyway, I'm done with this show now, and I just want to get out of Grand Marais with as little drama as possible."

"Okay, okay. I won't say anything about Fritz's ticket money at the party," Angie told her. "But I still want to find out if she was ever in Fritz's shows."

"Angie!"

"I'll be discreet about it. I promise."

Ruth sighed at her friend. *I just want this whole thing over.*

By the time she and Angie finished up in the women's dressing room and went over to the men's, Pastor Paul was almost done putting away all the men's costumes.

"Oh, Paul," Ruth exclaimed, "we would have done that! But thank you!" She introduced Angie, who told him he did a "really good job!" and that the show was one of the "best she'd ever seen!" After which they excused themselves and walked outside to Angie's car.

"I'm so glad this is over." Ruth breathed a sigh of relief as she got into the front passenger seat of Angie's new gray Toyota Camry station wagon. "Now we can really start our vacation." She patted the seat and said, "What a nice car! This must have been really comfortable to travel in."

"George only wants me to have the best!" Angie grinned as she started her car. "He says we might as well enjoy his money. I wanted a red one with white pin-stripes, but George told me it's better to blend in. He says I'm less likely to get a speeding ticket that way."

"George is probably right. I see he's also getting you to give up our local Goodwill, and shop in the Galleria. That's a beautiful outfit, by the way." Ruth admired Angie's green gauze tunic and matching pants. "That has a real 'Fawbush' look to it."

"Yeah." Her friend grinned again. "He loves driving me out there to shop." Angie pointed to her dangly artsy earrings. "See these? I got 'em at Fawbush's too, and they cost more than my whole outfits used to!" She preened. "And he insists I have my hair done at Aveda. Can you imagine? *Aveda!* They serve you hot herbal tea, and give you scalp massages!"

"You look just wonderful, Angie. Like some fashionable Minnetonka matron."

"Oh yeah, that's me." Angie put her nose up in the air and fluffed her hair. "Nothin's too good for Mrs. Van Snoot!"

Ruth laughed and hugged her. "You'll always be my Angie!"

Chapter 38

Blanche Is Up to Her Old Tricks

ANGIE PULLED HER CAR up to the East Bay. She asked Ruth, "Do you think we could stop in your room before we go over to the party? I need to use your bathroom and fix my makeup."

"I was just thinking we should do that," Ruth answered. "The boys and Annika are probably in Del's room, waiting for us."

Ruth was right. As they walked by Del's room, they could hear Annika's peals of laughter and Del singing "Poor Dead Skunk in the Middle of the Road," as an operatic aria.

While Ruth and Angie used the facilities in Ruth's room and fixed their hair and makeup, Angie continued trying to remember Edna's trouble with Fritz.

"This Edna's niece had a funny name, sort of like 'Wilma' or 'Wilbur,' or something ..." She mused.

Before Ruth could think fast enough to stop herself, she blurted out, "It wasn't 'Willy' was it?"

"Willy!" Angie nodded an emphatic yes. "That's it. Don't tell me she's up here, too!"

"She used to be." Ruth grimaced. "She got kicked out of the show. That's why Blanche had to play 'Carrie.'"

"What did she do? Steal money from the box-office?"

At Angie's insistence, Ruth filled her in on the details of Willy's bad behavior and subsequent leaving the show and the area.

"The police are looking for her," Ruth finally added.

"Oh, I remember her," said Angie, fluffing up her new fashionably styled auburn hair-do. "She was a 'mean girl.' The other gals in the cast gave her a wide berth. I told her off once. She knew better than to bother me again!" Angie pursed her mouth and applied some expensive-looking lipstick.

"People wouldn't dare go up against the famous Angie Corbello." Ruth laughed. "I'm sure glad you're on *my* side."

"Always and forever," Angie said. Then she hugged Ruth and promised, "We'll be friends until we're old and senile, and then we'll be *new* friends."

It was a lame old joke, but Ruth laughed anyway.

They picked up Del, George and Annika and headed for *Guston's*, which was only a few blocks away from the hotel. As they walked up to the front doors of the shiny, new restaurant and event center, Ruth noticed that someone—probably Sam, or one of his workers—had strung lights all around the entrance. And there was a huge sign that said, "Welcome Carousel Cast Members and Friends!"

"Oh no, I left my purse at the hotel!" said Angie. "I need to run back and get it. I'll be back in a few minutes. Ruthie, save me a seat by you?"

Ruth assured her she would.

Sam Guston had decorated the restaurant's party room with gold mylar balloons, and gold and silver mylar streamers hung from the ceiling. There were long tables, all covered in white linen tablecloths, tea candles, and arrangements of fresh flowers in crystal. On the beverage table were cans of pop on ice, along with silver-plated samovars of coffee and water. There was even hot water and an assortment of teas.

Good, they have tea, Ruth thought to herself.

The tables were set with fine china, linen napkins, pressed-crystal goblets, and gleaming silverware.

This almost beats Uncle Tony's party, thought Ruth, remembering that lavish cast party she had attended the previous summer. Tony, who had entertained the cast at his palatial mansion on White Bear Lake, had gone all out.

Sam Guston's buffet held a wonderful assortment of foods: shrimp cocktail, grilled chicken, dijon marinated pork loin, smoked lake trout, mini Beef Wellingtons on skewers, two big pots of chili (vegetarian and *con carne*), and a taco bar. There was a variety of salads, an assortment of cut veggies and cheeses, hot tortilla chips (made in-house), and every kind of dessert bar imaginable. The custom-printed vinyl banner hanging over the long table read, "Good Job! Cast of Carousel, We Love You!"

And in the middle of the room, on its own rose-festooned table under the big chandelier, stood a gigantic cake decorated to look just like a carousel. It even had little ceramic horses!

Sam Guston stood beside the cake and greeted everyone as they entered the room.

Ruth just blinked at it all, and finally said, "This is ... this is *amazing!*"
Del, eyebrows raised in appreciation, nodded.

Sam Guston reached out both hands and greeted the two of them as they approached him. His eyes met Ruth's and he nodded. "Do you approve?"

"I ... of course! I ..." Ruth wasn't sure what to say. "This is beyond anything I could imagine! You've done a wonderful job. Thank you so much!"

"I'm so happy you like it," said Sam, beaming at her. "Your approval means everything to me, I hope you know that."

"I'm sure the whole cast is very grateful for this party. This place is incredible!"

But inwardly Ruth was thinking, *He's acting like he and I are a couple. What's up with that?*

Del, who was beginning to look a little uncomfortable, extended his hand to Sam Guston and said, "My wife and I are so happy to be here. Thank you for the invitation."

"*Wife?*" Sam looked at Del. "You're *married?*" He gave Ruth a devastated look. "Excuse me, I ... oh, of course!" To Del he said, "You're a lucky guy." Then Sam appeared to suddenly notice someone across the room who needed him. He turned abruptly and disappeared through the gathering crowd.

Del looked at Ruth intently and asked, "How well do you know this fellow?"

Ruth was dumfounded. "I've hardly ever said two words to him! The first time I saw him was when Annika and I were having breakfast at the hotel. Then he was on the boat to Isle Royale, and I was terrified of him because Annika saw him drop a gun into the lake. Then you and I saw him meet Tony and Blanche at Sven and Ole's. And at the one performance you missed, he tried to follow me backstage, before Paul Ecklund stopped him. I really don't know what's going on here!"

"I do," Del said quietly. "And I can tell you in one word: Blanche."

"Blanche? What does Blanche have to do with this?"

"Don't you see? She's up to her old tricks."

"What tricks?" Ruth asked, looking around to see if Blanche and Tony had arrived yet. They hadn't.

"She's done it before." Del whistled through his lips. "She actually broke up the marriage of two people in one of our orchestras. She makes up 'romances' and gets lonely people to believe all kinds of things. She'll tell someone that someone else has a 'real thing' for them. And then when that person goes after the one with a supposed 'thing,' their spouse gets upset. Blanche loves this sort of drama. She thrives on it. And I'll bet she's doing the same here, trying to break us up."

"That's terrible!" Ruth stared at him. "I can't believe anyone would do something like that!"

"Believe it," Del said tersely. "I'll go talk to him, find out what this is all about."

"Oh God!" Ruth was miserable all of a sudden. "The food looks so good, but ... I've lost my appetite."

"Just find a table for us," he told her gently. "I'll see what's going on and be back shortly."

Del was gone about ten minutes. More guests were arriving, and a woman who looked a little like Sam came in from the restaurant's kitchen. She started ushering people to the tables, and got a buffet line going.

Sam's sister, perhaps? Jack Guston's mom? Ruth wondered, as she found a table and called Annika over to her.

"Where's Grandpa Del?" Annika asked her, taking a seat next to Ruth. "I want to go up and get some of that food. They have a taco bar!"

"Just wait, honey. He'll be here in a moment."

When Del returned, he had his arm around a very crestfallen Sam Guston.

They came over to the table. "I'm going to let Sam explain it to you," he told Ruth.

"Annika, there's Andrea," he told his granddaughter. "Why don't you go and sit with her?" Annika looked at him like she realized this was "adult stuff," and left the table to talk with her friend.

Sam began with, "Mrs. Mays, I'm so sorry! Blanche told me you were ... that you, ah ..."—he took a deep breath—"that you were *single*. And that you and Mr. Mays here were *just friends*. And that he was just 'stringin' you along.' She said you 'needed a good man like me, to love you.'"

Ruth stared and shook her head. "Del and I were married last fall. And Blanche knows that. I love Mr. Mays dearly, and he loves me." She reached for Del and held onto his hand. "And I don't know why on earth she would tell you those things, but—"

Just then Blanche and Uncle Tony entered the event center. They could see Blanche simpering and smiling, receiving accolades from the cast members. But when Blanche saw Del and Sam and Ruth together, she immediately knew they were discussing her. Blanche suddenly put her hands to her temples, as if she had a splitting headache, and after a moment, she and Tony left the party.

Del looked daggers at their backs and said, "Both Blanche and Tony are on my shit list."

"Ah, don't blame Ancino," Sam said to him. "Tony's a good guy, and anyway he was out getting us popcorn while Blanche told me all of this." He looked at Ruth again and said, "God, I'm such a fool! Geez, I'm so sorry!"

"It's okay, Sam." Ruth reached over and patted his hand. "Blanche can be very convincing. She's an actress, after all."

"And you would be a pretty nice catch for any lonely man," Sam admitted, tears in his eyes.

"Well, this lonely man caught her!" Del said.

"Yes sir!" Sam finally smiled. "I got that. Ancino's girlfriend had better leave town and go back to the cities; because if I catch up with her, she's getting a piece of my mind!"

Del patted him on the back. "She's not worth your trouble. And right now I'd like a piece of that cake!" He pointed to the carousel cake.

Annika came back to the table. "Are you guys done with the grown-up talk?"

Del laughed and hugged her. "We are, and we're ready to get some food."

Ruth, Del and Annika got into the buffet line. Sam, visibly upset, tried to go about the business of being a host.

"Poor guy," Ruth whispered to Del. "He's trying so hard."

"Well, at least he's got really good taste," Del whispered back. "But he shouldn't have listened to Blanche."

"Do you think they'll leave Naniboujou?"

"They'll leave tonight, if they know what's good for 'em."

"Are you going to confront Blanche when you see her again?"

"Nope." Del smiled at Ruth and chuckled. "When you and I get back to Boston, I'm going to completely ignore her. That'll bother her more."

I'm so glad we're going to the cabin tomorrow morning, Ruth thought, as she put a few veggies and some chicken on her plate and got some tea. She carried her plate and beverage back to their table.

"Cast parties," Del muttered as he sat down next to her.

Angie and George finally arrived, and got in the buffet line. Ruth waved and motioned to them.

Then she looked around. The whole cast had come, and were heaping their plates with delectables. She saw the Fuerlings too, and hoped that Angie would just forget about her *feeling* that she knew Edna.

But Angie apparently was having none of it. She was standing—her plate heaped with jumbo shrimp and smoked lake trout—in front of Edna and Norm, talking excitedly. There were so many people in the room and so much noise, Ruth couldn't hear what Angie was saying. But from the look on Edna's face, she could surmise what was going on.

Oh no, Angie, what are you doing? You promised you wouldn't!

Ruth watched in horror as Edna, a furious look on her face, got up and knocked Angie's plate right out of her hands. The jumbo shrimp and trout went flying! Edna stormed out of the room. A startled looking Norm followed his wife, stepping carefully over the spilled food as he did so.

All of a sudden there was dead silence. Angie looked over at Ruth's table and loudly announced, "I *knew* it was her. I *knew* it!" There was a brief pause, after which the party resumed, but never quite as loud.

People were either silently staring at Angie, or talking to one another in hushed tones.

Sam Guston's sister hurriedly cleaned up the mess. Angie, looking righteous, satisfied, and unconcerned, went back to the buffet for another plate.

Emmy walked over to Ruth, leaned over, and said, "What was *that* all about? Isn't that your friend? How does she know Mrs. Fuerling?"

I might as well tell her, Ruth thought, breathing heavily. *Everything comes out eventually.*

Ruth took a deep breath and said, "Angie and Edna were in a show together, years ago, down in St. Paul. I guess there was some trouble. Some money that went missing, or something. They thought Edna's niece took it."

"You mean, *Willy Guerin?*" Emmy glanced across the room to where her husband was chatting with a table of cast members. "*Willy* is Edna's niece, you know."

"So I've heard. But I didn't know that, until—"

"Willy stole money?"

Ruth felt acutely uncomfortable "I don't think anyone actually knows for certain—"

"Well, that answers something I was wondering about." Emmy looked at the side door, through which the Fuerlings had just exited. "During rehearsals I was getting donations from parishioners, to support the show. And I needed help to keep track of them. Both Edna and Willy offered to help me. They both seemed really happy to do it! But I remember Edna suddenly telling Willy, 'Butt out, I'll take care of this!' I was shocked, she was so curt with the girl! But maybe she knew something I didn't?"

"What happened to the donations? Are they okay?"

"I sure hope so. I left it all up to Edna."

Ruth just sighed.

Just then, Angie came to the table, sat down with her food and said, "Well, that was interesting!"

"Oh, Angie, what did you say to her?" Ruth asked.

"*All* I asked was whether she had been in one of Fritz Gerhardt's shows at Como Park. That's all I asked!"

"And what did she say?" asked Emmy, finally taking a nearby chair.

"She said, 'None of yer friggin' business!' and then she got up and bumped into me, knocking my plate of food right out of my hands!" Angie looked down at the front of her green silk tunic. "I sure hope this stain comes out. Geez, I bought this at the Galleria!" She glanced over at George, who was taking it all in. He nodded reassuringly, although looking perturbed.

"That was all you said?" Ruth shook her head, not believing what she was hearing.

"I might have said, 'So how's Willy, your niece?'" Angie sniffed as she tucked into her food with gusto.

"That would make a big difference," Emmy told her. "Willy is kind of *persona non grata,* right now. She got kicked out of the show for trying to blackmail my husband."

"Sounds like Willy," Angie quipped, before biting into another jumbo shrimp.

Ruth and Del caught each other's eye. What could they do? Angie was filterless. They loved her anyway.

Emmy spoke up first. "Well, it's a small town, and a lot goes on that we don't know about. People do the best they can. Sometimes it's not enough. My husband, Paul, and I have seen many unfortunate things happen to people. We just try our best to help them."

Angie looked over at her and said, "I think *you* should be a pastor."

"Paul tries to see good in everyone, even when ... even when it's not there. He believes that's what a small town does, inspires trust."

Del stood up and said, "Well, this small-town boy wants to go back to his room and get ready for bed, so we can get an early start tomorrow." He turned to Ruth. "What do you say, my love?"

Ruth immediately joined him and asked Angie, "Could you keep Annika for a little while? I know she wants to stay and visit with her friend, Andrea." (Annika enthusiastically nodded *yes!*) "Del and I have had quite a day and need to turn in. Maybe you could drop her off at my room in a couple hours? Or whenever you're ready to go?"

"Sure thing!" Angie said over a mouthful of food. Annika nodded affirmatively.

They said their good-byes to everyone at the table. And when Paul came over to shake hands with Del, he also gave Ruth a big hug, saying, "You're the best! I don't know what we would've done without you."

Del even shook hands with Sam Guston, who said to him, "Thanks, Mr. Mays, for being so understanding."

After Ruth told Annika to stay with Aunt Angie until they got back to the hotel, Del and Ruth walked hand in hand from *Guston's*.

As they walked down the sidewalk toward the East Bay, Ruth giggled.

"From now on, our time is our own!" she said.

Del grumbled, "And we won't tell anyone where we're staying. We'll finally have some privacy!"

About two hours later, Angie and George, along with Annika, knocked on Ruth's door.

Ruth was in her robe and slippers, but Angie was a good enough friend so she didn't feel embarrassed. "Thanks!" she told Angie. "Come on in for a bit?"

"Just for a moment," Angie said to her. "George and I are tired. That was a long drive up here. Do you think they'll ever build a tunnel through that stretch along Silver Creek Cliff?"

"Who knows? Annika was wondering the same thing."

"That road scared me silly."

Ruth told Annika to go in the bathroom and get ready for bed. Then she invited Angie and George to have a seat on the sofa.

"Del and I need to check out tomorrow, by eleven. But after that, why don't I pick up some groceries and we'll have a picnic lunch up at the cabin?"

"I'd love to see that cabin," Angie told her. "I wish we could stay there with you."

"I'm sorry, it's just not big enough. But I was thinking we could have sandwiches for lunch, and a wiener roast tomorrow night, when it's dark. We could even make s'mores! What do you say?"

"Oh, that sounds fun!" Angie gushed. "I'll buy the hotdogs, graham crackers, marshmallows and Hershey Bars. And you get the sandwich stuff?"

"I'll bring the sandwich fixings. Maybe you and George should follow us when we drive up to the cabin, so you can find it."

"Sounds like a plan," Angie said with a grin. George just looked adoringly at her.

Chapter 39

Angie's Got a Brand New Bag!

RUTH SLEPT PRETTY WELL, considering all that had gone on at the party. After Annika had fallen asleep, she had locked their door and walked quietly over to Del's room, to cuddle and talk over the day's happenings.

"I'll be glad to have our own room out at the cabin," Del told her, nuzzling her neck.

"I'll be glad to have it while Annika is staying with Angie and George," Ruth giggled.

They did some serious cuddling before Ruth slipped back into her room.

The next morning, Ruth, Del, and Annika packed up their things and then went in to have breakfast in the East Bay dining room. Ruth was glad that Pam was at the desk so she didn't have to face Loris.

I'll have to have a talk with her sometime, but not today, not until things calm down.

It was Sunday, so there was a special brunch.

"This looks just wonderful," Ruth said, looking over the long table.

It was full of breakfast entrees, including scrambled eggs and eggs benedict. The eggs were accompanied by crisp bacon and pork sausages. For the bread they had the blueberry muffins East Bay was famous for, cinnamon rolls, toast, and assorted jams. The fruits were a combination of sliced bananas, grapes, and blueberries. There were also orange slices.

"You mean we're not going to have this kind of breakfast every day, up at the cabin?" Del kidded her.

Ruth gave him a look.

"Grandpa Del," Annika told him, "I can cook really good eggs. I learned from my dad."

"Maybe you can cook for us some morning at the cabin?"

"I would love that," said Ruth, smiling at her. "We'll be sure to put eggs on our grocery list."

"He also taught me how to make bacon in the oven." Annika looked proud. "It's really good that way, but we have to have a cookie sheet and some of that parchment paper."

"Cookie sheet, parchment paper, got it," Ruth repeated.

In the buffet line, they each took a plate and dished up what they wanted. Then they sat down together at a table for six. Ruth hoped Angie and George would join them soon. She was not disappointed. The next minute Angie, resplendent in a hot pink velour jogging suit, and George, wearing a matching hot pink golf sweater with some dark gray pants, walked arm in arm into the dining room.

"They look like my Barbie and Ken dolls," Annika said over a mouthful of food.

Ruth Laughed. "They look nice. They match."

"Barbie and Ken look nice, and they match."

"Shhh."

Angie waved to Ruth. "Good morning!" she called out to them. George smiled and nodded.

Ruth pointed to the empty seats at their table and motioned to them to sit there.

Angie and George quickly filled their plates and came over to the table.

"This is quite a feast," George said first. "I won't need lunch after all this."

"But Ruthie is fixing us lunch," Angie interjected. "Remember? And I'm doing supper."

Ruth said, "Why don't we have a later lunch? And then we'll have our outdoor wienie-roast under the stars?"

"Perfect! What time are you checking out?"

"Right after breakfast. We've got our bags already packed. And after we check out, we'll shop for groceries, and then you can follow us to the cabin."

"Sounds like a plan!" said Angie. "Okay, George?"

George beamed at her. "Anything you want, my dear."

"Isn't he the best?" Angie beamed back. "We'll need to run to our rooms for our jackets, but we'll be at your rooms as soon as we can."

After eating breakfast, Angie and George went to get their jackets. Ruth, Del, and Annika stopped at the front desk to check out.

Pam looked up from her paperwork and asked them, "All ready for check out?"

"Be sure and put our breakfast this morning on our bill," Ruth told her. "Annika and I are through with the theatre group, so it's only fair."

"Will do." Pam added the cost of the breakfasts. She gave Ruth a piece of paper. "The phone number up at the cabin is on this sheet, along with some instructions about the electricity. You know, the fuse box and stuff." She looked at Del and added, "Be sure to open the damper on the fireplace if you have a fire. Otherwise, you'll get smoked out."

"Do you have a cookie sheet up there?" Annika asked, holding Loki up to the desk.

"I sure do." Pam smiled. "Are you two going to bake cookies?"

"Nope. Bacon." Annika grinned. "Loki likes bacon."

Del and Ruth both thanked her. Del paid the bill, while Ruth and Annika went back to their rooms to get the bags. Then they turned in their keys. Angie and George showed up as they were loading their suitcases into their respective cars.

"We'll follow you," Angie told Ruth. "But the grocery store first?"

"Yes," Ruth replied. "Just follow me." She waved as she got into her car. *I wish we only had one car up here, and that Del was driving it,* she thought, as they pulled out of the lot.

Annika was playing with her ring. "I'll grow into it in a few years," she told her grandmother.

"I'm sure you will," said Ruth. "In the meantime, though, try not to lose it. And please don't look at it if you're crossing the street."

"I won't, I'll be really careful, Gram."

They drove in tandem over to the grocery store. Even though it was smaller than the large chain stores in the Twin Cities, it was well-stocked and had lots of fresh fruits and vegetables. The prices were a little higher than Ruth was used to. *Probably because of the cost of getting the stuff up here,* she thought.

She encountered Angie in the produce aisle, putting a whole bag of ripe oranges into her cart.

"Do you remember when I couldn't afford to buy these?" Angie asked Ruth. "It's so nice to not have to think about the price of things." Angie wiped her eyes. "George just pays for it all. He never questions what I buy. I am eating so much healthier than I used to. I'm even losing some weight. I thank God every day for that man."

"You deserve him, honey." Ruth was moved by her friend's revelation. "You spent so many years not having enough, but you never complained, ever. You are always so full of love. You deserve the best."

"I've got the best."

"Oops," Ruth said to her, "I've got to get that parchment paper." And she went to find it.

They finished their shopping and went to the checkout. The men paid for the items and carted the groceries out to their respective cars.

Chapter 40

If I Had a Hammer ... I Would Hide It in the Woods

WHEN THEY WERE PULLING out of the grocery store lot, Annika asked Ruth, "Gram, did you remember to buy some matches? We'll need them for the fire tonight."

"I did," Ruth told her. "I got some tinfoil too, to wrap the leftovers. And just in case you want to cook bacon for us, I bought a roll of parchment paper."

"This will be fun!" Annika looked out the window at the lake. "Sort of like camping."

"I thought you wanted to stay back in the hotel with Angie and George," Ruth reminded her. "For the cable television?"

"Auntie Angie and I talked about it. We're all going home on Friday, right? So I'll stay at the cabin with you and Grandpa Del until Wednesday. Then I'll stay with Angie and George on Wednesday and Thursday. You can come and pick me up Friday morning." She looked at her grandmother. "Or should I just ride home with them?"

"I'll pick you up on Friday. I'll be so lonesome for you by then."

"Oh, Gram," she laughed. "You won't be lonesome with Grandpa Del there."

"But I still have to drive all the way home, alone. I'll need you to keep me company."

"Yeah, I forgot. We have two cars up here."

"I know." Ruth sounded regretful. "I wish we were all driving together."

"Me too," Annika acknowledged.

The cabin was just a mile or so past Naniboujou Lodge. As Ruth neared that grand old resort, she saw Uncle Tony and Blanche driving south, away from the lodge. They didn't even wave.

Good riddance!

Ruth drove carefully, keeping a look-out for the Biederman's cabin. She finally saw it and turned into the driveway, signaling for the others to follow her.

There was mostly sand and small rocks and very little grass around the cabin. Parking all three cars wasn't a problem. Ruth drove in first, then Del, then George and Angie.

"I'm afraid we're blocking you guys in," Angie called out as she got out of her car.

"That's okay," said Del. "We're in for the night."

Ruth whispered to him, "Did you see Tony and Blanche?"

"Yup, good riddance!" He whispered back.

They got their luggage and all their groceries into the cabin. While George was showing off Angie's new car to Del, Angie looked around. She looked at the small living room, then at Ruth.

"Did you see this place before you rented it?" she asked, frowning. Ruth chuckled and said, "It's not much, is it."

"I don't mind," said Annika. "It's only until Wednesday morning, right, Angie?"

"Right!" Angie high-fived the girl. "We'll come as soon as we have breakfast."

While Annika unpacked her suitcase in the smaller bedroom, Ruth and Angie put the groceries away in the little kitchenette.

Angie laughed and said, "I sure hope you didn't pay much for this place. It's really dismal."

"Oh, it's not all that bad," Ruth chided her. "Look, I brought my beautiful afghan from the car. Don't you think it dresses up the sofa?"

"You still have that?" Angie fingered the well-loved blanket. "My gosh, when did I knit that for you? Fifteen years ago?"

"I think so." Ruth arranged it over the worn sofa. "I love it. I take it everywhere. It's my 'blankee.'" She laughed.

The rest of the day and evening went smoothly. They all took a long walk down the shore, until they could see Naniboujou in the distance.

"Maybe we can all have lunch there on Wednesday," Angie said. "We can pick up Annika then, and take her home with us."

"I had tea there with Gram and Grandpa Del," Annika told Angie. "I'd go again. It was really good. And wait 'til you see the inside, it's got all these paintings all over the walls and ceiling. What do you call them, Gram?" She looked at Ruth.

"A combination of Art Deco and Native American, Cree, I think," Ruth replied.

Angie smiled at George and asked him, "How about it? Lunch at that ritzy place?"

"Sure," George said, putting his arm around her. "You're lookin' pretty ritzy yourself, lately." He grinned, obviously proud of her.

"Oh, George." Angie kissed her hand and rubbed it on his cheek.

When they came closer to the lodge, Del said, "Let's turn back here. I'm kind of getting ready for those sandwiches, and then maybe George and I can take that old boat out?"

"Sounds good," George told him.

They walked back to the cabin. Annika went to her room with a bunch of comic books. George and Del walked around the outside of the cabin, checking it out. Ruth and Angie busied themselves in the kitchen, making tuna-salad sandwiches.

"Let's not only put relish in them," Ruth suggested, "let's chop up some onions and carrots too. It'll give them more flavor and crunchiness."

They went to work, finely chopping the vegetables.

When the lunch was ready, Ruth put the sandwiches out. She had chips in a bowl, and some sliced cucumbers and tomatoes, and even some oranges, on a plate.

"Tell the boys it's ready," She said to Angie, who went outside to get Del and George. "Annika, lunch is ready!" she told the girl.

Del and George had gone to inspect the boat. Ruth could see them from the front window, walking around it, lifting the oars from the oarlocks to examine them. They both were shaking their heads. She could see Angie talking to them.

That boat doesn't look too promising, thought Ruth. *I bet they'll think twice about going out on this lake with it. It's not big enough.*

Annika came in from her bedroom and said, "Gram, look what I found in the bottom of the closet." She held up an old basket full of tools and nails. There was a towel covering it.

Ruth lifted the towel and noticed the hammer right away. She turned it over with the towel and saw the carved initials 'A H' in the wooden handle. Her heart began to pound.

Oh Lord, this must be Arvid's hammer—the one he lost, the one Loris used to kill ... and she hid it in this cabin! I can't say anything to Angie or Annika. I'll have to wait until Del and I are alone.

Ruth shrugged and said, as casually as she could manage with her heart pounding, "They're probably the Biederman's things. Cabins always need repairs, after all. Just put it all back in the closet where you found it, okay? We shouldn't be touching their stuff." She wrapped the tools up and returned the basket to the girl.

In spite of how Ruth felt, lunch went relatively smoothly.

I've just got to pretend everything's okay, she thought.

Angie finished eating and got up from the table. "George and I need a nap." She grinned meaningfully at George. "I think we'll go back to the hotel, and then drive up here again around six or so, for our weiner roast."

"And we'll bring stuff to make gin and tonics," added George with a smile. "We brought it up to Grand Marais with us."

"That sounds good," Del said, nodding affirmatively.

After they left and Annika sat down on the sofa to read, Del and Ruth lay down on the bed in the bigger bedroom.

"All right," Del whispered, "I can tell something's wrong. Please tell me what it is."

"Let's wait until Annika nods off," Ruth whispered back.

Annika called from the living room, "Gram! Can I go outside and look for rocks on the beach?"

"Sure! As long as you stay right by the cabin where we can see you from the windows." Ruth waited a moment, holding still until she heard the door slam.

Del reached for her. "Okay, what's wrong? I can always tell when you're worried."

"Annika found what I think may have been the murder weapon in her bedroom closet." Ruth hid her face in Del's chest.

"The *murder weapon?*"

"Shh! I don't want her to hear us. She doesn't know about Arvid's missing hammer, or my suspicions about Loris. But remember what I told you about the conversation I overheard at the church?" Ruth got up, went to the sofa, and wrapped herself in Angie's afghan. Del sat down close to her.

Very quietly, and with her eyes continually on Annika, out on the beach, Ruth reminded Del what she had overheard at the old church. She also reminded him of what she had said about Loris Biederman in her meeting with the police.

"I suppose Loris hid it here, not thinking anyone would think anything about some old tools way out here."

"You know we'll have to bring this in to the ... what are their names?"

"The Norstrands. God, I wish I could just forget I saw this."

"Maybe we can for now?" Del said quietly. "Angie and George are still at the hotel. If you brought this up now, we'd probably have to leave and go home." He sighed and shook his head. "I think it would be a firestorm. I can't tell you what to do, though. I don't even know myself."

"I've got to think about this." Ruth rubbed her eyes. "I don't want to be the lynch pin in all of this … this … trouble."

Del just sat there and held her. "You know what Mama Wilda would say?" He was referencing his mother-in-law, the matriarch and mainstay of his extended family.

Ruth chuckled and looked up at him. "I know exactly what she'd say. 'Put it in the Lord's hands.' I can even hear her saying it."

"Yes, ma'am, that's exactly what she'd say. 'Leave it all in the Lord's hands.'" He nodded, squeezing her tight.

Just then, they heard a car drive up. Then they saw Pam Biederman get out of an old 1980s dusty-blue Plymouth and say something to Annika before racing up the cabin steps and knocking frantically on the rustic pinewood door.

Chapter 41

We Shoulda Just Gone to the Police

RUTH RAN TO ANSWER the door. Pam looked distraught. Still in her waitressing uniform, with her thick dark hair pulled back in a hasty ponytail, she had no makeup on, just a panicked expression.

"What's the matter, honey?" Ruth asked the girl.

"I forgot something I was supposed to pick up at the cabin. Excuse me!" Pam brushed past Ruth and ran into the smaller bedroom, going straight to the closet. "Where is it?" She sounded desperate. "The tools! Where are the tools!" She was almost yelling.

"Um ... in a basket?" Ruth asked.

"Yes! They were in a basket, covered with a towel!" Pam didn't even pause when she bumped her elbow against the closet door.

"I told Annika to put them in our closet."

"So you saw it?" Pam finally exited the bedroom. She had tears in her eyes. "Arvid's hammer? You saw it?" She sounded resigned.

"Y-yes … ?" *Was there any reason I shouldn't?* Ruth entered the bedroom and opened the closet, where Annika had put the basket. She handed the basket to Pam.

"You know about Joey-Frank Jurak, don't you?" Pam's voice was almost a whisper.

"What I know is, you are a wonderful daughter, and your mom is a wonderful person." Ruth cleared her throat. "If your mom killed someone, it was because she had to. Maybe in self-defense?"

Del went to the sink and poured Pam a glass of water. She waved it away.

Pam was shaking her head. "You've got it all wrong. It was me. I killed Joey-Frank. I didn't mean to, but he tried to rape me. He showed up at the hotel dining room, just before we were closing for the night, and started arguing with me. He wouldn't shut up and he wouldn't leave me alone while I was finishing my shift. And when I tried to leave, he followed me through the kitchen to the back parking lot. Out in the parking lot, he … he grabbed me and covered my mouth! He dragged me and shoved me into my own car. I had the tools there, because I was going to work on the cabin. I just grabbed the hammer—it was the first thing I saw—and I hit him with it. I hit him as hard as I could, and I … I killed him." She sat down on the sofa and put her head in her hands. "I didn't mean to, I just wanted him to let go of me!"

"Oh, Pam!" Ruth sat down next to her, putting her arms around the shaking girl. "It's not your fault. It was self-defense." She rocked the girl in her arms. "He was a murderer, he killed Sally Merritt. You did a good thing."

"The minute I looked at him, I knew he was dead. I ran inside to get Mom. She said I'd lose my teaching job if anybody found out. That's why we didn't go to the police. Mom promised to help me, and she ... she helped me bury him on that deserted stretch of beach." Pam sniffed. "She said if he was found, she didn't want me to be the one in trouble. She'd say it was her that killed him. That's what she told my dad, that she 'took care of some nasty business.'" Pam shook her head. "What a stupid thing we did. We shoulda just gone to the police."

Ruth looked up at Del and said, "That's what I overheard at the church that day." To Pam she said, "I'm so sorry, but I had to tell the Norstrand's. I just couldn't keep that kind of thing to myself."

"We know. Bob and Roberta told my mom right away. I was there, and I blurted out the truth." She looked out of the window. "My mom was so pissed at me."

"I think she's mad at me, too."

"She was at first. But she knows you're a good person. Mom has always liked you."

"So, what's going to happen?" Del asked the girl.

"Nothing for now," Pam said quietly. "Joey didn't really have anybody that missed him, not even his sister. Bob and Roberta told us it was self -defense, and if it ever came up, they'd vouch for me. I was just so worried you'd find the hammer, and, you know, bring up my mom in all this."

"I really didn't know what to do. Your mom is such a wonderful person." Ruth was tearing up herself. "I'm so sorry I had to tell the Norstrands about what I heard."

"It's okay." Pam brushed gently at Ruth's tears. "Don't worry. You had to do that. My mom understands. Everything's okay."

"Can you take it with you, please?" Ruth pointed to the basket.

"Absolutely," Pam assured her. "I want you two, excuse me, you three, to have a wonderful vacation up here."

Annika came in just then, to show them the rocks she found. "What's going on?" She asked.

Ruth explained, "Pam needed her tools. She just came to get them." *She doesn't need to know all the rest,* she thought.

"And I wanted to know, how do you guys like my cabin?" Pam had recovered enough so that Annika wouldn't think there was anything wrong.

"Cable TV would be good," Annika told her, spreading all her rocks on the coffee table.

At this, Pam laughed. "I told Mom and Dad we should get a satellite dish. They're thinking about it." She patted Annika's shoulder. "I'm sorry, honey, you'll have to come back to the hotel for cable."

"I'm going to do that on Wednesday," Annika told her.

"She's going to stay with our friends from the cities until we all leave," Ruth explained.

"That's a good plan," Pam told the girl. "So, I'll see you and Loki in a few days?"

"Sure!" said Annika, grinning. "You remembered his name?"

"Of course! Loki the Trickster. Everyone knows about Loki."

"Not everyone. The lady in the store didn't."

They talked a bit more. Ruth was glad to see that Pam seemed relieved about everything.

I'm certainly relieved, she thought, sighing a deep sigh.

After Pam left, Ruth and Del sat on the couch and watched as Annika rearranged all of her "treasures," from the largest to the smallest.

"I suppose all of these round rocks are going home with you?" Del asked her.

"My mom loves rocks, and so do I."

Ruth just grinned at Del. "It's in our genes."

Chapter 42

Romance At High Falls

THAT NIGHT, THEY HAD a wonderful wienie roast with Angie and George. As good as his word, George made gin-and-tonics for all the adults, while Annika had a Coke. Angie had even brought all the fixings for s'mores, which according to Annika, was her favorite dessert.

As Angie started to pack for the return to the hotel, she noticed that Del and Ruth had their arms around each other. She turned to Annika and asked, "Sweetie, how would you like to come back to the East Bay Inn with us tonight? We have cable, and you could give your Gram and Gramps some vacation time alone." She smiled wickedly at Ruth and Del.

Annika gave Ruth a hopeful look. "Oh, Gram, can I?"

"Well, I suppose. Maybe Loki wants to watch cable too!"

Angie added, "We have a nice soft couch for her to sleep on, and we can get Dairy Queen, and all kinds of good stuff!"

"But I have one condition," said Ruth. "You need to call Hannah and Eric and tell them Annika is with you and George for a couple of nights." She got a piece of paper and wrote the numbers on it. "Here's Hannah's number, and the number for the cabin. In case you need to call us for anything. And one more thing"—she looked at Annika—"Call me when you get back to Grand Marais, and tell me you're safe and sound in Angie and George's room. Okay?"

Annika agreed. She kissed both Ruth and Del, and then took her suitcase and art bag full of comics and Loki, and piled into the back seat of Angie's new car.

The three of them took off for Grand Marais, and Del and Ruth were finally alone.

Half an hour later they got the promised call from Annika.

Angie got on the phone and assured them, "I'll watch her like a hawk. Don't worry. You just have yourselves a romantic night."

That night Ruth and Del lay in each other's arms and talked about anything and everything. Ruth talked about the people in the musical, and how she hoped Emmy would finally have a baby, and how sad she felt about Willy, who she thought "never had a chance."

Del mostly talked about his plans for a semi-retirement, and how they would work out their finances. Ruth, who had never been good at handling money, kept falling asleep.

"All that fresh air," she said. "I'm sorry, sweetheart, I know this is important, but I'm so tired I can't even concentrate. Maybe tell me tomorrow after some breakfast and tea?"

Del laughed. "You aren't much of a budgeter. But don't worry, I am. I'll take good care of us."

With that promise ringing in her ears, Ruth fell into a deep sleep.

The next morning, she got up and made cheese omelettes and toast for the both of them. Del made his coffee and Ruth made her tea.

While they were having a leisurely breakfast, Del said, "I would like us to take a drive north today." He picked up a map from the table. "I think we could see some of the scenery north of here and maybe have a picnic at that Pigeon River waterfall? I got this brochure at the hotel. I'll bet it's a pretty drive."

"That sounds like fun," Ruth agreed, looking at the map. "How long do you think it would take?"

"An hour or two."

"I still have some sandwiches left over from yesterday. I'll pack us a picnic!"

Del looked at his watch. "Can you be ready in twenty minutes?"

"You betcha!"

"We're finally having our vacation."

"I am really sorry about all the theatre stuff," Ruth said with a grimace. "We sure didn't need all of that trouble." She shook her head. "We could have been having our vacation as soon as you got here."

"But I can understand why you agreed to it." He patted her shoulder. "Helping out your friends, and especially helping that women's shelter, would be right up your alley." He smiled and looked into her eyes. "I knew you were a good soul the minute I met you. It's downright impossible for you to say 'no' if someone needs your help. That's one of the things I love most about you."

"Thank you. Your understanding is one of the many things I love about you."

They decided to take the beige Toyota, since Del's white Lexus still had all of the collected rocks in the back. He laughed when he told her, "Your car will be quieter."

They drove leisurely for about an hour, enjoying the scenery—the lake, the pines and birches, the rocky beaches. Ruth stopped several times to take photos for future paintings.

They arrived at Grand Portage, where Ruth and Annika had taken the Wenonah out to Isle Royale.

"I have not been north of this point," Del told her.

"I haven't, either," admitted Ruth. "Where do we go now?"

Del pulled over in the Wenonah's parking lot and studied his glossy tourism brochure. "I guess that waterfall is about eight miles north of here," he said, looking at it. "It's in Grand Portage State Park. That's where we can see the High Falls of the Pigeon River."

"Is it near the road?" Ruth was suddenly thinking of her left knee.

Del patted her left knee and told her, "I think you can make it. There's not too much hiking, according to this map. Maybe twenty minutes?" He grinned at her. "I'll carry you if it gets to be too much."

"Sure you will," she laughed. "I think it might be too early to eat our lunch, though. Why don't we leave it in the car, and we can eat it on the way back to the cabin? I did put a pack of ice on it, so it should be okay."

"Sounds like a plan! Come on, let's see this wonder of the northern world!"

A little later they arrived at Grand Portage State Park. They drove in and parked by the visitor's center. As they walked inside, Del, who read every sign, said, "This was where the French Voyagers made a portage from the Pigeon River to Lake Superior." He shook his head. "Can you imagine? They carried their canoes and supplies *and furs* through the woods until they reached the lake? Boy! Those guys must have been strong!"

"And here we are, fresh from the comfy seats in our car, thinking we are 're-living' that part of Minnesota history." As they entered the visitor center, Ruth exclaimed, "Murals! Oh my gosh, Look! They're wonderful!" She walked from one mural to the next. "I think I like 'Fall' the best. Yup, this one's my favorite."

Del agreed. "I like it too. I like the style of all of these." He glanced around the room. "I've always preferred realism; it shows a kind of talent I understand. It's what I liked about your work when I first saw it."

"Thank you." Ruth squeezed his arm.

"So, are you ready to hike? If the Voyagers could carry their canoes, and all their stuff, we can carry ourselves and our camera. How 'bout it?"

"I'm ready." Ruth braced herself.

They walked on a well-used trail through the woods. The only people they met were a young couple, obviously hikers, returning to the park. The hikers greeted them with "Keep going. It's just ahead, and it's awesome!"

Ruth and Del heard the falls before they saw it. The noise of the falling water made talking difficult. As the trail stopped and they got a view of the falls, Del and Ruth just stood there, transfixed.

"Wow!" Ruth said. "This has got to be the tallest falls I've ever seen!"

"It's the tallest falls in Minnesota," Del told her, putting his arm around her shoulder.

They took pictures and marvelled at nature. They experienced the majesty of the water cascading over the rocks. Del put his arms around Ruth and kissed her.

As they walked back to the car, neither of them said much.

Del finally broke the silence. "In the coming years, I hope you and I can do more of this sort of thing."

Ruth smiled at him. "We will," she said, nodding her head.

Stopping at a small stretch of pebbled beach, they got out and ate their lunch under some birch trees. Ruth took a picture of Del, hoping to do a portrait from it.

"Are you sure you don't want more rocks?" Del teased.

Ruth just laughed, playfully punching him. *What a wonderful day!* She thought.

Chapter 43

Michael, Row the Boat Ashore!

ARRIVING BACK AT THE cabin, they took a nice long nap. Waking up around six, Del tried to get some news on the television. He was too late, and there was only a game show on.

"Who needs the news anyway?" he said. "We can just forget about the world and go out and sit and look at the lake."

Neither of them was hungry for supper, but Ruth suggested popcorn.

Del happily suggested, "You know what I'd like?"

"What?"

"Popcorn and root beer! We can be like two kids tonight."

"I'm on it," said Ruth, as she got a kettle out and started to pour oil and popcorn into it.

That evening was lovely. There was only a sliver of a moon over Lake Superior, but the light from that and from all the stars over the dark green water was magical. It was chilly, and after a while, Ruth and Del both put on their jackets. They had pulled a couple of folding chairs from the cabin and put them out on the beach. They ate their popcorn and drank root beer like two teenagers. Soon the wind picked up and the waves got higher. The moonlight on the waves made the lake look like something from a fairy tale.

"It's really beautiful," said Ruth. "But I sure wouldn't want to be out on that lake."

"I wouldn't either. Especially not in the Biederman's boat. Somebody painted 'Lady Loris' on the side of it. I think they should have painted 'Titanic' instead," Del said, laughing.

Ruth laughed too. "Good thing we aren't going to have to go anywhere in it."

Just then, the phone rang.

"What now?" Del said, putting his can of root beer on the sand.

"I'll get it," said Ruth, getting up, hurrying to the cabin. *I hope Annika's okay*, she thought.

"I was getting cold anyway," Del said, as he followed her inside, picking up the bowls of popcorn and the root beer cans.

Ruth picked up the phone. "Hello?"

"Ruth! Oh, my God! You and your husband have to get out of there, quick!"

Ruth held the phone out so Del could hear. "Pam?" she said into the receiver. "Is that you, Pam? What's the matter?"

"You guys have to get in your car and drive away *now!*" There was hushed chatter in the background, then Pam Biederman added, "Mom says to drive north. She says Willy Guerin and her two thugs are on their way. They stole a car, and they're going to be at the cabin any minute. So please just get away from there! Drive north, okay? They have guns! They're on their way to the cabin!"

"Wait-wait-wait, what about Willy Guerin?" Ruth stared at the telephone receiver for a second, wondering if she had heard Pam correctly. "I don't understand. What do you mean, Willy and her thugs are on their way? What thugs? And are you sure it's Willy Guerin?"

"Ruth, I ... there's no time to explain it all. Just ... you have to *leave the cabin now.*"

"B-but how did they even know we're here?" Ruth stammered.

"They don't," replied Pam, obviously struggling to stay calm and coherent. "I'm pretty sure they think it's empty. Willy used to bring her druggie friends up there, even after I told her to stop. Even after Loris put new locks on the door. Her friends would just break in. Please, Ruth, just leave right now. I know what those guys with her are like; they'll shoot you if they see you. Get out!" Then she hung up.

Del said, "Grab the keys, we'll take the Lexus."

As they rushed outside they heard a car barreling up the narrow dirt driveway. There was yelling, followed by gunshots.

Del pushed Ruth down behind him and whispered, "We'll never make it to the car. We'll have to run for the boat."

"The *boat?*"

"Yep, let's go. This way!"

Running across the stones on the beach was noisy, but with the sound of the waves, no one could hear them.

"Get down," Del told Ruth as he pushed the boat out as far as he could. "Oof!" he said as he clambered over the side. "Pass me those oars ... thank you, hon." He maneuvered the small craft into the waves, taking them farther out on the lake.

"Can you see them?" Ruth crouched down as low as she could against the slippery wooden bottom. The fishy smell, as well as her fear, was making her nauseous.

"Yeah, I can see them stumbling around the cabin, looking for us, I guess. God, they look crazed!" Del rowed out farther in the dark waves. "I'm going to row us downshore to Naniboujou. We can get help there!"

Another gunshot rang out, whizzing past Del's head.

"Aw, Christ, they're shooting at us! They know we're out here!"

Ruth cried, "Get down before they hit you!"

"You get down! I'm harder to see!"

Thank God for that, Ruth thought, crouching as low as she could.

A couple more shots rang out, but none as close as the first.

"Come on, Laaaady Lorrrrris," Del sang to the boat as he worked the oars. "Save our butts todayyyyy!"

The next shot hit the stern of the boat, and Ruth screamed.

"Are you hit?" asked Del.

"No, but ... I think water's coming in!"

"Find something to plug the hole, while I keep rowing. I can already see Naniboujou in the distance. We just have to make it there!"

Ruth frantically looked for something to plug the bullet-sized hole. Finally, she took off her shoe and sock and plugged the hole with her sock. The incoming flow of water didn't stop, but it slowed considerably. She put her shoe back on and pressed her foot against the hole, to try and stop any more water from entering the boat. When it looked like that wasn't going to work, she removed her other shoe and added the second sock to the first. The water—about two inches deep in the boat now—was freezing cold.

"Lake S-s-superior, n-never gives up its dead!" she sobbed.

"Oh, stop now, sweetie. We're not going to die. Look! There's the lights of Naniboujou!" He pointed with one of the oars. "It's so close!"

"It looks far away!" Ruth cried. "I love you, Del!"

"I love you, too." Del kept rowing. "But the water is getting a little high in here. Can you find something to bail the boat out with? How about your shoes?"

Ruth took both her shoes and started bailing water out of the bottom of the boat. *We'll never make it!* She thought, panicked. But she kept on bailing.

Just then, a bigger wave hit them, almost swamping the boat.

"Hold on!" Del yelled.

"I'm holding, I'm holding!" Ruth yelled back.

"Aw, damn, I lost one of the oars!"

"No-no, you didn't," said Ruth, as the waves began to subside. "It's right here, in the bottom!" She handed it back to him and continued to bail.

Del put the oar in its lock and started rowing again. The lake had calmed down. They could see Naniboujou clearly now. And the cabin was out of sight.

Del was rowing as fast as he could, to reach the shore in front of the lodge. Ruth kept bailing water with her shoes. She worked hard, but the water kept coming in.

As they neared the shore they realize they were saved. Del looked up at the dark sky with its slivered moon and bright stars. "Thank you, Lord!" he cried to the heavens.

Ruth sent up a silent prayer, but with a sob.

"We made it, woman! Don't you get all weepy on me now." Then Del started singing in his wonderful baritone voice, *"Michael, row the boat ashore, Alleluuuu—iah! Michael, row the boat ashore, Al-lelu—eeee—iah!"*

Ruth started laughing in spite of herself.

A groundsman from Naniboujou heard Del singing, and shouted—as if there were drunks out on the lake—"Ahoy there! Bring that boat to shore, you crazy sons-of-bitches, before you all get killed out there!"

Del got close enough to the shore to get out and pull the boat the rest of the way. "We nearly were!" he shouted back to the man. "Call the police, please! We just escaped from some people who came onto our property we were renting. They shot up our cars, and tried to shoot us. We had to take this boat to get away." Del was breathing heavily and Ruth was shivering.

"Geez!" the man exclaimed as he approached. "We heard some police cars go by, just a little while ago."

"The people who shot at us apparently stole a car."

Ruth, shivering with cold, stammered, "C-c-can we p-p-please come in and get warm?"

"Oh, poor lady! Of course!" The man pulled off his jacket and wrapped it around Ruth.

He took them both into the lodge, and sat them in front of the giant fireplace. "I'll get you some hot cocoa," he told them. Then he disappeared into the kitchen. In a few minutes he reappeared with a tray with two mugs of cocoa. Then he disappeared again and a woman came out with two warm-looking blankets. She handed them to Del and Ruth and they thanked her.

"I've never tasted anything so good," Ruth said, sipping her drink and snuggling into her blanket. She gazed into the fire.

Del smiled at her and agreed. "It is good, isn't it."

"You saved our lives." Ruth looked at him in amazement. "Del, you actually saved our lives out there."

"Ahhh, ain't nothin'." He laughed. Then his hands started shaking and he quickly put the mug down, drawing his breath in harshly. "Delayed reaction." He had anguished tears in his eyes.

Ruth immediately got up from her chair and pulled her blanket around him and hugged him as hard as she could. "You're my hero," she whispered, holding him until he finally stopped shaking.

She held Del for a few more minutes until they both heard a commotion at the front desk.

They could see the Norstrands, and a couple of other policemen, coming toward them. They both stood up to greet them.

"Are you okay?" Sergeant Norstrand asked, concern in his eyes.

As Ruth and Del nodded *yes*, Bob went on. "We got Willy Guerin and her two, uh, *friends*. They're all on their way to some major jail time."

"Oh?" said Ruth.

"Selling drugs and destroying property is bad enough. But attempted murder? Much worse. You won't be seeing them for awhile."

"And don't forget extortion," Roberta added. "I'm afraid both your cars are pretty shot up. Let me take you back up to the cabin to get all your stuff. Don't worry, we can get you a loaner to get back home."

"I'm sure Angie and George can fit us all in their car," Ruth told him.

"Whatever works," said Bob.

Ruth and Del tried to give the blankets back to the staff at Naniboujou, but they not only gave them those blankets to keep, they even brought them two new ones, fresh from the hotel laundry and still warm! They also brought them more cocoa.

After thanking the staff, Del said to Ruth, "I'd like to stay here, sometime."

Chapter 44

Good To Be Alive

The Norstrands put Del and Ruth into the back of the squad car and headed for the cabin. Roberta turned the heat way up.

As the warm air blew over them, Ruth thanked her and added, "That feels so good."

"It sure does," agreed Del.

Between the warm blankets and cocoa, and the heated car, Ruth was starting to almost feel normal.

When they reached the cabin, however, all bets were off.

"Look at both our cars," said Del, incredulous. "Every doggone tire, shot clear through! I don't believe this!"

"Better than *you two* being shot clear through," the elder Norstrand reminded them.

Roberta said, "We'll get someone from Marathon to come up and replace all those tires tomorrow. It'll cost you, but at least then you can drive yourselves home." She turned to her dad, who was driving. "Can we get the guys to bring them to the hotel tomorrow afternoon?" He nodded affirmatively.

Ruth reached for Del's hand and said, "I'm so sorry this happened."

"It's not your fault." He hugged her. "You've done nothing but give back to this community ever since you came up here." To Bob he said, "Just tell them we'll be at the hotel, I guess, until they bring the cars down. Then we're all heading for home."

Ruth slumped in his arms and closed her eyes.

Their clothes and other belongings had been thrown all around the cabin. Ruth's purse was upended, with all of her money and credit cards gone, and her other items spilled out on the brown sofa.

"Don't worry," Roberta said as Ruth winced at the sight. "We emptied all of their pockets before we put 'em in the squad car. Your cards and money are safe."

"Thank you, that's a relief."

"How did they find out we were here?" Del asked Bob Norstrand, as he checked his now drying wallet, with all his cards intact.

"I don't think they knew anyone was up there," Bob told both of them. "My guess is they expected to hang out, do some drugs and party. That Guerin girl has been using this place off and on, because she knows it's usually empty."

"Pam has reported her a number of times," said Roberta. "But she's a slippery one." She snorted. "Until now. And by the way, we found out that her friends were the two guys that ran Roy Foley off the road. One of them told me, 'His slow driving pissed me off.' We are dealing with some really stupid, angry people here!"

"I'm sure glad you got up here so fast. Somebody must have called the police."

"Yeah, Tommy Sherman saw Willy and her friends in a bar. They asked him to join them for a 'party up at the cabin.' He knew about it, because he used to come up here, too. But instead, he stopped at the East Bay and told Pam that she needed to protect her place more. I guess Pam 'just freaked,' and told him you guys were renting it. Pam called to warn you right away, and then called to tell us to go up and help you. You were lucky."

"So, Tommy saved our lives." Ruth breathed a huge sigh.

"I think you saved his, too," Roberta told her.

"Pam and Loris are such good people, I hope they're ..." Ruth looked away.

"Oh, don't worry about them," said Bob. "We've got that whole thing under control."

They finished packing up their things. While the Norstrands were putting everything in the trunk and back seat of the squad car, both Del and Ruth took showers and changed clothes.

"It feels so good to be clean." Ruth fluffed her hair up.

"It feels so good to be alive." Del hugged her and kissed her cheek.

Bob came in and asked, "You folks got everything?"

"Everything except the groceries," said Ruth. "Maybe we can leave them? Maybe Pam can use them?"

"She said she's going to let that Sherman kid stay here a while, to watch the place for her. I asked her about it and she seemed okay with the idea."

"Well then, we'll leave them for Tommy." Ruth smiled.

"I got everything out of your trunks, except the rocks," Bob told Del.

"Leave the rocks," Del said. "We'll get those later."

Ruth just looked at him and smiled.

Before they left, Ruth put a 'Thank you, Tommy' note in the fridge, next to the vegetables. She also pulled a twenty dollar bill out of her purse and tucked it under the note. Del saw her do it, and did the same.

"I wish we could give him more," Del said, "but those tires are going to cost us a mint."

Chapter 45

All's Okay in Grand Marais

IT WAS ALMOST TIME for breakfast when the Norstrands pulled up to the East Bay with Ruth and Del. Pam and her parents ran out to meet the squad car. As soon as Ruth got out of the vehicle, Loris grabbed her in a huge hug.

"Oh, Ruth!" she was crying, "I'm so glad you guys are okay!"

Ruth started to explain about going to the police, but Loris *shushed* her.

"It's okay," said Loris. "They know everything." She looked over at the Norstrands. "And I'm glad they do. So come on in for breakfast. It's on the house. We've got fresh blueberry muffins!"

"Sounds wonderful!" said Ruth.

Loris called to Arnie, who was out on the porch, "Just put all their stuff under that tarp. It'll be safe there. Odie will watch it." The old lab thumped his tail as if in agreement.

There were already a few people in the dining room, eating breakfast. Ruth and Del sat down at their regular table. It wasn't long before Angie, George and Annika came into the room and joined them.

"Gram!" cried Annika. "Grandpa Del!" She ran over to their table, hugging them both.

"What?" Angie poked Del. "You don't trust us? Or your wife can't cook a decent breakfast?"

"Oh, Angie." Ruth shook her head. "You won't believe what happened to us!"

"Try me," Angie teased, as she pulled up a chair next to George and Annika.

Over cheese omelettes and blueberry muffins, and lots of coffee and tea, Ruth and Del described what had happened to them the previous night.

Angie was horrified, of course, and reacted just as Ruth expected her to. Ruth and Del even toned down their story a bit, because they knew Angie would be her usual filterless self.

"We know how much you love us, Angie, and we're okay," Ruth assured her. "That's the important thing. We're both okay."

"But ... you didn't even sleep last night! Both of you come up to our suite and take a nap. I'll ask Loris for extra cots."

"A nap sure does sound good," Del said. "I'm not sure I can drive home otherwise." He yawned.

Angie had two extra cots brought up to their suite. She put blankets and pillows out for Ruth and Del. She made sure the blinds and curtains were drawn.

"Come on, George, Annika ... we'll let these two people have a good nap." Angie grinned at George and asked, "Ya up for shopping?"

He smiled at her and nodded.

"I'm always up for shopping!" Annika piped up.

"Take a twenty out of my purse," Ruth said sleepily to her grand-daughter. "Enjoy yourself, because I think we'll want to leave for home this afternoon when we get up."

"I'm ready to go home. I miss Nefertiti." Annika fished the money out and put it in her jacket pocket. "Thanks, Gram. I'm gonna buy souvenirs for Mom and Dad, and maybe a lady fox for Loki."

"Have fun." Ruth was half asleep as she said it.

Del was already snoring.

Angie made sure the shopping spree included all the stores within walking distance of the East Bay. They went to the art gallery, Ben Franklin, the fudge store, the trading post, as well as Dairy Queen, where, to Annika's delight, they had lunch.

Angie wanted them to be gone at least three hours, so Ruth and Del could get a good rest. "I don't want them driving off the road because they're so tired," she told George.

"Maybe we should follow them home?" George suggested.

"Nah, they'll be fine."

When they got back to the hotel, Angie and George went into the dining room for a cup of coffee.

Annika stayed on the porch to introduce her new stuffed animal to Odie. "Her name is Freya," she told him. "She's a cat, but she likes dogs." Odie thumped his tail in response.

Loris stepped into the dining room and called to Angie from the doorway, "Can you take a phone call? It's the filling station."

"Filling station?"

"They have Ruth and Del's car."

"Oh. Sure, I can take the call." Angie excused herself from the dining room and went out to the front desk in the lobby.

A couple minutes later she returned and said to George, "That was the Marathon station. Ruth and Del's cars are both fixed and ready to go. They just have to get over there. It's gonna be expensive, though. All their tires had to be completely replaced!"

George looked thoughtful, then said, "How about I take care of this? For Del and Ruth?"

"Oh, George, you're the best!" Angie hugged him. "But we'll need to take someone with us, to get all the cars back to the hotel."

They divulged their plan to Loris, who offered to send Arnie along as a third driver.

While Annika waited on the porch, Loris brought her a glass of milk and two blueberry muffins. "I know they're your favorite," she said to the girl.

Annika was working on a large wildlife puzzle and sharing her muffins with the very appreciative Odie, when Pastor Paul and Emmy showed up.

"We heard what happened!" said Paul, shaking his head in disbelief. "Are your grandparents okay?"

"They're fine," said Annika, who wanted to finish her puzzle more than she wanted to talk to grown-ups. "They're taking a nap. Then we're going home."

Loris came out to the porch. "Oh, you two must've heard the news!"

"It's just horrible!" said Emmy. "I'm so glad Ruth and Del are all right!"

"Me too! And speaking of Ruth and Del, would you mind watching Annika on the porch for a little while? I'm busy with work, and her grandparents will probably be up soon."

"I'd love to. I'm going to miss all the new friends I made this summer."

Annika looked up at her and said, "Maybe we'll come back next year."

Paul cleared his throat, then glanced from Emmy to Loris.

"I, uh ... I've got a little secret," Emmy whispered to Loris.

"Ohh? Is it what I think it is?"

Emmy smiled and nodded as she reached for Paul's hand.

"You're having a baby, aren't you," said Annika knowingly.

"That's right. And if it's a girl, we're naming her Annika Marie."

"I've never had a baby named after me before."

Just then, Ruth came out onto the porch. "Who's naming a baby after you?"

Emmy turned to her and said, "I am! And we heard about your adventure last night. I'm so relieved you and Del weren't hurt!"

Ruth thanked and congratulated her and reassured her they were both fine.

Loris brought them all a tray of muffins and lemonade. "I figured if there was a party out here, I'd provide the refreshments."

"Thanks, Loris," said Ruth. "I think there may be a reason for a party." She smiled at Emmy and Paul.

"We're keeping our fingers crossed," Paul told everyone. "But we think sometime in late February we'll be parents." He put his arm around his wife, who grinned and nodded *yes*.

Loris turned to Emmy and said, "You just take it easy, hon. Let him wait on you." She looked pointedly at Paul. "Babies are lots of work, even before they're born. Trust me, I know."

Emmy said, "I'll get some practice when Amy Birdsong's baby comes. Her mom and I are going to take turns helping her on the days she has to work."

"You're a good person."

"And the Foleys have offered to help too. I've been helping Janet Foley with her kids while she goes back and forth to Duluth. I convinced her to put Norman in a day school that does wonders for kids with severe autism. It's in Duluth, so he goes there during the week. She and Roy have a small apartment there. Janet divides her time up between helping Roy go to his physical therapy and helping Norman. The three of them spend all their weekends up here, with Andrea." She sighed. "So far, it's working out. Andrea has made some new friends, kids who live near us. She doesn't want to live in Duluth, though. She loves staying at our house and then going over to her Grandma's house on the weekends. I don't know how long this arrangement will last, but I'm willing to help Janet and Roy. Besides, Andrea is such a sweetie."

"You are amazing," Ruth told Emmy. "And please drop us a line when the baby comes?"

"I already have some announcements." Emmy smiled at her husband. "And this time I hope I can use them!"

Paul made a praying motion with his hands. "Me too," he said.

Chapter 46

Coffee and Sandwiches for the Road

GEORGE, ANGIE, AND ARNIE finally returned with all three cars to the East Bay parking lot. The Eklunds left for home. Del finally woke up and, not seeing Ruth, came downstairs.

"Is my wife around?" he asked Loris.

"She's on the porch," Loris told him. "She and Arnie are putting everything into your cars. Arnie is on 'rock detail.'" She laughed.

"Rock detail?" Del was still a little groggy. Then he laughed too. "Oh yeah, rock detail. My wife had Lake Superior beach rocks rolling around in my trunk. She knows that would drive me nuts on the way home."

"Your wife is a good woman."

"That she is."

Ruth, Arnie and George entered the lobby.

Ruth joined Del and said to him, "As soon as you get some coffee, and maybe a sandwich, we can go. I'd like to reach the cities before it's too dark. Can we leave pretty soon?"

"We sure can," replied Del. "But where's Annika?" He glanced around.

"Angie took her upstairs to get her luggage. They'll be down in a minute, I'm sure."

Just then, Arvid Haakala came in from the porch. "You leaving for home?" he asked, shaking Del's hand.

"We are. And it was sure nice meeting you."

The larger man peered closely, grinning. "Ya sure you're not part Finn?"

"I could be. My great grandfather was kind of a 'mix.'" Del laughed.

"You're part Finn, I can tell." The man nodded, smiling. "I heard how you handled that boat out in those waves. Finns are good at that, ya know. Good job." He patted Del on the back and then walked down the hall.

"That's about the highest compliment Arvid has ever paid anyone," said Loris, dumbfounded.

Soon Angie and Annika arrived with all Annika's bags. While everyone was saying goodbye to Loris, Arvid returned. He looked questioningly at Annika's hand and asked her, "Where'd ya find that ring?"

"Up north, on a beach, under some bushes." She took it off and showed it to him. "Do you know whose it is?"

Arvid reverently turned the ring over and over. "It looks like one my wife had ... that I gave to my daughter ..." He spoke quietly, then noticed Annika's crestfallen face. "But ... it couldn't be! And even if it were, they'd both be happy knowing a girl as good-hearted as you was wearing it. So, I think it should be yours." He handed the ring back to Annika.

"Are you sure?" Annika looked up at him. "'Cause if it's your wife's ring, maybe you want to keep it for the good memories?"

Arvid bent down and kissed Annika on the top of her head. "I got plenty of good memories." Then he smiled at the group and left, walking back down the hall.

Ruth could see Loris wiping her eyes, while she was trying to write a check.

"This is because you couldn't stay the whole time at our cabin." She handed the check to Ruth. "Pam is up there now, cleaning it up for Tommy Sherman. I might have been wrong about him. Oh, and Pam said to tell you 'safe journey,' and she hopes to see you up here again."

Ruth handed the check back. "Just put it toward our next stay."

"Oh! Ah, well, thank you!"

"Speaking of money," said Del, looking all around the lobby. "Who took care of my Marathon bill?"

"Daddy Warbucks," replied Angie, poking George with her elbow.

"Just neighbors helping neighbors," said George, who was beaming with pride and delight. "After all, I'm gonna need help with a certain *wedding* that's coming up. You see, I'm having this famous opera singer sing at our wedding. But apparently he won't take any money for it!"

Angie quipped, "You're roped in now, Del, face it."

Del just stood there, shaking his head. Finally he said, "Thank you, George," and offered to shake his hand, but George hugged him instead.

After all the good-byes, Loris ran into the dining room kitchen and returned with a large takeout coffee for Del, tea for Ruth, and a Coke for Annika. She had also boxed up three lunches-to-go. Then they finally got into their cars, honked and waved, and left Grand Marais.

Their first "pit stop" along Highway 61 was in Tofte, for gas and snacks. They ate the ham-and-turkey sandwiches Loris had packed, and got right back on the road.

It was late at night by the time they arrived in Lake Elmo, both cars pulling into the dark driveway of their cottage-style home. A single light was on in the kitchen. The night air was warm.

"Annika?" said Ruth softly, peering into the back seat at the girl who had fallen asleep in her seatbelt.

Annika rubbed her eyes and blinked. "Are we home?"

"We're home, sweetie. You've been asleep since Elk River."

"What time is it?"

"It's pretty late," said Ruth, "but I'll bet Morrie and Griselda are still awake, just waiting for us!"

Annika closed her eyes again and muttered, "Good for them."

"Come on, sweetie. Let's get the luggage into the house. You can have a cup of hot chocolate before bed."

After Ruth and Del put a very sleepy Annika to bed, they called the girl's parents.

"You're home!" came Hannah's voice through the telephone receiver. "How was your trip? Did Annika like Grand Marais?"

"She had a wonderful time, and she can tell you all about it tomorrow. I just put her to bed."

"But ... but I thought you weren't coming home until next week."

Del cleared his throat and pressed his lips together as if sealing them shut. Ruth playfully elbowed him.

She said, "Well, we decided to come home early. And we'll tell you all about it tomorrow."

But Hannah's voice sounded suspicious as she said, *"Mom??* You'll tell us about *what* tomorrow?"

"Everything," said Ruth with a tone of finality.

"Did something happen in Grand Marais?"

"Oh, Hannah ... what could *possibly* happen in Grand Marais?"

"Mom! It better not be like *last* summer."

"Tomorrow!" repeated Ruth. "I promise I'll tell you all about it, at lunch. Okay?"

Hannah gave a loud *sigh* over the receiver. "Well, at least you're all okay. I'll see you tomorrow at lunch."

"See you then. I love you."

"I love you too."

After the phone call, Ruth joined her weary but happy husband in front of the fireplace. They both took their shoes off and put their stocking feet on the ottoman in front of the sofa, feeling the warmth of the fire on their toes.

Del had poured them each a glass of merlot. "It's good to be home," he said, raising his glass.

She sipped her wine. Then she put her glass down on the coffee table and leaned back in Del's arms. He was stroking her sides.

She looked up at him and asked, "You know how to tell when a Finn likes you?"

He chuckled. "How do you know when a Finn likes you?"

"I heard this from Loris. When a Finn likes you, he looks at your shoes instead of his own."

"Sigh."

"But! I think when a Finn *really* likes you ..."

"Yeah?" said Del.

"When a Finn *really* likes you, he tells you that he knows you have Finn ancestors, and he gives your granddaughter his late wife's ring."

Del just held her closer, as they watched the fire. "Yup," he said, wiping his eyes. "That Arvid is a great guy."

"It takes one to know one."

Chapter 47

EPILOGUE

As the weeks went by, Ruth could not get Willy Guerin out of her mind. Even when telling the authorities about their close call, she could not bring herself to believe that Willy had meant her harm.

"You're a good woman," Del said to her one November morning in the kitchen, while he was busy making a pan of scrambled eggs. "You want to see the best in everyone, but not all people deserve that kind of trust." He carried the pan over to their little kitchen table and spooned the eggs onto their plates. "We were almost killed because of her and her ... *friends*. Or whatever they were."

"I know, I know." Ruth sighed. "And you're probably right. But I told you how she was raised. That girl never had a chance."

"So, teach," he kidded her, "whatcha gonna do 'bout it?"

"I'm thinking of paying her a visit at that women's prison, down in Shakopee."

"Lord help us." Del gave her a stern look. "No. You. Are Not. You're staying away from that girl!"

"Is this going to be our first real argument as a wedded couple?" Ruth asked, looking up at him from the table defiantly. She took a bite of the eggs, then sipped her tea.

"Aaagh ... " Del backed off. "You know I'd agree to just about anything you wanted to do, but really! Have you thought this over?"

"I have. I'm driving down there on Wednesday."

Del was visibly upset. "You know I'm rehearsing that day with the St. Paul Civic Symphony. Can't you at least wait 'til I can go with you?"

"I'm sorry, Del, but I'm going alone. I don't want it to look like we're ganging up on her."

"*Hmph.* At least she'd understand *that.*"

<hr />

The trip down to Shakopee was fairly easy. Except for the traffic in and around Minneapolis, Ruth was comfortable driving it alone. It was fall, and she was thankful it hadn't snowed yet. The roads were clear.

Except for the big security fence surrounding the perimeter, Shakopee Women's Correctional Facility looked more like a college campus than a prison. Ruth had to leave her purse and coat in a locker, and her driver's license was looked over carefully by the staff. They asked her about the books she brought and the keyboard she was donating.

"I'd like to give it to Willy Guerin. But if I can't, then maybe I can donate it to the prison? Maybe she can use it sometimes?"

The guard looked her over. "You a teacher?" she asked.

Ruth chuckled and answered, "I taught in the public schools for twenty-five years. Yes, I'm a teacher."

"I figured. You look like a teacher."

"Can Willy have the keyboard?" Ruth asked again. "She's very musical and I think it will help her."

The guard shrugged. "We'll have to check it out, but yeah, she can have it, as long as she doesn't make too much noise and bother the other women."

"It has head phones. They're in the case."

"That'll help." The guard tucked the keyboard under her arm. "You can give her the books now, though," she said, as she walked away.

Not knowing what to do next, Ruth sat at the table and looked around the room. There were mostly women visitors, sitting at small tables, across from what she guessed were the prisoners.

The prisoners were dressed in street clothes—mostly sweatshirts and exercise pants. For the most part, they looked young.

After a few minutes Willy was escorted in by a female guard, to the chair across from Ruth.

She was also dressed in sweats and looked even younger, with her hair pulled back in a pony-tail and no makeup.

"Hello, Willy," Ruth said, looking hopeful.

"What are *you* doing here?" The girl did not look happy.

"I just wanted to see how you were doing?"

"How do you *think* I'm doing? I'm in a prison."

Ruth sat quiet for a moment. "I don't think you ..." Then she stopped, not knowing what to say.

"Well, just don't say to me, 'You didn't deserve it.' Because I do deserve to be here. I'm 'rotten to the core,' as Aunt Edna says."

"But you're not." Ruth shook her head. "The way you grew up, you never had a chance."

"How do *you* know how I grew up?" Willy was looking daggers at Ruth.

"Um ..." Ruth quickly changed the subject and pushed the books across the table toward the girl. "I brought you some books. And a keyboard, too! But ... I guess they need to check that out, first. But the guard said you could have it."

"You brought me a keyboard? Why? What do you want?" Willy sounded suspicious.

"I don't know. Maybe I just want you to have a chance at doing something good with your life."

Willy started paging through the books. There was a hymnal, a beginning piano book, and a book of Broadway songs. "You're giving me all these?"

"Y-yes. I thought ... I thought maybe, because you were a good singer ... maybe you could learn some other songs?" Ruth's heart was pounding as she tried to smile and look natural. "The keyboard was my son's. He said you could have it. He barely used it."

"They had a piano at school." Willy looked toward the window. "I used to play it sometimes, but I wasn't very good."

"Willy"—Ruth was hoping she was getting through to her—"take this chance to learn something new. I'll bet there's even someone here who can teach you to play."

"*Oh* yeah." Willy laughed derisively. "*Lots* of music teachers in prison."

"I can get you more books if you need them. I live in another city, but I'll try to visit once a month. That is, if that would be okay with you?"

Willy was starting to get tears in her eyes. "But … *why?* Why would you want to help *me?*"

"Because I was a teacher. And once a teacher, always a teacher. Also, I'm a mom. And I see the good in you. You're very talented, you know—"

Willy hurriedly got up, grabbed the books and started leaving the room.

Oh no! thought Ruth. *I really loused this up!*

As the girl walked away, she turned and said in a strangled voice, "That stupid gun wasn't mine, you know." Then she added, "See you again soon?"

In late February, Ruth and Del got a birth announcement in the mail for the six-pound twins—Annika Marie and David Andrew—born to *The Reverend Paul and Emily Ecklund.* There was a hastily scribbled note from Emmy included inside. It said: "We're up to our arm-pits in diapers. Be careful what you pray for! Ha ha!"

About the Author

Judith Johnson, who lives with her husband and cat in Eagan, Minnesota, has been performing in summer musicals at St. Paul's Como Lakeside Pavilion for many years. It all started in 1981 when her eldest daughter was in *The Sound of Music* and the director needed more nuns. Judith was hooked!

She has sung her heart out on that stage many times since, always as a member of the chorus and often joined by her children and grandchildren. This mystery (because she loves a good mystery) was written out of love for the directors, actors, musicians, and helpers who, every summer at the pavilion, say with gusto, "Break a leg!"